Praise for The Co

"A sparkling comedy of errors tucked inside a clever mystery. I loved it!"

— Susan M. Boyer,
USA Today Bestselling Author of *Lowcountry Book Club*

"Readers who enjoy the novels of Susan Isaacs will love this series that blends a strong mystery with the demands of living in an exclusive society."

— *Kings River Life Magazine*

"From the first page to the last, Julie's mysteries grab the reader and don't let up."

— Sally Berneathy,
USA Today Bestselling Author of *The Ex Who Saw a Ghost*

"This book is fun! F-U-N Fun!...A delightful pleasure to read. I didn't want to put it down...Highly recommend."

— *Mysteries, etc.*

"Set in Kansas City, Missouri, in 1974, this cozy mystery effectively recreates the era through the details of down-to-earth Ellison's everyday life."

— *Booklist*

"Mulhern's lively, witty sequel to *The Deep End* finds Kansas City, Mo., socialite Ellison Russell reluctantly attending a high school football game...Cozy fans will eagerly await Ellison's further adventures."

— *Publishers Weekly*

"There's no way a lover of suspense could turn this book down because it's that much fun."

— *Suspense Magazine*

"Cleverly written with sharp wit and all the twists and turns of the best '70s primetime drama, Mulhern nails the fierce fraught mother-daughter relationship, fearlessly tackles what hides behind the Country Club façade, and serves up justice in bombshell fashion. A truly satisfying slightly twisted cozy."

– Gretchen Archer,
USA Today Bestselling Author of *Double Knot*

"Part mystery, part women's fiction, part poetry, Mulhern's debut, *The Deep End*, will draw you in with the first sentence and entrance you until the last. An engaging whodunit that kept me guessing until the end!"

– Tracy Weber,
Author of the Downward Dog Mysteries

"An impossible-to-put-down Harvey Wallbanger of a mystery. With a smart, funny protagonist who's learning to own her power as a woman, *Send in the Clowns* is one boss read."

– Ellen Byron,
Agatha Award-Nominated Author of *Plantation Shudders*

"The plot is well-structured and the characters drawn with a deft hand. Setting the story in the mid-1970s is an inspired touch...A fine start to this mystery series, one that is highly recommended."

– *Mysterious Reviews*

"What a fun read! Murder in the days before cell phones, the internet, DNA and AFIS."

– *Books for Avid Readers*

COLD AS ICE

**The Country Club Murders
by Julie Mulhern**

THE DEEP END (#1)

GUARANTEED TO BLEED (#2)

CLOUDS IN MY COFFEE (#3)

SEND IN THE CLOWNS (#4)

WATCHING THE DETECTIVES (#5)

COLD AS ICE (#6)

COLD AS ICE

THE COUNTRY CLUB MURDERS

JULIE MULHERN

HENERY PRESS

Copyright

COLD AS ICE
The Country Club Murders
Part of the Henery Press Mystery Collection

First Edition | October 2017

Henery Press
www.henerypress.com

Trade Paperback ISBN-13: 978-1-63511-267-2
Digital epub ISBN-13: 978-1-63511-268-9
Kindle ISBN-13: 978-1-63511-269-6
Hardcover ISBN-13: 978-1-63511-270-2

Printed in the United States of America

For Matt, who occasionally peeks
through my rose-colored glasses

ACKNOWLEDGMENTS

Thank you. Thank you to my agent, Margaret Bail. Thank you to my editors at Henery Press, Kendel Lynn and Rachel Jackson. And thank you to the readers of the Country Club Murders—you're the reason I write.

ONE

November 1974
Kansas City, Missouri

The awful thing about murder—aside from the dead body, devastated families, and blood—is that one never knows when violent death will visit. For example, if one knew that someone would die on Tuesday night, one could pay particular attention to conversations and expressions and emotions. One might be able to stop a crime or unveil a killer.

Of course, it's impossible to know ahead of time.

But one does get feelings of impending Disaster! (with a capital D and an exclamation point).

I sensed Disaster! at precisely half past six on Friday night.

If I'd known what kind of Disaster! was coming, I would have ignored the doorbell and barricaded the door, or grabbed my daughter, Grace, and taken her on an impromptu trip to Timbuktu.

But I didn't know.

Happy in my ignorance, I opened the door and found Trip Michaels on my front stoop. He stood there looking like David Cassidy's more handsome younger brother. Brown hair, piercing blue eyes, corduroy pants, navy pea coat, and penny loafers.

No wonder Grace had fallen for him. At sixteen, I would have done the same. But hard-won experience had taught me that beautiful men were untrustworthy.

Lord knew Henry, my late husband, had been. Both beautiful and untrustworthy, he'd turned our marriage into a Disaster!!! (marriage to Henry was a Disaster with three exclamation points).

Trip cleared his throat.

I stopped ruminating.

He extended his hand. "It's nice to see you, Mrs. Russell."

Definitely untrustworthy. The boy was up to something.

That or the baggage I carried with me was coloring my view of a perfectly nice kid.

I shook his hand. "Come in, Trip. Grace should be right down."

Maybe. Grace had blasted through her closet in search of the perfect outfit and her room looked like the aftermath of an explosion, the casualties being tried-on and discarded clothes. How hard was it to decide what to wear on a date?

"Grace told me you're going to the movies. What are you seeing?"

"*Benji.*"

My dog, Max, eyed Trip suspiciously. His tail didn't wag nor did he offer his customary crotch sniff as welcome. Instead, he stayed glued to my side. Of late, I'd questioned Max's judgment. Should I trust his doggy sense now?

I crossed the foyer and called up the stairs, "Grace, hurry up. Trip is here."

"I'll be right down."

Trip's gaze traveled the front hall, taking in the sparkle of the chandelier, the flower arrangement on the bombe chest, and the painting that hung above it. "Is that one of yours?"

My gaze followed his to the Jackson Pollock hanging on the wall. My paintings weren't abstract. "No." And then, because standing around in uncomfortable silence made me itch, I asked, "What time does your movie start?"

"Eight o'clock. We're going to grab a quick dinner before the show." Innocuous words. Dinner and a movie. What could be wrong with that?

Plenty.

"So tell me, Trip—"

"I'm ready." Grace rushed down the stairs wearing a pair of jeans and a peasant blouse. For this she'd trashed her room?

Grace pulled a coat from the hall closet, turned, and noticed my dress. "Oh. Right. You have that cocktail party."

All I wanted was a glass of wine, my feet up, and an episode of *The Rockford Files*. Completely doable if I hadn't promised my friend Libba I'd go to the Brookfields' party with her. Libba had eagerly adopted *Sex and the Single Girl* as a personal manifesto, but she still couldn't walk into a party alone. She was counting on me.

"Will you be out late?" Grace asked.

"No. I'm exhausted. I'm just going to put in an appearance then come home." No need for Trip to think my house was empty and unsupervised. I'd already caught the two of them making out on the couch once. "When will you be home?"

"By eleven thirty." She coupled the world-weary tone of a teenager forced to answer a rhetorical question with an epic eye roll.

"Not a minute later."

That earned a second eye roll.

"I'll have her home on time, Mrs. Russell." Trip's smile probably inspired confidence with most mothers. Not with me.

"You two have fun." But not too much fun.

They slipped through the front door, leaving behind the scent of Grace's Love's Baby Soft and a lingering sense of unease.

I closed the door. "I don't know, Max. There's something

about that kid I don't like."

Max whined softly, reminding me I never liked any of Grace's potential boyfriends.

"Come on," I said. "I need a sandwich before I go." The Brookfields' parties tended to be heavy on liquor and light on food.

With the mere mention of a sandwich, Max followed me to the kitchen and carefully supervised the construction of turkey, Swiss, mayo, and a slice of tomato on rye.

He wagged his tail hopefully.

Ding dong.

I handed over the crusts of my sandwich to Max and hurried into the foyer.

Ding dong.

Ding dong.

I yanked open the door.

"I can't believe you made me get out of the car. I've been honking for ages."

I glanced at my watch and my smart retort faded away. Libba was early.

Libba was early.

Somewhere in Hell they were having a heckuva snow ball fight.

And somewhere at the Brookfields' was a man Libba fancied. I knew it as surely as I knew my dress was black.

"You're wearing that?" she asked.

I smoothed the silk jersey over my hips. "Yes." It was new. It was flattering. It wasn't low cut.

Now Libba glanced at her watch. "It'll have to do. Let's go." A smile lurked at the corners of her lips. The kind of smile a woman wears when she's infatuated with a man.

"Who is he?"

"Who is who?" Libba sounded innocent, but I wasn't fooled.

"The man."

"There's no man." The smile still lurked on her lips.

"Uh-huh." I smirked.

"Just drop it, Ellison."

I didn't need to pester her. The party would tell the tale. I slipped into a coat and picked up my handbag. "Let's go."

If the weather had been pleasant, we could have walked to the Brookfields' house. But the frigid air was heavy with impending snow. We climbed into Libba's car and she torpedoed us the few blocks to the Brookfields'. When we arrived, I opened the passenger door and put one grateful foot on the frozen pavement. "You nearly hit that Volvo."

"I did not."

She had. The Volvo's side mirror probably retained the cherry red kiss of her BMW's mirror. "Did too."

"You're in a mood." She got out of the car and slammed her door.

"I'm not the only one." I gently closed the passenger door. "I'm not staying late."

"Oh?"

"I'm tired. I'll stay long enough to be polite then call a cab."

"Fine." Libba didn't mind being at a party by herself, just arriving alone.

We walked up to the front door, anticipatory salt crunching beneath the soles of our shoes, and rang the bell.

Kay Brookfield opened the door wearing a stylish camel dress and a bright smile. "Welcome! Come in out of the cold."

We stepped into the warmth and light of the Brookfields' foyer, surrendered our coats, and accepted drinks from a waiter holding a silver tray (a stinger for Libba, wine for me).

"I'm so glad you got back from New York in time to come," said Kay.

"Me too." I'd had a successful gallery opening and only

arrived home that morning. "I wouldn't have missed this for anything." Except *The Rockford Files.*

"Everyone's in the living room." With a broad sweep of her arm, Kay indicated where she wanted us.

I lingered. "The house looks lovely, and the flowers—" I nodded at an enormous arrangement of mums, salmon-hued roses, and bittersweet positioned on a round table near the base of the stairs "—they're gorgeous."

"Thank you. I'm glad they turned out." A devilish grin lit Kay's face. "And I'm glad you didn't find any dead people on the driveway."

"The night's still young." Libba's comment wiped the grin clean off Kay's lips.

We left her with a worried furrow in her brow.

"That wasn't very nice," I said.

"Pish." Libba rolled her eyes with every bit as much drama as Grace. "You find a body nearly every week. I figure you're due."

God forbid.

Kay's living room wouldn't have been out of place in an English country house. A bottle-green velvet sofa edged in burgundy sat at a ninety-degree angle to a chintz sofa in shades of burgundy, cream, and that same bottle green. Above that chintz sofa hung a gilt frame, and in the frame hung a painting of dyspeptic sheep. The velvet drapes were hung high, closer to the ceilings than the actual windows. A fire blazed in the stone hearth and an arched doorway led to a paneled library.

Chester, the bartender who worked most of the parties I attended, was set up in the corner. He saw me and smiled warmly.

His expression was in stark contrast to Prudence Davies, who saw me, narrowed her eyes, and blew a plume of cigarette smoke in my direction. Prudence was one of the women with

whom my beautiful and untrustworthy husband had dallied.
Dallied.

Such a nice word. It sounded like springtime and sunshine and daffodils. The reality had been sordid.

Prudence was talking with Paula Staton and Jenny Woods, and neither of them looked happy about it.

I shifted my gaze, taking in the crowd.

Laird Williams, a friend of Henry's, clutched an old-fashioned filled with scotch and prognosticated about Saturday's football games with Tom Michaels, Trip's father. Laird's wife, Evelyn, stood with them. The poor woman looked bored beyond measure.

Laurie Michaels chatted with my friend Daisy and—my heart hiccupped—Hunter Tafft. Here? Tonight? Hunter Tafft was a thrice-divorced lawyer with silver hair, a silver tongue, and an abundance of charm. A man who wanted something from me I wasn't ready to give. A commitment.

As if she sensed my desire to turn on my heel and leave, Libba rested her hand on the small of my back and propelled me into the room.

"Paybacks are hell," I whispered.

Libba's smile was sugary sweet. "I'll take my chances. Besides, you're going to have to talk to him at some point. Look, Laurie's waving at you."

Laurie wasn't just waving, she was waving wildly, as if I was a long-lost relative she'd spotted in a crowded airport. That wave. That talk-to-me-first wave simply wasn't done. For so many reasons. Not the least of which was that if I didn't go to her, she'd look like a fool.

"Get it over with. Go talk to them," Libba advised. "Then trade the wine in for something stronger."

It didn't look as if I had much choice. Laurie wore a so-happy-to-see-you expression, Daisy looked bemused by Laurie's wild gesticulations, and Hunter—he'd noticed me. He raised a brow as if daring me to ignore him. I couldn't. Ever. He'd helped me too many times. I owed him.

My Italian pumps weighed more than a pair of anvils, but somehow I made it across the living room and presented my cheek for a kiss.

"Ellison, you look lovely."

And he looked handsome as ever. "Thank you, Hunter. It's nice to see you." That was it. I was out of words.

"The kids are out tonight," Laurie announced. She made it sound as if Trip was about to slip a ring on Grace's finger.

I smiled—a tight, wordless smile.

Laurie reached out and rested her hand on my arm. "We're so thrilled that Trip is dating a girl like Grace."

They were sixteen. It wasn't as if a few dates counted for anything. I found a few words. "Trip said something about dinner and a movie."

"That's what he told me." Her grip on my arm tightened. "She's a lovely girl. You've done a fabulous job."

Now I was supposed to say something nice about Trip. What? "Trip has impeccable manners."

Next to me, Hunter made a noise in his throat. A guffaw? Hard to tell since the polite expression on his face didn't waver. Trip wasn't the only one with impeccable manners.

"Daisy, how are your children?" I asked. A question guaranteed to elicit a ten-minute response.

Laurie removed her right hand from my arm and placed her left hand on Daisy's arm. "I'm dying to hear all about your children, but I must talk with Prudence. Would you excuse me? Please?"

"Of course," said Daisy.

Laurie hurried away.

"Do you really want to know about the kids or were you just

trying to get rid of her?" Daisy looked and acted as sweet as cotton candy. So much so that sometimes I forgot all that sugary fluff hid an actual brain.

"Of course I want to hear about the kids."

"Me too," said Hunter. It must be a terrible burden to have impeccable manners.

"Tom is playing basketball this year. Louis thinks he's the next Mark Spitz and wants to swim year-round. Susan is taking private art lessons. Mary loves third grade. And since his father took him to a game, all Matthew wants to do is wear his Chiefs jersey and talk about football."

Less than a minute. Something was wrong. "Wha—"

"I have a confession." Daisy's voice was small.

Oh dear. "What?"

She fixed her gaze on the carpet. "I invited Laurie to sub for Jinx at our bridge game."

"Where's Jinx?"

She looked up, glanced at Hunter, and said, "Resting." A euphemism if ever there was one. Of late, Jinx had been taking valium at an alarming rate.

"For how long?"

"Until the new year."

Oh dear Lord. "Is she all right? Was there another incident?" Incident instead of overdose. Two could play the euphemism game.

"No. Absolutely not. She's fine. Preston took her to a lovely place out in Rancho Mirage. I mean—I assume it's lovely. Everything in Rancho Mirage is." Daisy clasped her hands together. Her brows drew together and she bit her lower lip. "I hope you don't mind too much."

Mind that Jinx was resting? How could I mind that? My brain kicked in. Daisy was worried about my reaction to Laurie. "It's fine." It wasn't. Laurie's penchant for talking about "the kids" had already grown old. "It's only for the month of December." Please, God.

My gaze searched for and found Laurie. She was deep in conversation with Prudence. As I watched, Prudence shook her head and blew cigarette smoke out her nose. "You're nuts." Now that I was listening for it, Prudence's bray was easy to pick out among the voices filling Kay's living room.

Laurie said something, but unlike Prudence, she didn't bray. Her words were lost in the sea of conversations.

Prudence shook her head and turned her back.

Laurie grabbed her arm.

Prudence turned, stared at the hand on her arm, and curled the corner of her lip, revealing a few horse teeth. "If you can't keep him happy, someone else will."

Laurie dashed her martini in Prudence's face.

For a half a second, time froze.

When it resumed, Prudence spluttered, dropping her drink and her cigarette.

Shattering glass (the actual glass, not the coffee table) drew everyone's attention.

Prudence stood immobile, Laurie's drink dripping off the end of her long nose. Then she wiped away the drops of vodka with the back of her hand. "Bitch!"

"Adulteress!" With the buzz of multiple conversations gone, it was easy to hear Laurie's reply.

Tom Michaels stepped forward. "Laurie, what the hell—"

"Fire!" someone yelled.

The chintz couch was producing black, acrid smoke. So much smoke that the sheep behind it were lost in a haze.

Most of the people in the room stampeded toward the door to the hallway. Hunter raced over to Chester's bar and grabbed an ice bucket and a pitcher of water. He sped across the room to the smoking couch and dumped them both on the spot where

Prudence had dropped her cigarette.

Chester rushed after him with an armful of club soda and tonic bottles.

Hunter took bottles from Chester's arms and poured the liquid onto the smoldering fabric.

Our hostess pushed her way through the crowd, swimming against the stream. Her eyes were wide and her mouth pulled back in a rictus of horror. "What happened?"

"Prudence Davies dropped a cigarette on your couch," said Daisy. Like me, she'd remained rooted to the Axminster, watching Hunter and Chester pour nonflammable liquids onto Kay's couch.

Prudence had also remained. "Kay, I'm terribly sorry." She actually sounded contrite.

Kay's gaze traveled from the sodden remains of her couch to the smoke-darkened walls of her living room. Tears filled her eyes. "How?"

"It was Laurie's fault." There was the Prudence I knew—the woman who blamed others for her sins.

"You're the one who dropped a lit cigarette on a couch." It was Laurie who was braying now.

"After you threw a drink in my face." Prudence's cheeks were pale, her gaze furious. "I'm not sleeping with your husband. He doesn't have enough—enough imagination to keep me happy."

Prudence shifted her attention to me—just for an instant, just long enough to remind me my husband had not lacked imagination.

Daisy, God love her, moved closer to me.

Tom, the man without imagination, covered his face with his hand and collapsed onto the undamaged couch.

Prudence returned her gaze to Laurie. "You're pathetic. It's no wonder he cheats on you."

Tom, who apparently lacked backbone along with imagination, opened his mouth but said nothing.

"I could kill you." Laurie's hands were clinched at her sides and crimson flamed on her cheeks. She looked as if she meant what she said.

Again Prudence's gaze slid toward me. "Get in line."

"Get out!" Kay pointed to the door.

No one moved.

"I mean it, Prudence. Get out."

"Me?" Prudence's hands crossed over her chest. "She started all this."

Kay glanced at her ruined couch. "You are not welcome here."

"You heard her." There was more than a hint of gloat in Laurie's voice.

"You too, Laurie." Kay's shoulders shook as if hysterics lurked around the next corner.

Tom stood, moved to his wife's side, and took her arm.

She shook him off.

A dull flush rose from his neck to his face. "Let's go, Laurie."

She turned on him, her mouth parted—

"You're making a scene." His was the voice of an observer, one who didn't particularly care if Laurie made a scene or not.

She snapped her lips closed and regarded the handful of people still in the room with narrowed eyes. Her gaze caught on Daisy and me and she smoothed the expression on her face like a top sheet on a freshly made bed. Real emotion was replaced by polite dismay. She had caused a scene. An ugly one. "Kay—" she turned and faced our hostess "—I am so sorry about all of this." Presumably she meant the fire, the couch, and the scene. "Of course we'll go. And we'll replace the couch."

Tom blanched.

"Remember this," Daisy whispered in my ear.

"What do you mean?" I whispered back.

"This scene. Remember it."

As if I could ever forget. "Why?"

"We'll be questioned." She nodded toward Laurie, Prudence, Tom, and the tableau of ruined furniture. "This is the sort of thing that leads to murder."

TWO

On Saturday morning, I stumbled into the kitchen, pushed Mr. Coffee's button, and plonked myself on a stool while he worked his magic.

Grace wandered in and trilled, "Good morning."

I grunted.

"How was your party?"

"Memorable. How was your date?" A silly question, since animated songbirds perched on her shoulders and whistled.

"Fun." She opened the refrigerator door and peered inside. "Do you want some eggs?"

Mr. Coffee gurgled. The best sound in the world. I lurched off my stool and poured myself a cup of heaven. "Coffee?"

"Please. Do you want eggs or not?"

I took a second mug from the cupboard. "Give me a minute to wake up and I'll make the eggs."

"No, no." She spoke quickly. Insultingly so. "I'll do the eggs. Maybe you could put some bread in the toaster?"

"Fine." Cooking was not my strong suit. No one ever taught me scrambled eggs should be cooked at low heat. It wasn't really my fault when Henry chipped a tooth. I opened the bread box and found—"What's this?" With the tips of my fingers I held up a bag of raisin bread.

"Aggie bought it."

"Why?"

"I asked her to."

"Why would you want to eat something defiled by raisins?" I dropped the bag on the counter and took a step back.

"It's also got cinnamon in it. I tried it at Peggy's. It's good."

I raised a doubtful brow. "You can make your own toast."

Grace shook her head as if I was the one acting like a teenager.

That wouldn't do. "How was the movie?"

"Cute. It's about a dog who saves some kidnapped kids." She cracked eggs into a bowl then beat them with a fork. "What happened at the party?"

"Prudence Davies dropped a lit cigarette on a couch and started a fire."

"No way!"

"Way."

Grace put a shallow skillet on the stove and lit the burner. "Wow. I bet Mrs. Brookfield was upset."

"To put it mildly."

She added a pat of butter to the pan. "What are you doing tonight?"

I had a date. With Anarchy Jones. A date I didn't care to discuss. I hadn't yet consumed enough coffee to handle a teenage smirk. When Grace learned I was actually going out with him, she would smirk. When Mother learned I'd gone out with Anarchy, she'd sigh and sadly shake her head, and mention something about disappointment. Mother disapproved of Anarchy. He was a homicide detective, he had no people in Kansas City, and his parents had given him an unacceptable name. Mother preferred Hunter Tafft. "Why do you ask?"

Grace cocked her head and smiled. "I was wondering if Peggy, Kim, Debbie, and Donna could spend the night?"

"Of course." And then, because she'd relegated me to toaster duty, I added, "I'll make breakfast for you all tomorrow morning."

"Very funny, Mom." She poured the eggs into the pan and stirred them with the fork.

I dropped a slice of raisin-less bread into the toaster next to a piece of Grace's unspeakable bread, pushed down the lever, and sipped my coffee.

We ate our breakfasts (perfect eggs, burnt toast) sitting at the island. "What are your plans for the day?" I asked.

"Homework. If you'll give me some money, I'd like to go to the store for some snacks for tonight."

"Of course." I imagined the girls piled onto the couch in the family room, watching the late movie, chomping on popcorn, giggling. Meanwhile, I'd be—"How much do you need?"

"Is twenty too much?'

"Nope."

"Thanks, Mom. What are you up to today?"

"Painting." My fingers itched for the feel of brushes in my hands. I drained my coffee cup and stood. "Thanks for the eggs."

Grace did not thank me for the burnt toast. Imagine that.

I painted, breaking only for lunch and, at Max's insistence, a quick run. Then I painted some more.

The daubs on the canvas coalesced into real shapes and soothed every single one of my nerves. Painting did that for me—allowed me to express emotions best not shared with my friends at the club. Anger and sadness and joy all ended up on the canvas, transformed by swirls of paint. Usually anxiety joined those emotions. Not today. An anxious niggle refused to relocate to the painting.

I gave up, cleaned and dried my brushes, and headed downstairs.

Paint under my nails, a messy ponytail, and no makeup wouldn't do. I showered, dried my hair, and carefully applied my face. All the while, the niggle of nervous tension that had shadowed me all day grew.

I bit my lower lip and peered into my closet.

What to wear?

I held up a Diane von Furstenberg dress, gazed in the mirror, shook my head, and tossed the frock on the bed. I repeated that exercise with three more dresses. When the fifth dress joined the growing pile on the coverlet, I paused. I was behaving exactly like Grace last night. Unable to decide what to wear on a simple date.

I returned the dresses to the closet and donned slacks and a cashmere turtleneck.

Ding dong.

My heart ricocheted around my chest.

"Mooooom." Grace's voice carried from the foyer. "Detective Jones is here."

"Coming." I took a final peek in the mirror and grabbed my purse.

I paused at the top of the stairs. At the bottom, four teenage girls were gazing at Anarchy as if he were Steve McQueen and they were the presidents of his fan club. Grace was less impressed, but she was used to Anarchy's coffee-brown eyes, lean face, and killer smile. She gazed at me, passed judgment on my outfit, and ultimately communicated her approval with a tiny nod.

I descended, my gaze locked on the girls. Looking at them was preferable to looking at Anarchy. Just glancing his way made my mouth dry, made my lips twitch, made my spine tingle.

I reached the bottom of the stairs and he closed the distance between us, dropping a kiss on my cheek and whispering, "You look beautiful."

My heart, an unreliable organ, behaved like the ball in an

arcade machine. It bounced off other organs, tilted, and set bells ringing.

Predictably, Grace smirked.

Her friends gawked.

"I'll get my coat." The voice wasn't mine. It was too high. Too girly. I cleared my throat and added, "You girls have fun tonight."

"You too, Mrs. Russell." They sounded like a Greek chorus.

Anarchy and I stepped outside and the cold chilled the fire burning my cheeks. "Where are we going?" The squeak had returned. I cleared my throat.

Anarchy pulled open the passenger door. "Do you like steak?"

"I do." My regular voice was back. Thank God.

He circled the car and settled in behind the wheel. "We're going to the Ox."

"The Golden Ox?" The restaurant crouched next to the Kansas City Live Stock Exchange and was a favorite with the ranchers who brought their cattle to the neighboring stockyards. Legend had it that the Ox was the birthplace of the Kansas City strip. I'd never been.

"Best steak in town."

Who was I to argue? "Do you go there often?"

"Special occasions."

I was a special occasion? My lips twitched and a warm glow settled into my stomach.

"How was New York?" he asked.

"Good. The paintings sold well."

"I haven't been there in years. Usually when I travel it's to California."

"San Francisco?" I asked. Anarchy's father was a politics professor and his mother a fiber artist. He never talked about them.

He didn't now. Instead his lips thinned and he nodded.

"Are you going home for the holidays?"

He slowed the car for an upcoming red light. "I haven't decided yet."

"Is it just you and your parents or do you have siblings?"

"I have a brother and a sister."

"What do they do?"

He stared at a traffic light and said nothing. When the light turned green, he pressed the accelerator. "My brother is an environmental lawyer and my sister sings."

"Sings?"

"Songs." His jaw tightened and his gaze remained fixed on the road ahead. The message was clear. He didn't want to talk about his family.

"What are their names?"

"River and Journey."

That gave me pause. "Which is which?"

He snorted and the tight line of his jaw relaxed. "River is my brother and Journey is my sister."

River Jones? Journey Jones? "How...interesting."

"My mom wanted to name Journey Karma. My father liked Serenity. Journey was the compromise."

"What about River? Any discussion there?"

"Nope. They both love River." The tight line was back. With a vengeance. "Have you talked with your sister recently?"

"The surgery is coming up." My sister, in a selfless act no one had believed her capable of, was donating a kidney to my first cousin. "Mother and Daddy are flying to Akron to be with her. They'll stay for Thanksgiving."

"You're not going?"

"Maybe. It's up to Grace." Thanksgiving would be the first major holiday she'd spent without her father. All I wanted was for her to be happy, so I was following her lead. Thus far, she wanted to stay in Kansas City. "We may stay home."

He pulled into a parking lot filled with pickup trucks and slotted his car into a space. "Do you cook?"

"Not if we want to eat." Even I acknowledged that a turkey catching the oven on fire was a bad thing. "If we stay here, we'll get takeout from the club."

"Takeout for Thanksgiving?" He opened his door and the overhead light came on, illuminating the crinkles near his eyes.

"Don't judge."

Anarchy walked around the car, opened the passenger door, and extended a hand.

I had no choice but to take it. With his touch, an electric current raced from my fingers to my arm to my brain. My mouth dried. My tongue tied in knots. Somehow I got out of the car and let him lead me into the restaurant.

The carpet was a deep red patterned with ranch brands and the faces of heifers with attitude problems. The chairs were leather. One wall was papered with a rustic scene of a cattle drive on the plains. There were saddles and mounted heads and a pair of longhorns above the kitchen. It was a place by men for men.

"You've never been here before?" He sounded surprised.

Half the customers wore cowboy hats, a third wore leather vests—it was not the sort of place Henry would have taken me. Not the sort of place I'd lunch with girlfriends. "No."

"You're in for a treat."

I managed a weak smile.

We followed the denim-clad hostess to our table and sat.

I perused the menu. My choices involved cuts of meat, not types. The same range held true for sides. Potatoes—mashed, baked, or fried.

"You don't come to the Ox and order a salad."

"I wouldn't dream of it." I knew exactly what kind of salad

COLD AS ICE   21

I'd get—tired iceberg lettuce with a few strands of shaved carrots, a cherry tomato or two, and croutons, all smothered in green goddess or buttermilk dill dressing.

"Is this okay? We can go someplace else."

I stared across the table. Anarchy regarded me with scrunched eyes and worried lips. He was nervous too.

"Are you kidding? I love this place." Somehow I managed a smile. "Besides, I'm dying for a good steak."

He smiled back at me. My smile was a simple curving of lips. Anarchy's was something else entirely. Anarchy's smile warmed his eyes and broke up the austere lines of his face. Anarchy's smile set electric currents zinging and hearts tilting. Anarchy's smile left me breathless.

I took a sip of water, wished for something stronger, and shifted my gaze away.

There were men at the bar who looked like fixtures.

There were men in booths whose stomachs threatened to dislocate the tables.

There were golden ox heads on the walls staring at me.

We ordered. Steaks. Hardly a surprise.

The steaks arrived along with a bottle of red wine. The steaks and the wine were excellent and the anxious niggle at the back of my brain stopped worrying about the actual date and concerned itself with its end. With saying good night.

I wanted a good-night kiss. Long and slow and mind-melting.

If I told her, Libba would say that wanting a kiss was a positive step for me. Then she'd talk about empowerment and sexual liberation. And as soon as she said sex, I'd stop listening. Instead I'd recite the preamble to the Constitution in my head or think about football players in pantyhose or paunchy men streaking in the park.

"What do you do for fun?" The words spilled out of me,

infinitely preferable to thoughts of kissing or paunchy naked men.

"I have a motorcycle."

I knew it! I knew there had to be a hidden wild side to Anarchy.

His eyes narrowed slightly. "What?"

I blinked. "What do you mean, what?"

"You're smirking."

"I am not." I was.

"You're thinking *Easy Rider*. It's not like that."

"I am not." I wasn't. "I never saw *Easy Rider*."

Now Anarchy blinked.

"My husband had no interest in seeing movies like that." So, of course, we hadn't gone to the theater. Henry claimed the film glorified pot-smoking, LSD-dropping losers on motor bikes. He'd been much more interested in viewing *Bob & Carol & Ted & Alice*. Open marriages being more his style. I took a sip of wine. A large one.

Anarchy rested his forearms on the table and leaned toward me. "You didn't miss much."

It took me a few seconds to realize he was talking about *Easy Rider* and not wife-swapping. "I'm not exactly counter-culture."

"Neither am I."

But he could have been—his name was Anarchy. With a liberal politics professor for a father, he probably hung out in Haight-Ashbury or wherever it was that hippies hung out before the sixties. Me? I'd been groomed to be a wife from the moment my head rested in my cradle. Hardly a walk on the wild side.

He picked up his wine glass, turning it so the liquid within caught the light. "At some point in our lives, we decide what we're going to be. Who we're going to be." He lifted the glass to his lips but didn't drink. "My sister calls me a pig. My father too."

"I'm sorry."

"I'm not."

I would have liked to ask him more about his sister, but he frowned and his hand dropped to his waist. A second later he was peering at a small black box—his pager. "Would you please excuse me a moment?"

Something inside me—whatever it was, I refused to give it a name—deflated. "I thought you were off tonight."

Anarchy's frown deepened. "I am. I'm sorry about this. Excuse me." He crossed the crowded dining room, presumably to find a phone, and I leaned back in my chair.

Things had been going so well—I was close to learning something about his life, about him—and now, somewhere in the city, someone was dead and the dispatcher had paged Anarchy. He'd go. He wouldn't be Anarchy if he didn't. He'd go, and the leisurely kiss, the one dancing like sugar plums in my head, wouldn't happen. Not tonight. Not if Anarchy had to investigate a murder.

I sighed. Disappointment or relief?

Who was I kidding? Disappointment.

He strode back to the table with our coats draped over his arm. "Ellison—" He scowled down at the carpet. A heifer scowled back. "We need to leave. Now."

"A murder?" I stood.

He held my coat for me. "No."

"No?" I paused with my arm half in a sleeve, craned my neck, and looked up into his grim face. "What's happened?"

"Dispatch notifies me whenever a call comes in from your address."

His sentence hung there as real as the scent of grilling meat. As real as the hammering of my heart.

"A disturbance? Grace is home." The voice wasn't mine. It

belonged to a woman who couldn't catch her breath. A woman suddenly paralyzed by fear.

He dropped a few bills on the table. "Let's go."

THREE

My nose was inches from the dashboard and my right foot pressed an imaginary gas pedal as if that would somehow make the car go faster. "Did the dispatcher say what was wrong?"

"No."

Anarchy had bent the rules enough to put a flashy light on the top of his car and we were speeding through traffic. Not fast enough.

"But—"

"She didn't tell me anything. Just that there was a disturbance call."

A disturbance call? There was no way—no way—Grace and her friends had caused a disturbance worthy of a call to the police. My heart beat in my throat and I leaned even closer to the dash.

Anarchy slowed for a red light and I fisted my hands.

"Take it easy. Getting in a car accident won't get us there faster." He'd noticed my leaning or my clenched fists or my foot pushing its way to the pavement.

"Sorry." I settled back against the seat, forced my fingers apart, and eased up on the not-there gas. "You're right."

He looked both ways, saw no oncoming cars, and drove through the still-red light.

I leaned forward again.

"Ellison." His voice was velvet, meant to sooth. He reached across the bench seat, took my hand, and squeezed. Briefly.

Then he returned his hand to two o'clock on the wheel.

I closed my eyes and pressed my palms against my eye sockets. "What if—"

"We're almost there."

I peeked through the bars of my fingers. Anarchy was right. We were on my street. Cars lined the curb. Both curbs. Someone was having an enormous party.

Anarchy slowed the car to a crawl. I looked for the house flooded with lights and people.

Mine.

I was hosting an enormous party.

And if the police cars and scattering teenagers and empty beer cans littering my lawn were any indication, the party was a good one.

"She's grounded until she's thirty."

Anarchy snorted and pulled into the drive, parking at the bottom. The rest of the driveway was already filled with haphazardly parked vehicles.

I didn't wait for Anarchy to open my door. I was out of the car before he'd even turned off the ignition.

I charged up the drive in full Mother mode. Four friends to spend the night? Where was Grace? When I was done with her she'd wish for Mother.

"Ma'am?" A uniformed officer actually thought he could stop me.

My steps didn't slow. "My house."

He wisely got out of my way.

I pushed on the front door. It didn't budge.

Apparently the teenagers who remained in my house had decided their best course of action was to lock the door and wait out the police.

Too bad for the geniuses behind the door, I had a key. I inserted the gold Schlage and turned. The door swung open onto a world gone mad.

A mob of children holding beer cans stared at me with horrified expressions on their young faces. "Smokin' in the Boys' Room" blared from the stereo in the family room, loud enough for me to feel the bass rumble through the floor. The boys' room wasn't the only place people were smoking. Far too many children held cigarettes. My house smelled like a dive bar.

I stepped inside. "Where. Is. Grace?"

No one said a word.

"Out." I pointed toward the front yard.

No one moved.

I let my gaze travel. "I know who you are." I'd known most of the kids in my front hall since they learned to toddle. "If you're not out of here in one minute, I'll call your fathers." I paused, slowing my voice to deadly intent. "And send them bills for this mess."

The little delinquents flew out the door.

I felt a presence at my back and glanced over my shoulder. Anarchy stood behind me. "Wow." His voice was mild.

Wow? Maybe that was an appropriate response for a homicide detective who was accustomed to witnessing gruesome crime scenes, but as the unexpected hostess for this party, the words scrolling through my brain were much stronger. My fingers curved into talons and I stalked forward. At least thirty teenagers still lingered in the living room. And why wouldn't they? That was where most of the liquor was—had been. A group of five or six kids were spinning an empty bottle of eighteen-year-old Glenfiddich. The bottle had not been empty when I left.

They saw me and leapt from the floor.

"Out." I pointed toward the door.

Maybe it was the look on my face. Maybe it was the police detective standing behind me. They ran.

I strode toward the kitchen. The island was cluttered with

empty beer cans and glasses doing double duty as ashtrays. Three boys perused the contents of my refrigerator, a fourth pumped a keg.

The growl in my throat was visceral.

"Ellison, keep everything in perspective. No one's dead."

"Yet." Maybe not the smartest thing to say to a homicide detective.

The boys turned, saw me, and their complexions turned the color of wallpaper paste. The one pumping the keg looked as if he might pass out.

One of them spoke. "Sorry, Mrs. Russell."

"Out." I pointed toward the front door, my finger rigid, implacable as death.

I didn't have to tell them twice. They scurried away.

"Jungle Boogie" replaced the Brownsville Station song on the radio. I gritted my teeth and marched toward the source of the noise.

The lights were off in the family room. Only the light spilling in from the kitchen and the blue glow of the television pierced the darkness. Well, that and the cherry red ends of cigarettes. The house was going to smell awful for weeks. Which was the least of my worries.

The family room was dark because kids were making out.

I took vicious satisfaction in flipping the light switch.

Couples jumped apart as if the light had scalded them.

I took inventory. Plenty of kids I knew. Smeared lip gloss. Mussed hair. Untucked shirts. No Grace.

In a wingback, Peggy, one of the girls who was actually supposed to be at my house, struggled with a button on her blouse.

I pinned her with a stare worthy of Mother. "Where is Grace?"

"Um...I don't know. The study?"

"Peggy—" I shifted my gaze "—and Debbie, you two get a trash bag and start cleaning up in here. I want the rest of you out of my house."

"Bitch."

It was impossible to know who'd said it, but Anarchy stepped forward. "You heard the lady. If there are any more comments, you'll be going to jail instead of going home."

Someone—a girl—gasped. Hard to tell if she was worried about jail or just responding to the way Anarchy looked framed in the doorway.

"Out. Now." I stepped away from the door and let a bevy of sheepish teenagers file past me.

A few, those I knew well, stopped and apologized. None managed to look me in the eye.

When only Peggy and Debbie remained, I followed the kids back into the front hall and tried the door to the study.

Locked.

I knocked.

"Go away." It was a boy's voice. A chuckle followed. "We're busy."

I pounded my fist against the door.

"Don't," said Anarchy. "You're going to hurt your hand."

As if I cared. "Open this damned door right now or I'll have you arrested."

The boy on the other side of the door didn't respond.

"Let me try." Anarchy knocked on the door, a sharp purposeful rap. "This is Detective Jones with KCPD. Open the door."

The door opened.

Trip Michaels was on the other side. His shirt was untucked, his lips were swollen, and his expression was a cross between a smirk and ennui. "What seems to be the problem, Officer?" He shifted his gaze to me and his eyes widened. "Mrs.

Russell."

I brushed past him. The room was dim, but I could still see the girl, her face hidden by the shadowy curtain of her hair. With desperate fingers, she pulled at her clothes.

"Grace?"

The girl looked up.

Not Grace. Thank God.

"Who are you?" I asked.

"She's nobody," said Trip.

The girl winced as if he'd slapped her.

"This isn't what it looks like." Trip's voice had taken on a note of desperation.

"Really? Because it looks to me like you and this young lady were locked in the study doing things that require privacy."

"I'm so sorry." The words shook as if the girl was fighting tears. She swiped at her eyes and flipped her hair so that the curtain covered her face again.

"Go home, dear."

She didn't move.

"Do you have a car here?"

"No." Again she swiped at her eyes. Maybe. It was hard to discern features behind all that hair. She definitely sniffled.

Chances were good I'd kicked out her ride. I turned to Anarchy. "Could one of the uniformed officers take her home?"

His gaze shifted from Trip to the girl as if he was wondering why the boy she'd been kissing (please God let that be all) couldn't give her a ride.

As far as I knew, four hours ago Trip had been dating my daughter. Now he was canoodling with someone else.

"Let's find Grace," said Anarchy. "Then I'll take her home myself."

Grace. Did she know what Trip was up to in the study? The scowl I directed at Trip cut deep lines into my face. "See yourself out." I softened my voice and looked at the girl. "What's your name?"

"Dawn."

"Detective Jones or I will take you home."

Anarchy and I made a quick pass through the rest of the downstairs and found only a boy kneeling before a toilet with his head over the bowl. Upon consideration, I let him stay there.

We climbed the stairs.

The bedroom doors were closed. I opened each one. They were mercifully empty. Only my bedroom remained. I turned the knob and opened the door.

Grace, a large box of tissue, Donna, Kim, and Max all sat on my bed.

Max, who knew full well my bed was off limits, hopped off.

Grace looked up from her lap. Her eyes were swollen, her nose was red, and the remains of her mascara created black lines on her cheeks.

Donna and Kim shifted uncomfortably.

Apparently Grace knew full well what Trip was up to in the study. Still, I asked, "What happened?"

My question brought on a fresh wave of tears. Grace buried her face in her hands. "I said—" she hiccupped "—I said if he wanted that, he could find another girl." A fresh wave of tears wetted her cheeks. "And he did."

"At least you found out what kind of young man he is before you invested too much time." As opposed to me. I'd spent nearly eighteen years with a man whose "that" made me shudder.

Grace didn't take much comfort in my words. Her hands clenched into fists, which she held against her eyes. Poor child. The realization that a man's proclivities were more important to him than you hurt on so many levels. First there was the sense of betrayal. Worse was the realization that he put a higher value on cheap sex than you.

Henry had made me feel worthless. I understood exactly how Grace felt.

"Teenage boys are ruled by their hormones," said Anarchy.

Every female in the room, myself included, looked at Anarchy with narrowed eyes. Was he making excuses for Trip?

"They grow out of it," he added.

My husband had not.

Grace took a deep, wet breath and straightened her spine.

"Not that hormones excuse anything. You're better off without him."

"Exactly what I've been telling her." Kim's eyes were no longer narrowed. They were wide. They sparkled. Her lips were parted. Anarchy had that effect on women.

"How did the party happen?" I asked.

It was Donna who answered me. "Trip called and said he was coming over with a couple of friends."

A couple of friends? He'd brought the entire high school. "And?"

"It just sort of happened." Donna lifted her hands then let them drop into her lap. "First it was a few kids, then the house was full."

"There's a keg in the kitchen." That spoke of planning.

All three girls shifted their gazes to their crossed legs.

"People were smoking."

Donna sealed her mouth. She had nothing more to say.

"They've probably blown the stereo speakers."

Kim covered her ears. Apparently she'd heard enough "Jungle Boogie" to last her a long time.

"And they converted the family room into some sort of love den."

Grace groaned and covered her eyes.

What a trio. Speak no evil, hear no evil, see no evil. Meanwhile, my downstairs looked like the remains of *The*

Towering Inferno.

Worse, my next-door neighbor, Margaret Hamilton, was probably toiling over a bubbling cauldron of ill will and hexes. The woman was a bona fide witch and the occasional goings on at my house were the bane of her witchy existence.

"Do you have any idea how many calls I'm going to get?"

Grace kept her eyes covered.

"Debbie and Peggy are downstairs picking up. I suggest you join them."

Now Grace opened her eyes. "But—"

"The best medicine for a broken heart is to stay busy."

"But—"

"No buts." I crossed my arms and tilted my chin.

The girls crawled off my bed and filed past me, the very pictures of remorse. First Donna, then Kim, then Grace.

Grace I stopped. "We need to have a long talk."

"I know, Mom." She sounded world-weary.

"Go help your friends. There's nothing that needs to be said that can't wait until tomorrow."

She shuffled into the hallway, leaving me alone with Max and Anarchy.

Max sidled over and apologized for getting on my bed by rubbing his head against my leg.

I forgave him and scratched behind his ear.

"Don't be too hard on her. These things get out of hand quickly."

"No boys in the house when I'm not here. It's a rule." Anarchy understood rules. Followed them.

He nodded and shifted his gaze from me to the rest of the room.

My mouth dried. Anarchy Jones was in my bedroom. No male, with the exception of Max, had entered this room in years.

"Pretty room," he said.

It was. There were delicate chairs that looked as if they might collapse if a man sat on them. There were delicate fabrics that looked as if they might snag on the rough pads of a man's fingers. There were delicate colors guaranteed to make a man itch for something bold and manly.

"You shared this room with Henry?"

I stared at the delicate carpet on the floor. "I redecorated after he moved to the bedroom down the hall."

"I see."

Anarchy was familiar with my late husband's foibles and failings. Now he was familiar with just how alone I'd been in my marriage. Henry had cared more for his whips and handcuffs and sex games with endless other women than he ever cared for me.

"Your husband really was a total idiot." Anarchy spoke with complete conviction.

I continued my study of the carpet.

"He had you." Anarchy stepped closer to me. "And he let you go."

My breath caught and my mind went blank. I couldn't have answered him even if I'd had something to say.

He stroked my cheek with the back of his hand, and I looked up into his coffee-brown eyes.

This was happening. Anarchy and I were alone in my bedroom.

"I—"

"Shhh." His voice was a whisper, as soft as his fingers against my skin, as gentle as the lips he pressed against mine.

Who was I to argue?

His arms brought me flush with his chest.

My fingers, quite of their own accord, tested the softness of his hair.

I may have moaned.

He may have moaned.

Max, who didn't approve of affection that wasn't directed his way, nudged my leg. That nudge was all it took to remind me there were five teenage girls in the house and possibly a boy with his head in a toilet.

I pulled away. Well, as much as the bonds of Anarchy's arms would let me. "Is that a gun in your pocket or are you just happy to see me?"

Oh good Lord. Had I said that aloud?

Anarchy's brown eyes twinkled. "I'm very—" he kissed me "—very happy to see you."

"Mooooooom." Grace's voice carried up the stairwell and into my bedroom. "We need you."

"I need you." There was a new roughness in Anarchy's tone.

I laughed. What else could I do? I was a middle-aged single mother, not the object of desire. Again, I pulled against his arms.

"She'll come up here and find us."

With seeming reluctance, he loosened his hold on me. "I get a do-over."

"A do-over?"

He nodded. "This isn't how I hoped tonight would end."

"We're alone in my bedroom."

Max yawned, an activity that included a yowling sound.

"We're not skipping steps, Ellison."

"Pardon me?"

"The next time we're alone in here it'll be because we can't wait another minute."

My skin, my pulse, my heart rate—they all plotted to prove that spontaneous combustion was a reality. "I'd better check on Grace," I croaked.

Anarchy's smile was amused, and knowing, and enough to curl my toes.

"Mom!" Grace's voice was louder—and pitched high enough to make Max cover his ears. "I think I found a body."

FOUR

Anarchy and I raced down the front stairs and found Grace and her friends jammed into the guest bathroom.

The young man who'd been puking up his guts lay on the floor.

My heart resumed beating. "He's just passed out." I crossed my fingers behind my back.

Anarchy pushed through the bevy of girls, knelt beside the boy, and searched for a pulse. "He's not dead."

I exhaled.

"But we need an ambulance."

Oh dear Lord. The child had alcohol poisoning from drinking at my house. "Grace, who is this?"

Rather than answer me, she glanced at her friends.

"Who?"

She shifted her weight and her gaze.

Anarchy removed a wallet from the boy's back pocket and pulled out a driver's license. "Sherman Westcott."

I collapsed against the door frame. "He's older than you." Grace, not Anarchy.

She nodded—a tiny jerk of her chin. "He's a senior." Her voice was as tiny as her nod.

I had to be sure. "This is our Sherman Westcott's son?"

"Yes. Everyone calls him Wes." Her voice was barely audible.

"Hold off on that ambulance," I said to Anarchy. "I'm going

to call his parents."

I trudged into the kitchen, pulled the Junior League directory out of a drawer, looked up Jeannie Westcott, and dialed.

The phone rang...and rang. Seven rings and then, "You've reached the Westcotts. Please leave your name and number at the beep and we'll call you back."

Beep.

"Jeannie, Sherman, this is Ellison Russell. The kids had a party while I was out tonight and your son drank too much. We're taking him to the hospital to have his stomach pumped. I'll call again as soon as I know more." I hung up and glared at the ceiling. Dammit. Wes's father, Sherman, managed the banks my husband had left to Grace. I needed Sherman Westcott. Grace needed Sherman Westcott. And we were taking his son to the hospital.

I returned to the powder room. "His parents weren't home. I left a message."

"He needs medical attention."

"I know. I said we were taking him to the hospital."

Sherman moaned.

"Do you want to drive him or should I call an ambulance?"

I considered. What was one more set of flashing lights in my front yard? Besides, young Wes was likely to throw up on the trip to the hospital. "Ambulance."

Anarchy stood. "I'll have one here in a few minutes."

I backed out of the bathroom and eyed the girls—six of them if one counted Dawn hovering nearby.

"You heard that?"

They nodded as one. Emphatically.

"I'm going to the hospital with Wes. When I get back I want every trace of this party erased from this house. Got it?"

Another group nod. This one with less enthusiasm.

Anarchy strode past us, disappearing through the front door. Presumably police dispatch could get an ambulance to my house quicker than a mere phone call.

The door opened almost immediately. "There's an ambulance here already." Anarchy stepped inside. "Some kid fell and hurt his ankle running down the driveway."

If I got through this night without being sued, it would be a miracle. "Is he okay?"

"Just a sprain." Anarchy edged past me into the half bath and hauled Wes off the floor. The boy was as limp and crumpled as linen on a hot, sweaty day.

Anarchy half-dragged him toward the front door.

I took one last look at the girls. "I mean it, every trace gone." Then I followed Anarchy and Wes out into the cold.

Dawn trailed after us.

Dammit. What was I going to do with her?

I stuck my head back inside. "Grace!"

"What, Mom?" She sounded properly contrite.

"Take Dawn home."

This directive was met with silence. Asking Grace to take home the girl with whom Trip had dallied was asking a lot. I didn't blame Grace for her silence, but I didn't have much choice.

"Just do it." I turned to Dawn. "Grace will take you home."

She crossed her arms over her chest. French nobles being led to the guillotine looked happier.

Two disgruntled teenagers. My work was done.

The EMTs loaded Wes into the ambulance and I climbed in behind them. The ride to the hospital was blessedly short, just long enough for the EMTs to take Wes's vitals and start a drip of some kind.

We arrived and they wheeled him away, leaving me to deal with the admitting nurse. I recognized her. She recognized me.

After all, I was a regular customer.

"Good evening, Mrs. Russell."

I peeked at her name badge. "Good evening, Mary."

She picked up a pencil. "Who brings you in this evening?"

"Sherman Westcott, Jr."

"Oh?"

"He's had too much to drink."

She looked up from her form. Drunkenness was a new reason for me to be at the hospital. "Parents' names?"

"Jeannie and Sherman Westcott." I glanced around the busy ER waiting room. "Senior."

"How much has he had to drink?"

"No idea."

Her lips thinned.

"Ellison!" The cry came from the entrance to the ER and was loud enough to turn heads. Certainly mine. Jeannie Westcott wore a mink coat, leather gloves, and a distraught expression.

Next to her, Sherman looked gray. New lines cut through his cheeks and the skin beneath his eyes sagged.

Jeannie rushed toward me. "How is Wes?"

"They just took him back."

"How could this happen? Wes has never been in any kind of trouble."

Sherman's eyes widened at his wife's statement.

"I have to see him." Jeannie rushed over to the admitting desk, leaving me with her husband.

"I'm sorry about this, Sherman. I went out for the evening and when I got home—" I pushed a stray hair away from my face "—there was a party."

"It's not your fault, Ellison. Don't give it another thought." He glanced around the waiting room. "Thank you for getting him help."

Unlike his wife, Sherman didn't seem worried.

"Has Wes done this before?"

Sherman answered with a grim nod. "His throat will be sore, but he'll be fine."

One would think that having one's stomach pumped once would be enough.

I stood next to Sherman and watched the anxious mother confer with the admitting nurse. Jeannie looked over her shoulder at us and beckoned her husband.

Sherman stepped toward his wife then stopped and looked at me. "I need to speak with you."

"Of course."

"It's about the bank." He sounded serious. Deadly serious.

My heart sank. Was he going to resign? "All right. Monday?"

"How about tomorrow?"

A banker who wanted to talk business on a Sunday? My heart took up residence next to my toes. "Fine. Do you want to come by the house? Say ten o'clock?"

Sherman nodded. "I'll be there." He glanced at his waiting wife. "I'll see you tomorrow."

I stopped him from walking away with a hand on his sleeve. "You're not leaving the bank?"

He barked a laugh. "Not unless you fire me."

That didn't sound good. "Wha—"

"Sherman!" Jeannie's hands were planted on her hips. Any moment now she'd start tapping her foot. "Are you coming?"

I released Sherman's arm. "Go. I'll see you tomorrow. I hope Wes is okay."

The exit beckoned. I gathered my coat around me, tightened my grip on my handbag, and walked toward the door.

Anarchy entered. "I'm sorry. It took forever to find a parking space."

"I wasn't sure you'd followed me."

His face broke into a grin. "Of course I followed you."

Looking at Anarchy made me feel marginally better. "Wes has been admitted and his parents are here."

"Do you want me to take you home?"

"Yes. Please."

This time, as we drove, I didn't worry about Grace or what was happening at my house. I worried about what kind of banking disaster would bring Sherman Westcott to my home on a Sunday.

Anarchy pulled up the drive and parked just a few feet from the front stoop. The flashing lights and scattering kids of our first arrival were gone. The beer cans were not. They glinted in the headlights.

He got out of the car, opened my door, and escorted me to the front door.

Thank you for a lovely evening didn't seem quite right. I swallowed. "Thank you. For dinner. For being here. For the ride home."

"Anytime." He dropped a kiss on my cheek and took a step back.

A kiss on the cheek? That was it? Then I saw the face pressed against one of the glass panels that flanked the front door. Not Grace's face. One of her friends. A lookout. I sighed. "I guess I'd better go in."

"I'll call you tomorrow."

I nodded, raised up on my toes, and kissed his cheek. The trace of a whisker tickled my lips. "Good night." I stepped inside.

The girls had been busy. A trash bag filled with God knew what sat next to the bombe chest. The rumbling of the attic fan told me the smoke-fouled air was being sucked from the house. A broom leaned against the bannister.

Max came forward to greet me. I scratched behind his ears.

"You're back quickly." Grace spoke from the kitchen hallway.

"Did you get Dawn home?"

She pursed her lips and offered a curt nod (shades of Mother). "Yes."

I glanced around the foyer and exhaustion settled onto my shoulders. "I'm going to bed."

"You're not going to help?"

I lifted my foot to the first tread. "This is one mess I didn't make."

"Moooom."

"Good night, Grace. We'll talk tomorrow."

She snapped her mouth closed.

Bed never felt so good. I slept like the dead, woke up at seven, and stumbled downstairs for my morning rendezvous with Mr. Coffee.

Max whined softly. I let him out into the backyard.

Eight bulging trash bags sat in a neat line on the back patio. Max stopped and smelled each one before heading into the grass.

Finished with his doggy business, he trotted back to the house and looked at me expectantly.

I handed over a biscuit. "There you go."

He took his prize to the corner and ate it with apparent relish.

"Good morning," I said to the coffee maker.

Mr. Coffee didn't answer. He was the strong silent type.

I filled his reservoir, scooped coffee, and waited for him to work his magic.

A cup of coffee could make the whole world look brighter. I took my mug and toured the house with Max at my heels. There were ring marks on multiple tables where Grace's guests had left sweating beer cans and plastic cups. The liquor cabinet was decimated. Someone had spilled a beer in the living room and a brewery stench filled the air. One of a pair of majolica candlesticks my grandparents bought on their honeymoon was broken. The giant stain on the couch in the family room didn't look as if it was coming out. Ever. And then there were the pants. Neatly-folded-over-the-back-of-a-chair pants. How-does-one-leave-a-party-without-their-pants pants.

I sighed, sipped my coffee, and reminded myself it could have been worse. The house didn't catch on fire. Wes Westcott managed to make it to the bathroom before he lost the contents of his stomach. No one died.

It was at moments like these that I actually missed my late husband. Not because I wanted his company (I didn't), but because being a single parent was hard. Henry at his worst had still been a decent father. He would have had opinions about Grace's punishment. Decided opinions.

Me? I had no idea how to handle her. There was no part of me that believed Grace had planned for last night's disaster. I blamed Trip Michaels. I bent and picked up an empty beer can peeking out from beneath the couch.

Grace knew darned good and well she wasn't allowed to have boys in the house when I wasn't home, but she'd welcomed Trip and his friends. What was the punishment for that?

I returned to the kitchen, tossed the empty can, and refilled my mug.

I could forbid her from seeing him, but I suspected (hoped) she was already through with the boy who'd used her house for a pubescent blowout then disappeared with another girl. I could ground her. I could take away her car. I could make her pay for the damage her guests had caused. All of the above?

Undecided, I trudged up the stairs and got ready for the day.

Sherman Westcott arrived at precisely ten o'clock. He was dressed for church in a gray suit, white shirt, and rep tie.

I wore jeans and a sweater.

"Coffee?" I asked.

"Please."

"How's Wes?" I led him toward the kitchen.

"He'll be fine. Thank you again for getting him to the hospital."

"I'm just glad he's all right." I poured coffee into a mug. "How do you take it?"

"Black."

I handed over his mug and settled onto a stool.

Sherman glanced at the open door to the back stairs. Bits and pieces of a conversation between Grace and one of her friends drifted down from the second floor. He took a sip of coffee, shifted his gaze to me, and cleared his throat. "This is a fairly delicate matter."

Oh dear Lord. "We can chat in the study."

He glanced again at the stairs. "I think that would be best."

Sherman followed me to the study.

I claimed the desk chair for two reasons. The first being that it loaned me some power. The second—well, Lord only knew what Trip and the girl he'd brought in here had been up to on the couch.

Sherman sat across from me. "There's a problem."

That I knew. I waited.

"It's about the Michaels' line of credit."

"Tom Michaels?"

He nodded. A serious nod. "The line is renewable."

Still I waited.

"It's a business line, but it's always been secured personally. When Tom's father was alive he pledged certificates of deposit as collateral. When he died, Tom's mother, Lorna, kept the arrangement in place." Sherman glanced at his lap. "Tom has been a customer for so long..."

At this rate, Sherman would still be telling the story tomorrow. "What has happened?"

"Mrs. Michaels—Lorna—has been cashing her CDs as they come due."

"So the secured line of credit is now unsecured?" Unfortunate, but not the end of the world. There had to be more.

"Tom hasn't made a payment in six months."

That gave me pause. "A principle payment?"

Sherman's skin looked grayer than ever. "No. Nor an interest payment."

"How big is Tom's line?"

A few seconds passed. Long seconds. Sherman glanced at his hands in his lap. He glanced at Henry's collection of Toby mugs. He glanced at the floor. "He owes us a million dollars plus interest."

I thudded my near empty mug onto Henry's blotter. Surely I'd misheard. Sherman had been mumbling. "One million? Dollars?" One million dollars was an enormous sum for an unsecured loan. "How much does Lorna have left in CDs?"

"Twenty thousand."

"Have you talked to Tom?"

Again Sherman's gaze wandered. He looked at anything but me. "He's not taking my calls."

"What about other assets in the bank? Checking? Savings?"

"The checking account is overdrawn and there isn't a savings account."

"How badly overdrawn?"

"Five thousand." For most people, that represented nearly half a year's pay.

I stared at him, gaping.

Sherman shook his head. "Mrs. Michaels always kept so much money in the bank we didn't worry. Her CDs—" he clenched his hands into fists "—renewed automatically."

"Until she moved the money." I planted my elbows on the desk and lowered my head to my hands. "Who released assets used as security on a loan?"

"One of the girls in the lobby. She didn't realize."

The bank didn't have girls in the lobby. Grown women sat behind desks and helped customers. But I wasn't about to split sexist hairs with Sherman or ask why in the devil someone hadn't checked with the loan department before giving Lorna her money. I'd do that later. I lifted my head. "Did Lorna say where she was moving the money?"

"No. She asked for cashier's checks made out to herself."

"Have the checks been cashed?"

"Not yet."

"What will happen to the bank if Tom defaults on the loan?"

Sherman bent his head. His skin was so gray and the lines in his face were etched so deeply that he looked like a concrete statue come to life. He lifted his hands from his lap then let them drop.

My heart dropped with his hands. "Are you telling me one bad loan could put us out of business?"

"There are others."

The coffee in my stomach gurgled, threatening to make a reappearance. I covered my mouth with my hand and closed my eyes. The bank was Grace's inheritance from her father. The bank represented dependability, safety, a solid rock amidst a stormy sea. The bank represented the way I wanted her to remember her father. She couldn't lose the bank. Could not.

"How?"

Sherman lifted and dropped his hands again.

"I mean it." My voice acquired a Mother-like edge. "How?"

Sherman's hands stilled and his Adam's apple bobbed. "We could weather the other loans."

"But Tom's is the straw?" The damned camel and its damned back.

Sherman nodded.

"This has been a problem for a while?" I demanded.

Another nod.

"Then why am I just finding out about it?"

Sherman leaned forward in his chair. "We didn't want to bother you."

I closed my eyes. Mainly to hide their I-could-lunge-across-the-desk-and-kill-you expression. "I'll call Tom today. And Lorna." The steady drumbeat of an impending headache whacked against my temples. "I want a list of every outstanding loan."

"Most of them are perfectly good credits." Now Sherman sounded defensive.

I opened my eyes. Narrowed my eyes.

He shifted in his chair.

"Every single loan, Sherman. Denote those that are past due for payments."

His face was shuttered and unhappy, but he nodded. A resentful nod, as if he didn't appreciate a woman telling him what to do.

"I want the list in my hands by six o'clock tonight."

"That might be a..." His voice petered out.

Perhaps the expression I allowed into my eyes stilled his tongue. It was one of Mother's best. It spoke of impending pain and suffering and icy fury. "Tonight. Six o'clock."

"Fine." He stood.

I did not. I regarded him from behind the massive expanse of Henry's desk. All that polished wood lent me power—no wonder Henry had liked having a desk the size of Rhode Island.

"Sherman."

"What?"

"Call a board meeting as soon as possible."

He paled. "Now, Ellison, if you'll call Tom, we can get this straightened out."

It was the verbal equivalent of a pat on the hand. Lord save me from patronizing men.

"Be that as it may, call the meeting. Or I will."

"Fine. I'll see myself out."

Probably just as well. Either anger or adrenaline had turned my knees to gelatin. I reached for the phone, heavy, black, and somehow reassuring. Tom probably had a perfectly reasonable explanation. My hand hovered above the receiver, and I remembered the sick look on Tom's face when Laurie offered to buy Kay Brookfield a new couch.

I couldn't imagine anything much worse than the bank going under. Was this the cause of the dread that had been following me around like a lost puppy? And yet, the sense that the other shoe had yet to drop wouldn't leave me. Something else was going to happen. I felt it in the air and my bones and the queasiness of my stomach.

I sat behind Henry's mammoth desk and stared at the wall.

Yes, the bank had made a mistake releasing the securities, but did we have legal recourse? I knew the man who'd have that answer. With fingers that felt heavier than lead, I dialed Hunter Tafft.

FIVE

I hung up the phone from calling Hunter and returned to the one man who was always available when I called. Mr. Coffee. My rock amidst a stormy sea.

But not even Mr. Coffee could stop Mother. She barged into the kitchen, kissed the air next to my cheek, asked for coffee, sniffed the cream before she poured, then stared out the window at the trash bags on the patio. "I've left complete instructions for my funeral."

"Pardon me?"

She turned her gaze from the trash to me. "The instructions are in the safe deposit box at the bank."

"What brought this on?" Why was she here? And still in her church clothes? A navy suit with a double row of brass buttons, a polka dot silk blouse with a bow at the neck, and sensible pumps.

"I served at Myra Whitcomb's funeral yesterday."

Ahhh. "You didn't approve?"

Mother sniffed. "'Nearer, My God, to Thee.'"

A stickler about hymns, that's Mother.

"Make sure the priest wears proper shoes."

As opposed to flip-flops?

"The priest yesterday wore Hush Puppies under his cassock."

She'd rendered me speechless.

"What's more—" she wagged a finger at me "—make

absolutely certain the priest is a man. You were traveling so you may have missed it, but the Episcopal Church ordained women priests in Philadelphia this summer. Lord only knows what's next."

Chaos, bedlam, a woman as president, her daughter dating a police detective. I swallowed. Hard. "Promise."

She lifted her coffee to her lips. "Services this morning sounded like a zoo."

I bit. "A zoo?"

"There was a child who sounded like an exotic bird. Another was growling. In my day, parents controlled their children. Especially at church."

As if I needed reminding. Mother had a way of grabbing unsuspecting shoulders (near the neck) with her talons (okay, nails) that could incapacitate a child without leaving a mark.

She sipped her coffee, wrinkled her nose, and put the cup back in the saucer. "How long has it been since I've seen you in church?"

"We go to different services." I made sure of that.

"Yes, well, one hears things."

That I knew all too well. Had she heard about my date with Anarchy?

I braced myself. My hands gripped the edge of the counter. My toes curled around the rung of the stool. Tension tightened every muscle from my neck to the tendons in my heel. I was not in the mood for a lecture about men.

"I understand Grace had a party last night."

"She did." My neck relaxed ever so slightly. It had to. If it didn't, it would snap.

"I also hear she's dating Lorna's grandson."

I made a noncommittal sound and studied a spot on the countertop.

"Watch out for that boy."

The tension returned. "Why?"

"One hears things," she said airily. Mother was never airy.

"What things?" I demanded.

"Things, Ellison." Her eyes flashed. Apparently she didn't appreciate my tone.

"Does Lorna know about these things?"

Mother pursed her lips. "I never raised boys."

I was aware. I'd been there. "That doesn't answer my question."

"Boys are different."

There was an understatement. Unbidden, the lyrics of a song popular a few years ago popped into my mind. Something about boys taking rich girls out to dinner and doing whatever they wanted with poor girls.

"Mother, I have to ask you something, but I need you to keep it to yourself."

"Of course, dear." She sounded airy again.

I reached out and wrapped my hand around her wrist. "This is serious."

Her gaze traveled from my hand on her arm to my face. She paled. "Did that no-good boy get Grace in trouble?" "Trouble" she whispered, as if even the euphemism was too awful to say at full voice.

"No! Of course not."

Color returned to her cheeks.

"I think she broke up with him." I hoped she'd broken up with him. "This is about Tom."

"Tom?"

"Lorna's son. Trip's father."

"I know who Tom is, Ellison."

"He owes the bank a lot of money." I half-hoped she'd tell me not to worry. That the Michaels had more money than God.

She didn't. She paled again. "How much?"

"More than a million."

Mother held her hand over her heart. "Do you have collateral?"

"We did."

"Did?"

"Lorna's certificates of deposit. But one of the women in the lobby cashed them."

With her hand still on her heart, Mother stared into her coffee cup. A moment passed. She lifted her head, her expression grim. "You need collateral for that loan."

My right hand mirrored Mother's. It clamped against my heart. As if a mere hand could keep my heart from plummeting to my ankles. Although both my heart and my ankles should be used to the sensation by now. "What do you know?"

"I know Laurie spends faster than Tom can make. Lorna told me. He's been to her for money."

"And?"

"She helped him the first time." Mother gave up on her heart and pinched the bridge of her nose. "And the second. Now, she's cut him off."

We sat. Quiet. Silenced by possible repercussions.

Mother stirred first. "Your father will know what to do."

By all means, we should call a man in to solve the problem. A man had caused the problem.

Then again, who was I to throw stones (even silent ones) at Mother's suggestion? I'd called Hunter Tafft. His machine had answered and I'd hung up. If the man himself had picked up the phone, I'd have spilled my guts and begged for help.

"I'm going to talk to Tom." Resolute. Confident. That was me. Not. "Will you talk to Lorna?"

"What exactly are you going to say to Tom?"

"I'll ask for other collateral. His house."

"Mortgaged to the hilt. Lorna told me."

Dammit. "Surely he has other assets."

Mother shook her head, as cheerful as the Grim Reaper. "What do you want me to say to Lorna?"

"Those CDs were pledged. If necessary, the bank will sue."

"You want me to tell my oldest friend that my daughter is going to sue her? Lorna's like a sister to me. Closer than Sis." Mother and her real sister had been estranged for years. Their rapprochement was of recent vintage. "Do you remember when you kids were children? Lorna and I hoped that either you or Marjorie would marry Tom."

How could I forget? I cringed even now.

"And then—" A cloud darkened Mother's expression.

"And then?"

"And then I found Tom filling a flask with your father's good scotch." She adjusted her already straight shoulders. "I can't abide sneaky."

I'd spent most of my life thinking Mother gave up on the Tom and Ellison dream because it embarrassed me.

"At any rate," Mother continued, "Tom's behavior never affected how I felt about Lorna. She's been with me through thick and thin."

"Thin?"

"Every marriage has its challenges."

What?

"And then there's your sister's husband. That was a blow." Mother's face took on a stony quality—like Mount Rushmore but harder. "Not to mention you and all your bodies."

I held the pads of my fingers against my eyelids and pressed. "Can we get back to the bank?"

"How did this happen?" There was the tone I'd been waiting for. The accusatory one.

"I don't know."

"Why did you give Sherman Westcott the authority to loan

so much money?"

"I didn't. This is Henry's mess." I opened my eyes. Across from me, Mother opened her mouth and closed it. Twice. Three times. A fish deprived of water. A woman deprived of her belief that men were better at running things.

She recovered quickly. "As soon as your father gets back from the club, I'm going to tell him everything. He'll know what to do."

We were back to depending on a man to save us—save me.

In a surprise move, Mother reached across the space that divided us and took my hands in hers. "What happens if he defaults?"

"The bank could go under."

She paled still further, her skin turning the shade of cauliflower or maybe a virgin golf ball.

"Grace and I would be fine, but—" my voice caught "—the bank is her inheritance from her father. I'd hate for her to lose it."

Mother squeezed. A reassuring squeeze. "Then she won't." She spoke with total authority. Lending laws, federal bank examiners, Tom's fecklessness, Sherman Westcott's poor management—none of it mattered. Mother had issued a decree.

And somehow, I felt better.

"Talk to Tom," Mother instructed. "If that doesn't work I'll talk to Lorna."

It was almost a plan.

The lump in my throat made answering her an impossibility. I nodded.

"In the meantime, I'll talk to your father and you—" her grip on my hands tightened "—you should call Hunter."

I nodded, but I couldn't call him again. That I'd dialed his number the first time spoke of my desperation. *Hello, Hunter. This is Ellison. I know I rejected you, but now I need your help.*

But now we had a plan. Calling Hunter a second time was a last resort.

Mother finished her coffee, patted me on the back, and left.

I poured myself more coffee and stared at the phone. Sixty seconds ticked by on the kitchen clock before I reached for the receiver. I did not dial Hunter Tafft.

Tom Michaels proved to be an expert at ducking my calls. No one answered his home phone. Not all day Sunday. Not Sunday evening. Not early Monday morning.

I called his office. "May I please speak to Tom Michaels?"

"Mr. Michaels is out of the office today. May I take a message?"

"This is Ellison Russell calling. It's urgent that I speak with him."

"If he checks in, I'll be happy to give him the message."

I gave the receptionist my phone number and hung up, more on edge than I ever imagined possible. Not even a fresh cup of heaven, courtesy of Mr. Coffee, helped. Instead, I sat, stared into my cup, and stewed.

Brnng, brnng.

I lunged for the phone. "Hello."

"Ellison?" The voice did not belong to Tom Michaels.

I swallowed my disappointment with a sip of coffee.

"It's Daisy."

"Good morning."

"Did I catch you at a bad time?"

I forced a smile into my voice. "Of course not." Yes! "How are you?"

"Fine, but I can't meet with the chef tomorrow after bridge."

Why was she telling—oh. "Libba's birthday party."

"Can you come on Wednesday morning? I'm happy to call and change the appointment." Better her than me. This was the third time she'd rescheduled and the chef at the club thought of himself as an artist, not an employee. He wouldn't be pleased.

"No problem."

"Thank you. I have a parent-teacher conference tomorrow."

"I thought those were earlier in the year."

"They were. This one is impromptu."

Daisy had more children than the old woman who lived in the shoe. Her life was a round-robin of carpools, conferences, pediatrician appointments, and unscheduled visits to the principal's office.

"Wednesday is..." My voice trailed off. "Wednesday is fine. Is Laurie still subbing for Jinx tomorrow?"

"As far as I know. Why?"

"I have a question for Tom and I've been unable to reach him. I thought maybe they were out of town."

"No," said Daisy. "I saw them last night."

"Where?"

"Nabil's."

How lovely for them. While I'd been home worrying about Sherman's failure to bring me the files, they'd been sipping cocktails. While I'd been pushing a piece of grilled chicken around with my fork because my stomach was too knotted to eat a single bite, they'd devoured a delicious meal. At a nice restaurant. Where they'd spent more of the bank's money.

"They were there with Lorna."

Hopefully Lorna had bought their dinners. "Oh?"

"They all looked—" She searched for a word.

I wrapped the phone cord around my little finger and waited. And waited. "They all looked?"

"Tense," she replied. "Or angry. No. Both. They looked tense and angry."

Lorna being angry at her son was not good news for me. "Angry?"

"Definitely. Laurie didn't table hop or anything. Not like she usually does. She—" another pause while she searched for a word "—glowered."

"At Tom or Lorna?"

"At both of them. Oh my gosh! Is that the time? I've got to go. My errand list is three miles long."

We said goodbye and hung up.

I poured myself still more coffee and resumed my staring. Unfortunately, there were no solutions to be had in my coffee mug. I looked up when Aggie, my housekeeper, bustled into the kitchen. She carried a bucket of cleaning supplies in one hand and an empty liquor bottle in the other. She held up the bottle. "This was stuffed under the cushions on the couch."

I couldn't manage the energy for ire. I simply shook my head.

"You look like your dog died."

My dog, who was sprawled in a patch of sunlight, lifted his head from his paws, proving he was very much alive.

"Did you find a body I don't know about?" She rinsed the bottle and threw it in the trash.

"No."

"Then what?" Aggie's late husband was a private investigator. She assisted him with his cases. The experience had left her ever inquisitive.

The seed of an idea sprouted.

Aggie stowed the bucket of cleaning supplies in the closet. "You're looking at me like I'm Red Riding Hood and you're the Big Bad Wolf." She was wearing a crimson caftan. And she had skills I needed.

I rubbed the hungry expression away with the back of my hand.

Aggie sashayed up to Mr. Coffee, borrowed his pot, and refilled my mug. "What is it?"

"I have a problem."

She poured herself a cup of coffee. "That much is obvious." With a sigh, she settled herself onto one of the stools at the counter and rubbed her lower back. "How can I help?"

"There's a customer at the bank to whom we've lent a great deal of money."

Her bright eyes narrowed slightly, but she remained silent, waiting for me to continue.

"I'd like to know what he's done with our money."

"Didn't he have to tell you that before you loaned it to him?"

She was right. The very first thing I should have done was call Sherman and demand the files. I stood so abruptly I upended my stool.

My fingers flew around the phone dial.

A receptionist answered the phone. "First Missouri Bank. How may I help you?"

"Sherman Westcott, please."

"I'm sorry. Mr. Westcott is in a meeting."

"This is Ellison Russell calling."

"May I take a message, Miss Russell?"

"No. You can interrupt him."

"I'm sorry, ma'am, but...oh. Mrs. Russell?"

"Yes."

"Please hold."

I glanced over at Aggie in her caftan. If I tried to clean house in a caftan, I'd drag the sleeves through furniture polish or catch the hem in the vacuum. Not Aggie. Her caftan was pristine.

"Hello." Sherman sounded harried and annoyed, as if I'd just pulled him away from something important.

"Good morning, Sherman. You didn't bring the files."

"They were locked up. I couldn't get them."

"I presume you can get them today. I want them all by the end of the day, and I want someone to bring the Michaels' loan file to my house immediately."

He cleared his throat, a patronizing sound. "Now, Ellison—"

"Send the file, Sherman."

"That's not how we do things—"

I channeled Mother. I channeled the Rhode Island desk. I channeled the successful artist who knew her stuff. "I decide how the bank does things. I expect the file to be here within thirty minutes." Then I hung up.

The file arrived twenty-five minutes later.

Aggie and I opened the thick manila folder together. Immediately numbers started running together like watercolors in the rain. I blinked. Narrowed my eyes. Rubbed my forehead.

"I'll review this and tell you what's in it," said Aggie. Amusement shaded her voice.

She didn't need to tell me twice.

Unfortunately, my ability to pay attention to anything else had shrunk to nothing. I picked up the newspaper and scanned the headlines without reading them. I sat at the counter and fidgeted like a five-year-old in church. I stood and peered out the window at the backyard.

"Why don't you take Max for a walk?" Annoyance replaced amusement in Aggie's voice.

Max, hearing his name and "walk" in the same sentence, yawned, stretched, and looked at me expectantly.

"Fine." I snapped a leash onto his collar and put on a coat and gloves.

We made it to the bottom of the driveway.

"Mrs. Russell." The voice was somehow both strident and creaky. Just what you'd expect of a witch.

I turned. "Mrs. Hamilton." Margaret Hamilton and I had lived next to each other for nearly a decade. We were not yet on a first-name basis.

"I believe you owe me an apology."

She was right.

"I'm terribly sorry about the party Grace hosted. She did not have my blessing."

Her mouth opened slightly and she stared, as if she couldn't believe she'd extracted an apology without hexing me first.

"If there was any damage to your property, we'll reimburse you."

"Tituba was traumatized."

Tituba was a cat.

"So was I. I'm sure both Tituba and I will recover without any long-term effects."

Max growled. He didn't like Margaret Hamilton and all this talk of her cat was upsetting him.

"If you'll excuse me, Max needs his daily constitutional."

She sniffed. "Tell that boy to keep his car off my lawn."

"What boy?" Heart. Ankles. This had to stop.

Her smile was almost gleeful. Definitely gleeful. With a side of malice. "The one who snuck into your house at eleven o'clock last night."

SIX

"What do you have to say for yourself?" I'd been sitting, waiting, stewing at the kitchen island for hours.

Grace dropped her backpack to the kitchen floor and regarded me with a Mom-belongs-in-a-mental-institution expression. "What are you talking about?"

My hands tightened to fists. Tight fists. My nails cut crescents into my skin. "You know exactly what I'm talking about."

"No, Mom. I don't." She used an eye roll for punctuation.

"Who was over here last night?"

"Oh." More of an exhalation than an actual word. "That."

"That." I forced my fingers apart. "Who?"

"Do you want some coffee? Can I make you some coffee?"

As if I could be deterred with a wonderful, rejuvenating, delicious, steaming cup of..."No." Besides, I'd had plenty of coffee. If the shaking in my hands was any indication, I might—maybe—have had too much. "Who was here?"

Grace's arms crossed over her chest and she gazed at the floor. "Trip."

"Trip?" The pitch of my voice was high enough to disturb Max's nap. He gave me a baleful stare then ambled off to find a patch of sunlight.

We watched him go.

One, two, three, four—someone once told me to count to ten when I was angry—five, six. "I cannot believe you let that boy back in our house. Not after the way he treated you."

"He came over to apologize."

"Words."

Grace's eyes narrowed. "Pardon me?"

"Words. It's easy to apologize when the mess is cleaned up, when the girl in the study...What was her name?"

"Dawn," Grace supplied, her eyes mere slits.

"It's easy to apologize when Dawn's not around. It's easy to apologize when—"

"I get it." She raised her hands as if to ward me off, as if I was being unreasonable. "You don't like Trip."

"I don't like the way he treated you." Nor did I like that his father's misfeasance might cost Grace her father's bank.

"He's sorry about Saturday night. He told me."

"What about Dawn?"

She blinked. A slow blink. "What about her?"

"He cares about you, but he used her for—" I had to say it "—sex. What about her? I guarantee you that girl has feelings for him. I saw the way she looked at him. He took advantage of her."

"She let him!"

"She loves him. What did she say to you when you took her home?"

"We didn't talk. She was crying."

"Told you so."

If Grace's expression was any indication, she didn't like hearing "told you so" from me any more than I liked hearing it from Mother. "He broke up with her. Why are her feelings my problem?"

"They're your problem because she's going to be available every time you say no to him. You deserve a young man who won't cheat on you."

She combined an eye roll and a head shake. Paired that

way, they communicated clearly: I had zero idea what I was talking about. "You don't understand," she insisted. "Things are different than when you were young."

"I recall saying the exact same thing to your grandmother when I was your age."

"Doesn't make it any less true."

"Nor does it make my point less valid."

"What is your point?"

"Trip Michaels is a boy who can't be trusted. He does what he wants without thought for the feelings of others. And you are better off without him."

"Are you forbidding me from seeing him?

And make him ten million times more attractive? "No, but I trust you to look at this situation with clear eyes. If you do, if you judge Trip by his actions, you'll see the same things I do."

"That he's no good?" Yet another eye roll. This one with more feeling. "Fine, Mom. Whatever you say."

"Also, you're grounded." I crossed my arms. "And you can forget about the ski trip in December. I'm canceling the reservations."

She bent, grabbed her backpack strap, and hefted the bag off the floor. "Whatever."

She tromped up the backstairs, each heavy fall of each foot expressing her extreme displeasure.

Aggie peeked her head around the door to the hallway and grimaced. "I didn't mean to eavesdrop."

"I handled that all wrong."

"I don't think there's a right way to tell a woman, no matter her age, that the man she's with is no good."

I planted my elbows on the counter and dropped my head into my hands.

"You can't keep her from getting her heart broken."

"She's had such a hard year." Losing her father, bodies

turning up at our home, family revelations. Now Trip. "I wish she could see what I see."

"What I see is a girl who's strong enough to withstand a knock or two. Grace will be fine no matter what she decides."

I raised my head and offered Aggie a grateful smile.

"I finished with the file."

The file. My other enormous problem. "And?"

"And either someone at the bank wasn't doing their homework or—" Aggie bit her lip and shifted her gaze away from me. "They loaned Tom $25,000 for a piece of equipment that cost less than a thousand. More than once."

Fraud.

"Who was the loan officer?"

Aggie's cheeks flamed as crimson as her caftan. "Your late husband."

There was only one explanation. Tom and Henry had some sort of shady deal going. Sometimes I wished Henry was still alive—so I could kill him myself.

"I'm going over there." I had to do something. Waiting by the phone for a call that didn't come was getting me nowhere.

"Over where?" asked Aggie.

"To the Michaels'."

"Do you think they'll talk to you?"

Probably not, but I needed to do something. Driving to the Michaels' was exactly that. "Maybe."

She nodded. "I may be late tomorrow morning. I plan on swinging by Tom Michaels' business and doing a little snooping."

One wouldn't think of "Aggie" and "snoop" together. Not with her sproingy hair and crimson caftan. Maybe that was why she was so good at being sneaky—she was so obvious no one could believe she was up to anything.

"Be careful." I grabbed my handbag and a coat.

"I will. Promise."

The drive to the Michaels' wasn't even long enough for the car to warm up. I parked at the curb and looked up and down the street. Empty except for a red Volkswagen Karmann Ghia. Unfortunately, the Michaels' driveway was empty as well.

I got out of the car and hurried up the front walk, the wind whipping my hair.

The front door was large and solid and very much closed. I rang the bell and waited.

And waited.

"They won't answer."

I leapt out of my boots.

Dawn, the girl I'd caught with Trip in Henry's study, stood behind me. Her hands were jammed in her coat pockets and her nose was red from the cold. "They just won't."

"They're home?"

"I saw Mrs. Michaels drive in a little while ago."

I poked at the bell a second time.

Dawn stood at my shoulder, her breath a cloud at the corner of my vision. "They might answer if I go away."

I wrapped my head around the idea that Laurie Michaels had let Dawn stand out in the cold. Actually, it wasn't that surprising.

Maybe Dawn's nose was red from crying.

"You stay right here." I jabbed at the bell a third time.

The front door stayed resolutely shut.

"I just need to talk to him." Using the back of her mitten, she wiped at her eyes. The rims were as red as her nose and her lashes were spiky. She had been crying.

How could Laurie leave a crying child alone on her front stoop?

"Let's go sit in my car for a minute. You can get warm." I waved toward the Triumph waiting for me at the curb. Not that my car was warm, but it would be out of the wind and I could listen to her.

She nodded. "Okay."

We climbed into the car and I turned on the engine. "It heats up fast."

Dawn's body was angled away from me, toward the Michaels' front door. She made no comment.

Cold air blasted from the vents.

I stared out the windshield at the empty street with its stately homes, denuded trees, and dormant lawns. "Did you and Trip date for a long time?"

"Long enough." Dawn sounded as jaded and cynical as Libba after a bad breakup. A sixteen-year-old girl had no business sounding like that. A single tear tracked down her cheek. "He's not a good guy. I know that. I just need him..." She dropped her face to her hands and fell silent. When she lifted her head, she did it slowly, as if it weighed two tons. She stared out the window at the Michaels' home. "I need him to tell me that I mattered. That we mattered." She swallowed something that sounded suspiciously like a sob and her chest heaved. Her left hand pressed against her throat. Her right opened the car door. "Thank you, Mrs. Russell. I'm going home now."

Dawn walked to her car with her shoulders slumped. The wind tugged at her hair and the hem of her coat. The elms towered above her. She looked small, and cold, and on the verge of breaking.

Poor kid.

I stayed up all night worrying about the inheritance of a girl who wasn't speaking to me. Her sole form of communication was eye rolls. And, wow, did those eye rolls communicate. I was unreasonable. And lame. And not worthy of her teenage bon mots.

Grace left for school in a flurry of injured silence, slammed doors, and yet another eye roll.

I sat down for some one-on-one time with Mr. Coffee. I needed him. My brain ached with the gritty nails-on-a-chalkboard feeling that followed a sleepless night.

With my fingers wrapped around a mug, I took stock.

Members of the Michaels family remained elusive. I had my doubts about Laurie showing up for bridge.

Until I talked to Tom, Mother wouldn't talk to Lorna.

Grace was furious.

Aggie, God love her, was off snooping.

And Anarchy hadn't called me in two days.

I poured myself a second cup. "What would you do?" I asked Mr. Coffee.

Mr. Coffee said nothing, but Max whined softly.

I crouched next to him and wrapped my arms around his neck. "You still love me, don't you, boy?"

He pulled free of my embrace and shook his head until his ears whapped against the side of his head.

No love.

With a sigh and a third cup of coffee, I climbed the stairs and got ready for bridge.

I arrived at the club early and was immediately waylaid by Jenny Woods. "Ellison," she whispered. "You must tell me what happened Friday night."

Friday night? Friday night. The fire. Why was she whispering? And why was she asking? She'd been there.

"Prudence Davies and Laurie Michaels got into an argument and Prudence dropped her cigarette on the couch."

"What was the argument about? I've heard conflicting stories."

The decibels had surpassed a jackhammer's. The

Brookfields' next-door neighbors had probably heard Laurie accuse Prudence of sleeping with her husband.

"Laurie thought that Tom and Prudence were—"

Her eyes widened and she held up her hand. "Tom and Prudence? Seriously?"

"Prudence did deny it."

"I can't believe Laurie would think that Tom—" Jenny rubbed her chin and shuddered "—with Prudence." She shook her head as if shaking off an unpleasant thought. "Are you here for bridge?"

"I am."

"How's Jinx? I heard her health has been poor."

I searched Jenny's face for any hint that she was taking joy in Jinx's troubles and found none. The question was sincere. "Jinx is on the mend. I imagine she'll be back soon."

"That's good news."

"Ellison!" Libba's voice carried down the hallway.

Hollering like a pig farmer in the halls at the club being frowned upon, I replied with a properly quiet wave.

The click-clack of Libba's heels on the wood floor made further conversation impossible. We waited.

Libba kissed the air next to Jenny's cheek. "What a delicious sweater."

"This old thing?" Jenny smoothed the ribbing at her waist.

"The color is divine," Libba insisted. "It brings out your eyes."

"Thank you. I'll wear it more often."

Libba turned her attention to me. "I saw Daisy in the parking lot. She's actually on time."

"Good. Did you see Laurie?"

"She's riding with Daisy."

That was a surprise. I'd been certain Laurie would stand us up.

Jenny glanced at her watch. "Listen, I've got to run. It's wonderful to see you both. Drinks soon?"

"Absolutely." Libba never turned down a drink.

"Hope you both have good cards." Jenny kissed the air next to our faces then hurried down the hall.

Libba and I followed at a more sedate pace.

"Jenny really does look fabulous." Libba nodded sagely. "I bet there are a lot of worried wives."

Jenny was that rare divorcée who'd come out of her marriage with enough money to pay the club bill. No spritzing perfume or hunting and pecking on a typewriter for a paycheck for her. She spent her days playing tennis and golf and bridge and doing good works. Just like when she was married. But without a husband.

"I never saw Jenny as an adulteress."

"You never see anyone as an adulteress."

I couldn't argue Libba's point, so I changed the subject. "I'm glad Laurie showed up."

"You had your doubts?"

"I've been trying to reach her for days."

"Oh?" Libba raised an interested brow.

The walls had ears. "I'll tell you later."

We claimed our usual seats at the card table.

I picked up a deck and shuffled, suddenly nervous. What was I going to say?

Daisy and Laurie breezed in. Well, Daisy breezed. Laurie followed her. She looked like a washed-out version of herself. To be fair, no one looked good in orange.

Daisy took her usual chair.

Laurie lowered herself into Jinx's spot. "Thank you for letting me join you."

"We're glad to see you." It was God's truth. I'd been looking for a member of the Michaels family (anyone but Trip) for two days.

I fanned the deck across the table and we drew for deal.

"Ellison." Daisy held up a three of clubs. "You look pale. Are you feeling all right?"

"Fine."

"Are you sure? There's something going round the kids' school."

There was always something going round her kids' school. That was the nature of cold weather, lots of kids, and lots of germs.

I turned over the jack of hearts. "I'm fine. But thanks for asking."

Libba drew the ace of diamonds.

Laurie's hand ventured into the deck and pulled the eight of spades.

"My deal," said Libba. "Who wants to keep score?"

"I will." Laurie and I spoke at the same time.

She giggled. A nervous sound. "I'm sure you're better at numbers than I am."

I was sure of that too.

I claimed the pad and a short pencil with a lethal tip.

"Shall we say a penny a point?" Laurie asked.

Daisy, Libba, and I stared at her. Gaped.

"We don't play for money," said Libba. She turned the word "money" into something soiled. Something she wouldn't touch without gloves.

"Then what do you play for?" Laurie's expression belonged to a child denied a trip to the ice-cream shop.

"Glory," I replied. Any pennies Laurie had should be directed to the bank, not a bridge kitty. "I've left several messages for Tom."

"Oh?" Now Laurie was the pale one.

Libba pushed the deck toward her. "Do you want to cut?"

Laurie took a few cards off the top and put them on the table.

"He hasn't returned my calls."

Tom's wife inspected her manicure. "He's terribly busy."

"Is he?" I desperately wanted to demand answers. Sharp words took up residence on the tip of my tongue. But the bank's other customers—the ones who actually paid off their loans— might not appreciate hearing that I was discussing private banking business over the bridge table. "Business must be good." Sharp words ceded to a sharp tone.

Her gaze remained fixed on her hands. "It is. Never better."

Liar, liar, pants on fire.

I picked up my cards. "I really do need to speak with Tom. Do you suppose I could stop by the house this evening?"

Across from me, Libba raised her brows.

If Daisy thought my request was odd, she didn't react. She was too busy arranging the cards in her hand, her brow slightly furrowed and her tongue caught between her teeth.

Laurie fanned her unexamined cards then snapped them shut. "Tonight is no good. We have plans. You should call his office."

"I have."

"I don't know what to tell you."

"Perhaps we could call him together. From here. Wives always get put through."

Daisy nodded her agreement and moved a card from the far left to the far right of her hand.

"Maybe that's how things worked for you and Henry, but Tom gets so wrapped up...I'm sure he'll get back to you as soon as he has time." Her voice had an edge to it. The kind of edge usually reserved for a determined toddler who has asked for a cookie seventy times in a row.

"So—" Daisy looked up from her cards and smiled. An

encouraging, can't-we-all-get-along smile. "I heard Grace had a party."

"It was an impromptu affair." I slid my gaze toward Laurie, who was arranging cards as if her life depended on it. "A boy she was dating invited over a few friends."

"Was dating?" An amused smile flitted across Libba's face. "Did you tell her she couldn't see him anymore?"

"Not at all. He disappeared into Henry's study with another girl."

"Who?" asked Daisy.

Laurie stared at her cards as if her life depended on the hearts and spades in her hand.

I turned my gaze to Daisy. "His ex-girlfriend. Her name is Dawn."

Laurie dropped her cards.

"Laurie," the concern in Daisy's voice was genuine, "are you all right?"

"I don't feel well." Her skin had turned a delicate shade of celadon. "Maybe I should go home."

"Seriously?" Libba loved bridge and we hadn't even played a hand.

Daisy hurried round to Laurie's side of the table and helped her from her chair.

"I hope you feel better," I said. "Please have Tom call me."

Laurie responded with a weak wave. "I will. Thank you."

Daisy and Laurie disappeared down the hallway, shuffling as if Laurie was knocking on death's door.

When they were out of hearing range, Libba leaned toward me. "Do you want to tell me what the hell is going on?"

"It's bad."

"Bad enough for Laurie to fake an illness?"

"I guess so." I squeezed my eyes shut and found Laurie's slumped shoulders and pathetic shuffle burned on the back of my eyelids. Somewhere, deep in my gut, the feeling that Disaster! approached took hold.

SEVEN

Brnng, brnng.

My hand snaked out from under the covers and reached for the phone. "Ellghah." Hello.

"Mrs. Russell, it's Peggy calling. May I please speak to Grace?"

"Peggy, do you have any idea what time it is?" I didn't. I cracked an eyelid and peered at the clock next to my bed. "It's five in the morning."

"I know. I'm sorry." She sounded beyond sorry. She sounded miserable. "I wouldn't call if it weren't important. This is an emergency." Peggy was one of the level-headed friends. Emergencies for her constituted more than whether to wear the flowered or plaid blouse to school. Something had happened.

"Jussaminn." Just a minute.

I left the embrace of my warm bed, where dreams of Anarchy kissing me still lingered, and staggered down the hall to Grace's bedroom. The door was cracked open, so I poked my head inside. "Grace, Peggy is on the phone for you."

"Ellghah." The way the lump under the covers said "Ellghah," I doubted she meant hello. "Garray."

"Garray?"

"Go away."

My daughter, the morning person.

"Should I tell Peggy you'll call her back?"

An arm extended from under the covers. A hand tightened

around the receiver of the princess phone. The receiver disappeared under the covers.

I returned to my room and picked up the phone.

"That can't be true." Grace's voice was still sleep-filled. Sleep-filled with an edge of disbelief.

"I swear to God."

What truth had Peggy discovered at five in the morning that couldn't wait till school? I hung up the phone. Grace was already mad at me. If she caught me eavesdropping, her face might melt.

I crawled back into bed. Sadly, both the warmth and the dreams of Anarchy's kisses had dissipated. As had my ability to sleep. I flipped on the light. On my bedside table rested a copy of *Tinker, Tailor, Soldier, Spy*, but I didn't possess the concentration needed to follow Le Carre down his rabbit holes. I reached for a sketchbook and pencil instead.

The gentle friction of charcoal on paper soothed some of my worry. That first dark line could be anything. A face, a bank building, a bridge table. I got to decide. I smiled at the paper and added a second line.

"Mom?" Grace stood in the doorway with tears streaming down her cheeks.

I dropped the pad but not the charcoal pencil—charcoal is hell to get out of sheets. The pencil I put down on the table. "Honey, what is it?"

"It's...it's...it's—" A sob stopped her. "Mommy."

I opened my arms and she ran into them as if she were still five years old and a hug from her mother could solve all her problems.

I squeezed my arms around her, wishing I could solve all her problems. "What is it?"

Her body shook and her tears drenched the shoulder of my nightgown. "I—" hiccup "—I—it's my fa-a-a-ault."

What could be so awful? I stroked her hair. "Honey, what's happened?"

"D-d-d-d—"

I rubbed circles on her back, the flannel of her Lanz nightgown warming beneath my hand. "Just calm down. Whatever it is, it'll be okay."

"No." She sucked an enormous amount of air into her lungs then expelled a ragged breath. "It won't."

"Grace, what happened?"

"Dawn."

"Dawn?" Now that Congress had finally shifted the country out of daylight savings, dawn appeared around seven.

Grace pulled away from me and sank her head into her hands. "She tried to kill herself."

Dawn.

"It's my fault."

"No, it's not." The words rushed from my lips.

"It is," she insisted. "I was really mean to her."

"It's not your fault." A mother's knee-jerk reaction.

"How do you know?" Her voice cracked.

I didn't. Not for certain. "I just know. What happened? Is she all right?"

More tears ran down Grace's cheeks. "An ambulance took her to the hospital. I have to go see her. I have to apologize."

Dread nipped at my heels. "What did you say to her?"

A tremor seized Grace's body. Her head shook. Her torso shook. Her hands shook.

"What did you say?" My voice was sharper than it should have been.

"Nothing."

"Nothing as in nothing, or nothing as in you're not going to tell me?"

"Nothing. I didn't speak to her." She directed her wet gaze

to her lap. "And I made sure no one else did either."

So Dawn had been ostracized. By my daughter. "Grace." Disappointment crept into my tone. And my heart.

Grace must have heard it. A fresh round of sobs racked her slender body. I hardened my heart and let her cry.

"She shouldn't have gone off with Trip." Grace sounded defensive.

There was no tip-toeing around Grace's feelings. Not if she was blaming Dawn. "Grace—"

"I know, Mom." A hint of attitude, the verbal equivalent of an eye roll, made her lengthen "Mom." "I shouldn't have made her feel isolated. I was wrong." An enormous tear plopped onto my comforter. One hundred thirty-seven more followed. "I am so, so sorry."

Max ambled over to the bed, rested his head on the edge of the mattress, and regarded Grace with worried amber eyes.

I shared his worry.

"You're right. You do need to apologize to Dawn." I brushed the back of my hand against her damp cheek. "I'll go to the hospital with you."

"You will?" She lifted her gaze from the soaked comforter.

"Of course I will. I'm supposed to be at the club at nine. It won't take long." I pulled a tissue from the box next to my bed and handed it to her. "When I get home, we'll go. We'll stop and buy flowers on the way."

She blew her nose and crumpled the used tissue in her hand. "What about school?"

"I'll call you out." Hanging around with a bunch of emotional girls wouldn't help Grace one bit.

"Really?" Her voice sounded more alive.

"Really."

That earned me another hug.

"What did Dawn—?" All the horrible things girls could do to

themselves ran through my head. Razors and ropes and exhaust pipes.

"Peggy says she took her Mother's valium."

"And how does Peggy know all this?"

"They live next door. The sirens woke them."

I knew the scene too well. Neighbors in their pajamas and bathrobes huddled on the sidewalk watching—speculating. Although, given the temperatures, Dawn's neighbors probably wore overcoats over their nightclothes. Boots instead of slippers. Maybe even gloves.

"How much of her mother's valium did she take?"

"A lot."

Enough to nearly kill her.

"I need coffee." The hour was far too early for me. "I need it now."

Together we descended the stairs to the kitchen. Mr. Coffee, dependable and cheery, waited for us. I filled his reservoir and thought about the girl I'd seen at the Michaels' house. She hadn't struck me as someone contemplating ending her life.

Then I remembered her bent head and slumped shoulders as she walked toward the red Karmann Ghia.

Why were teenagers so secretive? Why didn't they just ask for help? Didn't they realize secrets could be deadly?

From the sound of things, Dawn had come very close to discovering that truth.

Thirty minutes later I discovered a truth. Chef Paul didn't appreciate having the people for whom he cooked in his kitchen. There was no other explanation for the stool. I shifted my rump on the uncomfortable seat (hopeless—the springs had long since begun their relentless push through the naugahyde). Of course Daisy was late. And frankly, I found Chef Paul with his large knives and large mustache so intimidating that I'd suggested we review the menu rather than wait for her.

I tapped a nail on the paper he'd put in front of me. "Libba can't stand Brussel sprouts. Asparagus?"

He scowled at me. "What about green beans?"

"Maybe."

The chef pulled on the tip of his mustache and his scowl deepened. He shifted that scowl to a young man wrapped in an enormous apron. "Have you made the pies?" he snapped. I got the distinct impression he wanted to snap at me. "Are the crusts defrosted?"

The sous-chef paled and dropped his whisk. "Right away, Chef." He dashed across the room to a walk-in freezer. "Still locked."

Chef Paul dug in his pocket, withdrew a set of keys, and tossed them to the sous-chef. "English peas." A small smile appeared beneath the mustache.

"No. No one likes chasing them around a plate." Why was I even negotiating? I was paying for the damned luncheon. If I wanted asparagus, he ought to cook asparagus.

But Chef Paul was known to be temperamental. Rumored to have thrown a saucepan of over-browned roux at a sous-chef. It was dangerous to annoy him. I'd annoyed him. He pulled the tip of his mustache again. "What did you have in mind?"

I'd already told him. I took a deep breath and watched the sous-chef jam a key into the padlock that secured the freezer. "Asparagus."

My request was met with another scowl. What did the man have against asparagus?

Across the room, the sous-chef jiggled the lock free, pulled the silver door open, and disappeared into the freezer.

"Asparagus is better in the spring," said Chef Paul.

I opened my mouth, an argument on my lips.

That's when the sous-chef emerged from the walk-in freezer.

His face was whiter than cake flour and he stumbled over his feet as if he'd been tippling cooking wine. He grabbed the edge of the counter and looked at us with enormous eyes. His mouth moved but didn't produce any actual words.

"What?" demanded Chef Paul. "What's wrong?"

The sous-chef's eyes rolled back in his head and he collapsed like a soufflé.

Chef Paul rose from his stool (no springs poking through the seat—I checked) and hurried to his fallen comrade. "Merde."

Really? Merde? Chef Paul was about as French as Graham Kerr.

What could be awful enough to make the sous-chef faint? I hopped off the torture device masquerading as my stool and poked my head into the freezer.

Most freezers held ice cream, and ice, and a frozen pie crust or two. Commercial freezers held those things too. They also housed boxes of frozen vegetables and chicken cutlets and plastic containers of sauces. This freezer held all that and a woman.

She sat propped up against a shelf, her ankles crossed, and her hands folded neatly in her lap. Her skin was a soft gray tinged with lavender, and her eyes stared sightlessly at the shelf across from her as if, in her last moments, she'd become fascinated with bags of Brussel sprouts and English peas. There was no question. She was dead.

Merde.

A hollowness bloomed in my stomach and threatened to expand. Threatened to consume me. I took a deep, cold breath and emerged from the freezer. "Where's the phone?"

"The phone?" Chef Paul looked up from slapping the unresponsive sous-chef's cheeks.

"The phone. There's a body in your freezer."

Chef Paul stared at me, his expression as blank as Laurie's.

"I need to call the police."

"The police?"

"Unless you'd like to keep the body in there." I sounded like Mother. Like Mother would sound when she heard I'd found another body. I blamed the cold from the freezer that clung to me like a shroud. That or the cold that settled around my heart. Or maybe it was the hollow space in my core where my stomach used to reside. Another body? Seriously? "The phone?"

He paled, his skin tone matching his chef's coat, and pointed to the corner.

With shaking fingers, I dialed Anarchy's number.

"Jones."

"Anarchy, it's Ellison."

"Hello." His tone was warm enough to defrost the freezer. "I'm sorry I haven't called. I had a case."

"I understand."

"But it's wrapped up. Are you free for lunch?"

If only we could stop our conversation there. I could say yes. We could make eyes at each other over a table filled with good pasta and better wine. We could hold hands. We could...We couldn't. "Ummm..." There was a hitch in my "ummm." A lesser man might have missed the incipient nervous breakdown in my voice, but Anarchy was a detective.

"You found another body." It wasn't a question.

Did he have to sound so resigned?

"Yes."

"Where are you?"

"The kitchen at the country club."

"Who is it?"

"Laurie Michaels."

"I'm on my way."

We hung up and I leaned against the wall. Chef Paul and the unconscious sous-chef's positions on the floor were hidden by the stainless tables that filled the kitchen.

Laurie Michaels. Dead.

I picked up the phone a second time, dialed Mother's number, and waited.

"Ellghah." Well, not exactly. But she didn't answer with her usual crispness either.

"Mother." Some might argue that what I was about to do was calculating. That Laurie wasn't yet cold (she was extremely cold). That it was grasping and rapacious. I didn't care. Not when Tom Michaels owed Grace's bank more than a million dollars. I lowered my voice. "I just found Laurie Michaels' body. Can you find out if she was insured?"

Mother was silent for so long I wondered if she meant to answer me. Finally, she asked, "Where are you?"

"The club."

That bit of information engendered a second silence.

Mother, being Mother, was weighing the satisfaction of scolding me with the possibility of getting a lien placed on an insurance settlement, thereby saving Grace's bank.

Grace won. "I'll see what I can find out."

"Thank you. I've got to go."

We hung up and I ventured forth a few steps. "Chef Paul?"

The man grunted at me.

"We should probably get out of the kitchen."

"I have prep work."

"I think the police will be here all morning. You won't be serving lunch today."

Chef Paul's head appeared above the edge of the table. "But—"

"Crime scene." I didn't have the heart to tell him that the stores in his freezer were probably evidence.

"There are reservations."

"Someone will have to call and cancel them. Also, you should probably inform the club manager about this."

"Merde!"

I didn't argue.

"Who is it?" he asked. "In the freezer?"

I was one hundred percent sure he'd been eavesdropping (hopefully he hadn't heard my whispered conversation with Mother), but I told him anyway. "Laurie Michaels."

"You were friends?"

"Not really."

"That explains it."

"Explains what?"

"You seem almost blasé."

I was sorry Laurie was dead. Sorry a life had ended. Sorry for the husband she left behind. Sorry for her son. But actual grief? The kind that twisted guts and woke one up in the middle of the night? No. "I'm not remotely blasé," I explained. "I just have an unfortunate habit of finding bodies." Although, strictly speaking, the sous-chef had found Laurie's remains. "We really ought to get out of here. Can your assistant move?"

Before he could answer, the kitchen door swung open and Anarchy's partner, Detective Peters, strode in.

Peters scanned the room, his hands jammed in the pockets of his disreputable raincoat. He took in Chef Paul, the bowls on the tables, and me. His eyes narrowed when his gaze landed on me. The detective was not one of my fans.

"Good morning, Detective Peters." It never hurt to be polite.

He curled his lip.

The door swung again and Anarchy entered (he did not scowl at me). The hand-wringing general manager followed him.

"Where's the body?" Peters demanded.

"The freezer."

The detectives entered the freezer.

A groan from the floor suggested the sous-chef had returned to consciousness.

The general manager, who had a thankless job, folded his hands as if in prayer then whacked himself in the forehead. Repeatedly.

Anarchy emerged, his face firmly set in cop mode—eyes sharp, lips thin, all traces of humor wiped away. "What time did you open the freezer this morning?"

"Right before Mrs. Russell called you." Chef Paul hauled himself off the floor using the edge of one of the work tables. He looked down at the floor as if surprised he'd been there. "It was Chris who opened the door. I gave him the keys."

Chris moaned.

"The freezer was locked?" asked Anarchy.

Chef Paul nodded. "The kitchen closes at nine on weeknights. We clean and lock up." He pointed to the hanging padlock. "The freezer's locked by ten."

"And last night?"

"Last night? I don't know. I wasn't here."

"Who was cooking?"

"Chris."

Chris wasn't talking. Chef Paul prodded him with the toe of his clog.

Anarchy looked back at the spot where Laurie died. "Why do you lock the freezer?"

"We lock the refrigerators too," said the club manager. "We've had whole sides of beef disappear."

Really? That never made it into the club newsletter.

Anarchy reached into his jacket pocket and took out a small notepad. "There's staff in the kitchen until ten?"

"Always." Chef Paul added an emphatic nod.

I leaned against the wall. Sometime after ten, someone had locked Laurie in the freezer. What had they been doing in the kitchen?

"How late is the club open?"

"On Tuesdays? The bar is open till eleven."

All gazes shifted my way. Perhaps I should have kept my mouth shut.

Anarchy made a notation on his pad. "I'll need a list of everyone who was in the clubhouse last night."

"You can't think one of our members did this," the club manager spluttered.

If you asked me, he was laying it on a bit thick. The idea that a stranger would sneak into the clubhouse and lock a woman in the freezer stretched the bounds of credulity.

"We need to talk to everyone. Members and staff." Anarchy's voice was mild. He glanced back at the freezer. "Who has keys to the lock?"

"Chef Paul and me."

"No one else?"

"No," said Chef Paul. "No one."

"Do you need a key to secure the lock?"

Three gazes swung back to me. Four. Although, strictly speaking, Detective Peters' gaze was more of a glare. One he leveled my way from the entrance to the freezer. Why couldn't I keep my mouth shut?

"It's a simple padlock," said the manager, the one man with a vested interest in keeping me happy. After all, my father was on the club's board of directors.

So no key needed to close the lock.

All gazes, including mine, shifted to Chris's supine body. He was the only one who knew for sure if the lock had been secured. And when.

"How long has he been out?" asked Detective Peters.

"Since he found the body," said Chef Paul.

Anarchy rubbed the back of his neck and returned his gaze to me. "Who wanted her dead?"

EIGHT

"You're late." Grace sat on the third from the bottom step of the front stairs. She coupled her words with a glare. A teenager ready to point out her mother's flaws.

I'd forgotten all about our trip to the hospital. "I'm sorry." I put my handbag on the bombe chest and tugged on my left glove. She would hear about Trip's mom. Her death would be prime gossip within an hour. "There was a..." Another murder. There was no way Laurie accidentally locked herself in the freezer. "...a situation at the club."

The left corner of her lip lifted slightly. "A situation? What could be more important than visiting Dawn?"

"Trip's mother, Laurie."

Grace tilted her head to the side like a curious robin. "What about her?"

I pulled off my other glove and joined her on the stairs. She smelled of Tame Crème Rinse and Love's Baby Soft. A precious child struggling to grow up. I looked down at my knees. "She's dead. I was there when they found her body."

The air in the foyer stilled, grew heavy.

Bewilderment replaced curiosity. "That can't be right."

"I saw her, honey. She's gone."

She tilted her head farther and wrinkled her nose, giving her face an air of put-upon disbelief. "You're not funny, Mom."

I never joked about finding bodies. "I'm not trying to be." There was no sugarcoating this. The gossip was just too good.

Whispers and innuendos would be melting phone lines within the hour. "Someone locked her in the freezer. It looks as if she was murdered."

Who knew eyes really could grow as big as saucers? Grace stared at me. Unmoving. Mute.

A moment passed.

And then another.

"Do you think Dawn did it?" Grace had used those silent moments to make an enormous leap.

The hinge holding my jaw closed went on a sudden vacation. I gaped. "What?" In a million years I wouldn't have connected Laurie's murder and the hospitalized Dawn. But now that Grace mentioned it...a death and a near-death on the same night? Could it be a coincidence? Maybe. But a teenage killer? I couldn't see it.

Using the bannister, Grace pulled herself to standing. "I have to call Trip."

"No!"

"What?" Spoken with teenage intonation, the word was not a question but an attitude.

"Trip may not know his mother is dead."

"Oh." A tiny sound. And then a thud as her bottom hit the stair. "I guess I'll call him later."

"Speaking of Trip, the night he came by, what exactly did he want?"

She shrugged as if sneaking boys into the house on a school night was nothing. "He was upset."

"And you let him in?" My voice held enough outrage for ten Mothers.

"For like five minutes. It was too cold to talk outside."

"What did he want to talk about?"

"He apologized."

"And?"

"And I sent him away."

Thank God.

"That's it?"

She nodded.

"Do you still want to go and see Dawn?"

She lowered her head to her knees, considering. "I can't see her as a killer. I want to go."

"Okay." I needed some help from Mr. Coffee first. "Is Aggie here?"

"In the kitchen."

"Give me five minutes. Are you all right?"

Grace looked pale. Almost as if her mother had told her about another murder. "I'm fine."

"Five minutes." I hurried into the kitchen.

Aggie wore a teal caftan with small gold medallions alternating with bouquets of flowers. It looked nice with her red hair. It looked nice with the yellow rubber gloves that covered her hands and lower arms. It even looked nice with the sterling spread across the kitchen counter.

Aggie held a candlestick and a blackened rag. She looked up when I walked in. "Good morning."

"Good morning. Is the coffee fresh?"

"Of course."

I grabbed a mug and poured.

"Your hand is shaking." Aggie was nothing if not observant.

"I found Laurie Michaels' body this morning."

Aggie put down the candlestick. "Murdered?"

"Yes." I brought the coffee to my lips. *Sweet mystery of life, at last I've found thee.* I took a sip or four then recounted everything that happened at the club.

"The husband did it." Aggie spoke with complete authority.

Every so often those closest to me forgot that when my husband died I was a suspect. They hopped on the surviving-spouse-did-it train then sat back and watched the scenery. I stared at Aggie over the rim of my coffee mug.

She flushed. "I poked around his company and found none of the equipment he claimed to have bought."

"That doesn't mean he murdered his wife." But it did mean the bank was in a world of trouble.

Unconvinced, Aggie picked up the candlestick and rubbed. "Something's rotten in the state of Denmark."

"We'd better hope he didn't kill her."

"Oh?" Her brows rose.

"Tom would definitely default on that loan from jail."

A few more pensive rubs on the candlestick. "Do you think she was insured?"

"That's another reason to hope Tom didn't kill her. I'm pretty sure insurance companies don't pay claims when the policy holder murders the insured." I drained my cup and put it in the dishwasher. "Mother's checking on all that. I've got to take Grace to the hospital to visit a classmate. Will you tell me more about what you found at Tom's company when I get back?"

She squinted at a smudge on the candlestick and rubbed harder. Out damned spot! "Of course."

"Grace," I called. "Grab your coat. Let's go."

Outside, flakes fell from a sullen sky. I pulled my collar tighter and hurried to the car.

Grace climbed into the passenger seat. "It's supposed to snow ten inches."

"Ten?"

She nodded. "I saw it on the morning news."

I sped down the drive. "Let's get to the hospital and get home before the roads get too bad."

By the time we reached the hospital, the flakes had asked friends to join them. A solid wall of white muted the world.

Walking into the lobby felt like walking into a blaze of color—albeit an overcooked oatmeal-colored blaze.

We approached the information desk. "We'd like to see Dawn—"

"Hathaway," Grace supplied.

The woman at the desk regarded our snow-covered shoulders. "Is it getting bad out there?"

"It's coming down hard."

Next to me, Grace fidgeted with impatience.

The woman ran her finger down a list, her lips moving as she searched for Hathaway. "Room 406."

"Thank you." I turned to Grace. "Shall we stop by the gift shop and get her some flowers?"

We'd meant to buy flowers before we came, but poor Laurie and the bad weather had cleared those good intentions from our minds.

We backtracked to the gift shop. One wall of the tiny shop held a glass-fronted cooler with flowers inside. A second wall was given over to magazines and word-search books. All manner of candy bars and chocolates were on display on a rack in the center. The morning edition of the newspaper sat next to the cash register. The woman behind the register smiled at us. "May I help you?"

"Just looking," Grace murmured.

I selected a box of peppermint Dynamints and put it on the counter.

"How are the roads?" The woman patted the near-lavender of her hair. Someone had been over-generous with the bluing.

"Not good." This needed to be a short visit. "Grace, are you ready?"

Grace added a bouquet of yellow roses and daisies in a white vase and a crossword-puzzle book to the counter.

I paid for our purchases and we rode the elevator to the

fourth floor in silence.

A woman clutching a handkerchief stood outside Dawn's door. She watched us make our way down the hall and seemed surprised when we stopped next to her.

"May I help you?" she asked.

"I'm here to see Dawn," said Grace.

"You are?" The woman emphasized "are," as if she couldn't quite believe someone was there for a visit.

I thrust my hand forward. "I'm Ellison Russell and this is my daughter, Grace."

"Pleased to meet you, Mrs. Russell. I'm Edith Hathaway."

She in no way looked like an Edith—but maybe that was because when I heard Edith, I pictured Archie Bunker's wife in her house dresses and tight perm. Edith Hathaway, despite her red-rimmed tired eyes, was pretty. If Grace attempted suicide, I wouldn't look pretty. I'd look like something Max threw up.

"Go on in, dear. I'm sure Dawn would love to see you."

Grace slipped through the doorway.

"How is she?" I asked.

Edith's red-rimmed eyes filled. "The doctors say she'll be okay." She waved her hands in front of her eyes. "They say she needs counseling and—" *Hiccup.* She clapped one hand over her mouth. The other hand waved the air in front of her eyes. "Excuse me, I'm having a hard time with this."

"Anyone would. May I buy you a cup of coffee?" It was the only comfort I could think of. A trip to the coffee shop was at odds with my mission to get in and out of the hospital quickly, but Edith looked as if she needed coffee. Coffee and someone to listen to her.

She bit her lip and considered.

I waited. And waited. I'd asked her for a cup of coffee, not a lifetime commitment.

Finally, she nodded. "That would be nice. Just a minute."

Edith poked her head into the hospital room and told Dawn and Grace she was stepping away but would be back soon.

We walked to the elevator in silence.

We rode the elevator in silence.

We chose a table in the coffee shop in silence. Maybe she didn't need someone to talk to.

We had to speak to the waitress. We both ordered coffee.

The waitress put our mugs on the table and we both reached for the cream.

"Go ahead," I said.

She selected one of the little plastic cups from a ramekin filled with melting crushed ice, peeled back the top, and poured the contents into her cup.

I did the same.

Edith stirred her cup, staring at its contents as if they possessed the secrets of the universe. "We never should have sent her to that school."

My mother and father attended Suncrest, my husband and I attended Suncrest, now Grace was there. For us, it wasn't a choice, it was a tradition. "Oh?"

"We don't fit in there. We're not country club people." She looked up from her coffee and offered me an apologetic smile as if she'd used naughty words in polite conversation. "We're not from here. And we won't stay here."

"What brought you to Kansas City?"

"My husband's job. Arch runs the Midwest division."

I didn't ask of what. I was too busy keeping my jaw off the table.

Edith noticed. "When we got married, we had no idea there would be a television show that used our names." She took a sip of coffee. "The next step for us is moving to Chicago. As much time as he's been spending at the home office, I'd say we'll be moving sooner rather than later. He's there now." She pulled a paper napkin from the dispenser and daubed at her eyes. "It snowed so much, the airport closed. He can't get home."

"He must be wild with worry."

"He is." Her mouth thinned and she glared at the snow on the other side of the window. "I told him public school would be fine, but he wouldn't listen. He had to send her someplace elite." She returned her gaze to me. "And she met that boy."

"Trip Michaels?"

Edith nodded. Slowly. As if she was reluctant to acknowledge his existence. "Things were going all right until she met that boy. I took one look at him and knew he'd break her heart. She wouldn't listen to me."

"Teenage girls never listen to their mothers."

The sound she made was somewhere between a laugh and a sob. "Isn't that the truth? I never listened to my mother."

"I still don't."

She gave me a rueful smile. At least I'd made her smile.

"Of course, she fell in love. Hopelessly in love."

I made a sympathetic noise in my throat.

"And I didn't realize just how serious things were." She pulled another napkin from the dispenser and blew her nose. "Sorry."

"It's quite all right."

"I should have been paying attention." She put down the used napkin and clutched her coffee mug. "I wasn't. I was down at the cathedral serving lunch."

"Serving lunch?"

She nodded. "The cathedral provides a free lunch to anyone who's hungry."

I knew that. I'd raised money to help them buy food. I'd just never dreamed of passing out the actual sandwiches or making the Jell-O salads. "I see." My voice was faint.

"I also teach people to read as part of their adult literacy program."

Edith Hathaway was a hands-on volunteer. No chairing galas for her. She was the type who actually worked with those in need. How very admirable. The closest I came to hands-on volunteering was pricing donated clothing at the Junior League Thrift Shop.

"I should have been home with my daughter."

"Is Dawn your only child?"

Edith nodded.

"Grace is an only as well."

A small connection. We smiled across the table at each other.

"It was very nice of Grace to come down here to see Dawn."

"She insisted."

"Why?"

The unvarnished question stopped the coffee cup halfway between the table and my lips. "Um..."

"Dawn has never mentioned her." Edith wiped beneath her eyes with the tips of her index fingers. "She never mentions any of the girls from school."

"She doesn't have friends?"

"There's a girl named Donna who calls sometimes." Edith stared into her coffee mug apparently unaware of the tears trickling down her cheeks. "Mostly it was just Trip." She pursed her lips and said no more.

"I'm so sorry." And I was. My heart ached for the woman sitting across from me and for the girl lying in a hospital bed on the fourth floor. Grace should have been kinder, more welcoming. Grace shouldn't have rallied the troops and ostracized a girl who had no friends. "After Dawn and Trip broke up, he asked Grace out."

She gazed at me with her red-rimmed eyes. "That boy is no good." Her shoulders shook. "And his mother is worse." A hardness settled onto Edith's pretty face and she wasn't pretty anymore. "It's really coming down." Edith jerked her chin toward the plate-glass window. On the other side, snow hid the sidewalk and the street and the world. She pushed her chair away from the table. "I should probably get back to Dawn, and you should probably head home before it gets any worse."

I dug a few dollars out of my purse and left them on the table.

"Thank you for the coffee."

"It was my pleasure."

"And thank you for listening. Sometimes it's easier to talk to a stranger than a friend." It was a rather deft way of telling me there'd be no more coffees in our future.

"I understand."

We rode the elevator to Dawn's room in silence.

I tapped on the door and stuck my head inside Dawn's room. "Grace? We should probably get going."

Dawn was propped up in her bed. She looked tiny and fragile and way too young to be so sad. Her skin was whiter than her sheets. "Hi, Mrs. Russell."

"Hi, Dawn. How are you feeling?"

She lifted her hands from her lap and let them fall. "I've had better days."

"Well, you just concentrate on getting better." If I'd tried I couldn't have come up with anything more banal to say.

If Grace's eye roll was any indication, she agreed.

Grace looked almost as pale as Dawn. What had the two of them been talking about?

"We should go," I said.

Grace's coat was draped over the arm of the chair. She stood, picked it up, and smiled at the patient. "Take care."

Dawn stared at Grace with an unsettling intensity. Her pale lips thinned. Her eyes welled. She glanced at her mother then returned her gaze to Grace. A look passed between them. One fraught with meaning.

Grace nodded and slipped her arms into the sleeves of her coat.

I turned to Edith. "Please let us know if you need anything."

"Thank you for coming."

Everyone was so polite. Why did I get the feeling I was the only one who couldn't see the elephant in the room? A secret hidden from me like the snow hid the world outside.

"Let's go, Mom."

I followed Grace into the hall and to the elevator. "What did you and Dawn talk about?"

Grace pulled her ponytail free of the collar of her coat. "I can't tell you."

"Pardon?" I jabbed at the button for the ground floor.

"I promised Dawn I'd keep her secret." She stared up at the lit numbers above the elevator door. Four, three, two, ground.

We stepped out onto slippery tile floor (visitors were tracking in snow) and Grace turned to me and clutched my arm. "One thing I can tell you. I promise I'll never go out with Trip Michaels again."

NINE

Getting a teenager to divulge a secret to her mother is like getting a chimpanzee to speak Latin. A hopeless task, unless you count annoying the chimp as a win.

"Forget it, Mom. I'm not telling you." Grace crossed her arms and stared out the passenger window at the thick snow.

"Dawn tried to kill herself. If there's something that's making her that unhappy, an adult should know what it is."

Grace cut her gaze my way. "Her mother knows."

"In that case, I'll drop it." Curiosity. Cat. The last time I was curious and cat-like, I stuck my head in a walk-in freezer and saw Laurie. If Edith knew what was bothering her daughter, I'd turn my attention elsewhere. There was a bank that needed saving and the chimpanzee could definitely live without *amo*, *amas*, *amat*.

The back tires spun on a slick spot. I tightened my hands on the wheel and said a silent prayer that we'd make it up the snow-packed hill near our house. "Snow day tomorrow."

"You think?" Enthusiasm gave life to Grace's tone. She even turned her head toward me.

"If this keeps up? I think."

She grinned and for a moment she was six and not sixteen. Six, when her biggest problem was missing teeth. Six, when boys had cooties. Six, when she couldn't keep a secret for more than five seconds without bursting. "Can we make cocoa and roast marshmallows in the fireplace?"

"Of course." I loved six. I loved sixteen too. Six was easier. Fewer secrets.

We slipped. We slid. We played pat-a-cake with a snow-filled curb. And finally, we made it home.

A strange car was parked in the drive. I pulled the Triumph around back and parked it in the garage.

"Is that Detective Jones' car?" Grace took her first step in the deepening snow.

"I don't know." Anarchy drove different police cars. All of them American made. All of them slightly disreputable. Who else could it be? The thought of him waiting for me in the house gave me flutters. Stomach butterflies and snow don't mix. I slipped. The snow broke my fall.

I struggled to my feet, brushed off my white-coated hiney, and shuffled to the back door.

The kitchen was filled with light, the smell of a cake baking, and Anarchy Jones. He sat at the kitchen island nursing a cup of coffee while Aggie, yellow gloves still in place, washed dishes with singular fervor. "Hi." My voice was faint.

"Hi." His voice was as delicious as s'mores made in the fireplace on a snow day. Melty and warm and addictive.

I dragged my gaze away from the detective. "Bundt cake?" I asked Aggie.

She nodded. "If the roads clear, you can take it tomorrow."

Tom Michaels would be inundated with Bundt cakes and casseroles—egg noodles and tuna mixed with cream of mushroom soup or hamburger meat and peas in cream of celery. Someone would bake a ham. And, as if the poor man wasn't suffering enough, he might even get a few Jell-O salads. Daisy made one with pimiento stuffed olives, sweet pickles, and walnuts in lemon gelatin. And people said I was a bad cook? I shuddered just thinking about those olives staring at me like lost souls locked in a jiggly prison.

Grace shrugged out of her coat. "Can I take that for you, Mom?" She held out her hand and I slipped off my wrap and gave it to her.

Grace and the coats disappeared down the hall.

"I thought you'd be investigating," I said to Anarchy.

"I figured you could tell me as much about Laurie Michaels as anyone."

Did he really want to know about Laurie or did he want to see me?

I looked at him more closely.

Anarchy was in cop mode. He'd come for information and not my company.

I hid a sigh. "What do you want to know?"

"The usual. Her friends. Her enemies. The state of her marriage."

"You don't ask for much, do you?"

He answered me with a grin.

He came for information, not to see me.

"Let's start with the state of her marriage," he said. "What can you tell me?"

"Give me a minute." I poured some coffee, wrapped my hands around the mug, and let the warmth seep into my fingers.

Anarchy fixed his coffee-colored gaze on me. "Was Tom Michaels having an affair?"

"Not that I'm aware of."

"Do you know Jenny Woods?"

"I do."

"Is it possible that Mr. Michaels and Ms. Woods were involved?"

"Anything's possible." I sipped my coffee, visualized, and couldn't see them together. "I don't think so."

"Mrs. Michaels accused Ms. Woods of sleeping with her husband."

"When?"

"Last night at around nine thirty."

"Pfft."

"Pfft?"

"Laurie accused Prudence Davies of the same thing last weekend."

He pulled a small notepad out of his jacket pocket and wrote in it.

"What are you writing?"

"Ms. Davies was at the club last night. She said she and Mrs. Michaels were friends."

"Pfft."

His lips quirked. "She exaggerated?"

"She lied."

Anarchy looked down at his notepad. "Do you know a man named Salvatore O'Hearne?"

"Good gracious, no."

"A Rocky or Rocco O'Hearne?"

Aggie turned away from her soapy water to face us. "Sal O'Hearne is a bookie. His brother, Rocky, is an enforcer." She offered me a rueful smile. "My Al met all kinds."

"I have not made the O'Hearnes' acquaintance." I sounded starchy—starchier than Mother. I softened my tone. "Why do you ask?"

"Rocky O'Hearne was escorted off the club property last night."

"Oh?" I kept my voice neutral and my gaze on Anarchy. If Aggie and I exchanged glances the same question would appear in both our eyes. Had Tom gambled away the bank's money?

"So you have heard of him?" Not much gets by Anarchy. My innocent "oh" must have been a shade too innocent. Fortunately, he'd reached the wrong conclusion.

"I can honestly say I've never heard of the O'Hearne

brothers until you brought them up."

The look on his face said he didn't quite believe me. "Did Laurie Michaels gamble?"

"Of course no—" My voice quit and my mind returned to her penny-a-point suggestion at bridge. I cleared my throat. "I don't know. Maybe."

Anarchy waited. His pencil poised. His expression curious.

"She wanted to play cards for money the last time I saw her."

He wrote on his pad. "Did you?"

"Play for money? Of course not."

"Do you know Edith Hathaway?"

"Yes. Why?"

"She was also at the club last night."

Really? The woman who'd said country club people with such disdain? "With whom?"

"Apparently she came on her own." He looked down at his notes. "She and Mrs. Michaels had a heated discussion just before ten."

"About what?"

He shook his head. He didn't know.

Someone had heard them. He just needed to ask the right person. I could find out. Easily. I might already know. "Laurie's son and Edith's daughter dated. She was the girl in Henry's study at the party."

Anarchy scribbled a note.

"Dawn is in the hospital. She tried to kill herself with her mother's valium."

"When?" Direct, slightly harsh, very cop-like.

"According to Grace's source, the police were called around four thirty this morning."

"Grace's source?"

"One of her friends lives next door to the Hathaways. She

called before school." Grace's earlier enormous leap that Laurie's death and Dawn's suicide attempt were related no longer seemed so far-fetched. "Was Dawn at the club with her mother last night?"

"If she was, no one mentioned it."

I tipped my head and swallowed my coffee in one gulp—as if it was a shot of vodka and not a shot of caffeine.

Aggie stepped forward, took the empty cup from my hands, and refilled it. "Seemingly the country club was the place to be last night."

I took the mug from her. "Thank you. Who else was there?" I asked Anarchy.

He flipped back in his notes. "Prudence Davies."

I wrinkled my nose.

"Your parents. They had dinner with Lorna Michaels." The tip of his pencil moved the next names on his list. "Your friend Libba, Pamela and Gordon Moore, Marilyn and Warren Ellsworth..." He continued listing names. There must have been thirty or forty.

"How many of those people were there after ten?"

Aggie's brows rose in question.

"There was staff in the kitchen until ten," I explained. "They would have noticed someone locking Laurie in the freezer."

"Your parents and Lorna Michaels left after Laurie Michaels' argument with Jenny Woods." Again he checked his notes. "Apparently Mrs. Michaels, Lorna Michaels, was upset that her daughter-in-law had—" he read from the page "—'made a spectacle of herself like some two-bit whore.'"

"She said that to you?" Lorna would never speak of her son's wife like that. Not to a police officer.

"No." Anarchy squinted at the tiny handwriting. "She said that to Marilyn Ellsworth."

Lorna and Marilyn were cousins. And Marilyn wasn't nearly

as discreet or loyal as Lorna.

"So everyone was there after ten except for my parents and Lorna."

"I'm afraid so." Anarchy sounded grim.

"Who was the bartender?"

"Billy Ryan."

"That explains it."

"Oh?"

"Billy pours generously, and if he likes you, the drinks don't necessarily appear on your monthly statement." Or so I'd heard. Billy had never forgotten a single sip on my behalf.

Then again, I wasn't much of a drinker.

I closed my eyes and pictured the full bar at the club. "No one noticed Laurie was gone?"

"No."

"What about Tom? Surely he wondered what had happened to his wife."

"The Michaels drove separate cars. He assumed she'd driven herself home."

"But what about when he got home and Laurie didn't show up?"

"The Michaels slept in separate bedrooms. Mr. Michaels claims he didn't realize she was missing."

In the last years of our marriage, Henry and I lived in a similar fashion. I never knew where he was or when he'd come home. And I hadn't cared. "That's possible." Tom couldn't be the killer. He. Could. Not. His being arrested for murder would be the end of the bank. "What about this O'Hearne person? What time was he at the club?"

"He was escorted off the premises at ten thirty."

"There you go! He's your killer."

"Possibly." Anarchy's voice gave nothing away. If he liked the bookie as the killer, he wasn't tipping his hand to me. "We're bringing him in for questioning."

I circled the island and settled onto a stool. "Last night the dining room and bar were full?"

Anarchy nodded.

"Where did Laurie accuse Jenny?" I asked.

"In the hallway." Meaning that anyone in any of the rooms that opened off the hall would have heard her accusations.

"What was Jenny's response?"

"Ms. Woods told Mrs. Michaels that she was mistaken."

I doubted Jenny phrased her reply quite like that. "Where did Jenny go after Laurie accused her of sleeping with Tom?"

"She joined your friend Libba in the bar."

Libba had probably bought Jenny a stinger and told her to forget the whole thing. I pictured them in the club chairs in front of the fireplace. In my mind, they cupped their drinks in their hands as firelight gilded their faces. "What about Laurie? Where did she go?"

"She appeared in the bar a few minutes later." He flipped a page in his notes. "She joined her husband at the actual bar."

"Where was she in between the argument and appearing in the bar?"

"No one can account for her whereabouts."

Interesting.

"And Edith walked into the bar just before ten?"

"Yes."

"They argued in the bar?"

"No. Mrs. Hathaway requested a word." Again he looked at his notes. "It seems Mrs. Michaels was reluctant to go with her."

"But she went?"

"Mr. Michaels insisted."

"Where did they go?"

"Apparently they went to the ladies' lounge."

"Apparently?"

"Marilyn Ellsworth passed them in the hallway."

"Ah." Marilyn had eavesdropped. "What did they say?"

Anarchy's lips twisted into the wry approximation of a smile. "Mrs. Ellsworth was deeply offended that I even suggest she had listened to a conversation that wasn't hers."

Piffle. Marilyn had probably stood right outside the door devouring every word like Max devoured leftover steak. Voraciously. "Did Laurie return to the bar after their conversation?"

"Yes."

Lucky for Edith.

"She had a whispered conversation with her husband then left again. Mr. Michaels finished his drink and left."

"What were they whispering about?"

"Mr. Michaels says she told him she was tired and was going home. He replied that he planned on following her soon."

Why whisper that?

"Did she talk to anyone else?"

"No."

Things didn't look good for Tom.

"What about Rocky O'Hearne?"

"At ten fifteen, Jane Addison returned from a trip to the powder room and reported there was a man who didn't belong wandering around the club. The busboy went and found him."

"Who was bussing?" The word "busboy" conjured up images of scrawny sixteen-year-old boys with scratchy collars and ill-fitting service jackets.

Anarchy scanned his notes. "Gus Finn."

Definitely not a boy. A man. A man with a bicep bigger than my head.

Even with Gus's brawn, I couldn't imagine an enforcer for a bookie just handing over his identification. I said as much.

"A few of the men in the bar followed Gus."

"Oh?"

"One of the men, Judge Winslow, recognized O'Hearne." Anarchy stared into the empty depths of his mug.

"More coffee?" I asked.

"No, thank you."

"So Terrence recognized O'Hearne," I prompted. "Presumably from his court room?" Terrence Winslow was as straight an arrow as there was in the quiver. Imagining him owing money to a bookie was an impossibility.

"Exactly. Judge Winslow demanded to know what he was doing at the club."

"And?"

"Rocky said he was considering becoming a member."

At least Rocky had a sense of humor.

"Did anyone detain him?"

"No. They asked him to leave."

"He was wandering around the club after ten o'clock and no one knows why."

"Exactly."

"And by ten fifteen, Laurie had left the bar."

"Yes."

"Had Tom?"

"No one is sure."

That was better than a definitive yes.

"It seems to me O'Hearne is your suspect."

"Every member of your club would agree with you."

"You don't?"

"I'm not discounting O'Hearne, but a busted nose or broken ribs are more the brothers' style. Anyone there after ten is a suspect."

"What if someone else came in and killed her? Someone no one saw."

Anarchy turned the empty coffee mug in his hands. "That

someone else snuck into the club is highly unlikely." He sounded certain. "Besides, how would they know where to find Mrs. Michaels?"

"Maybe Laurie saw something she shouldn't have." That would clear Tom.

"Like what?"

"A judge doing cocaine. A CEO tipping off a buddy about stock prices. A couple...coupling...when they're married to other people."

A slow smile transformed his face. "You've given this some thought."

Not really. I'd seen two out of three.

Aggie snapped the damp dish towel and hung it over the oven handle. "The snow is really coming down. Do you think you'll make it back to the station in this?" Aggie didn't do subtle hints.

Anarchy grinned at her. It was a be-my-friend grin. A we're-all-in-this-together grin. A you'll-come-around-eventually grin.

How did Aggie resist?

She scowled, pulled off her gloves, donned oven mitts, and pulled a perfect cake from the oven.

The scent of warm sugar and cinnamon was mouth-watering.

She put the cake on a warming rack, gave me a get-rid-of-him glance, and said, "I'll be back in a moment. Would you make sure the beast doesn't eat the cake?"

The beast lifted his gray head off his paws and looked innocent.

No one was fooled.

"Of course."

She disappeared down the hall in a swirl of disapproving teal caftan.

"Ellison, I want you to make me a promise."

I returned my attention to the man at the counter. "What?"

"Stay out of this investigation."

I was more than happy to comply as long as he stayed away from Tom. "I never purposefully get involved in any investigation." That wasn't strictly true.

Anarchy raised a single brow but didn't comment.

"I don't."

"And yet trouble arrives at your door more often than the mailman."

I couldn't argue.

His hand erased the distance between us and his thumb grazed my cheekbone. "All things being equal, I'd prefer it if no one tried to kill you. Promise?"

What woman on earth could argue? "Promise."

He stood. "Aggie's right. I should hit the roads before the weather gets worse."

I climbed off my stool. "Who's your top suspect? Rocco O'Hearne?" Did I sound too hopeful?

"I thought you weren't getting involved." He stepped closer to me and a fluttery butterfly feeling winged its way through my stomach. "I know you don't like hearing this, but the killer is usually the surviving spouse."

"That wasn't involvement. That was a question." A question with an answer that reacquainted my heart with my ankles. And, thanks to Anarchy's nearness, my heart was beating double-time. It was an odd sensation to have near my feet. Extremely distracting.

He leaned forward and brushed his lips across my cheek. "I'm holding you to your promise. No involvement." He straightened. "I'll call you later."

I followed him down the hall to the foyer.

He pulled on a shearling coat and opened the front door.

Outside, the snow swirled.

"Drive safely."

"I will. Remember your promise."

"I remember." I'd promised. I'd stay as far away from Anarchy's investigation as possible—unless Laurie's death had something to do with the money Tom owed the bank. If Laurie had been murdered because of that money, all bets were off.

TEN

The white stuff piling up outside changed the light inside. Snow light. Brighter, cleaner, purer than regular light.

I leaned against the front door, listened to Anarchy's car slide down the driveway, and told myself I should go to my studio, take advantage of the light, and paint.

I went to the kitchen instead.

Aggie looked up from wiping an already spotless countertop. "He's gone?" She was not as enamored with Anarchy as I was.

"He's gone." My gaze bounced between Mr. Coffee and the refrigerator.

Aggie threw away her paper towel. "Would you like coffee? Or I can make you a bowl of soup and a cheese sandwich."

"Soup and sandwich would be lovely."

If Aggie looked surprised by my decision, Mr. Coffee looked positively taken aback—maybe even hurt. I never chose food over him. Never. But my stomach was rumbling with an emptiness that threatened to spread. I couldn't run on empty. Could not. Not when Tom Michaels might default on that loan.

"Grace is probably hungry too." Aggie pulled a loaf from the bread box and cheese and butter from the fridge. "Will she eat tomato soup?"

"It's her favorite. I'll grab a few cans."

Before Aggie, the soup in the pantry lived a chaotic life. Chicken noodle cozied up to cream of mushroom. Italian wedding knocked cans with cream of celery. Vegetable whispered in the corner with beef barley. After Aggie, the soup lived in orderly red and white alphabetical rows. T for tomato.

Brnng, brnng.

I emerged from the pantry, put the soup on the counter, and answered the phone. "Hello."

"Ellison, I'm worried." Mother's voice was strident.

I clutched the phone so hard my nails cut crescents into my palms. "Laurie wasn't insured?" I expended my allotment of air, but my lungs refused to re-inflate.

"What? That? Of course she was insured." Mother made my fears sound ridiculous. "For more than a million dollars."

Good news. Excellent news. I leaned against the wall, my knees weak with relief. My lungs resumed normal operations. Breathe in. Breathe out.

"Are you all right?" asked Aggie.

"Mother," I mouthed. One word explained all.

I loosened my death grip on the receiver and asked, "If it's not insurance, what are you worried about?"

"The weather. We're supposed to fly to Ohio the day after tomorrow."

"I'm sure they'll have the runways clear." Runways, shmunways. Laurie was insured! As long as Tom didn't kill her, nothing could cloud the sun shining in my heart.

"The storm is headed east and you know how your father is about flying."

He needed a valium and a strong scotch to fly on a perfect day.

"I'm only telling you this because we may be at your house for Thanksgiving."

And there it was, a thunderhead that blotted out all sunshine. I squeaked.

"If we come, I'll bring a pie."

Oh dear Lord.

There was no way I'd ever, ever deny my parents a seat at my table on a holiday, but—I swallowed. "I'm sure you'll be able to get to Ohio. Marjorie is so looking forward to your visit." The tip of my nose itched. Badly. Sniffed-a-bouquet-of-poison-ivy badly. The way it itched when I told a whopper. I scratched.

"Yes, well. Maybe we'll go for Christmas."

"Henry's sister is coming for Thanksgiving."

Mother could transform silence into something solid and disapproving. So much so that her silence had weight. Weight that grew heavier with each passing second. The ponderous silence that emanated from her end of the line spoke volumes. She did not like or approve of Henry's sister, and I was supposed to fix this new hiccup in her holiday plans.

I wrapped a coil of the phone cord around my finger, admired my new rubberized ring, and said nothing. I could use silence too.

"Isn't she a vegan?" Mother spat the word "vegan."

Gwendolyn Russell made my Bohemian aunt look more conservative than Gerald Ford. "Yes. Or at least she was when she informed me she was coming in September."

An audible breath reached through the phone lines. "What religion is she now?"

"Hindu."

Mother made a strangled sound.

"But she goes through phases," I added. "She might be a Buddhist or a Jainist."

"A what?"

"A Jainist." If I closed my eyes, I could see Mother. She was sitting at her desk with her ankles crossed and her lips pinched in a tight line. She held a pen in her right hand and with it she drew neat three-dimensional boxes on the pad positioned next to her phone. No free-form doodles for Mother. Just boxes.

Boxes with precise angles and clean lines.

A put-upon sigh traveled from her house to mine. "If she doesn't want to be an Episcopalian, why can't she be a Presbyterian?"

"I think Gwen is looking for meaning outside the constructs of Christianity. I'll ask her over Thanksgiving dinner."

"Ellison Walford Russell! You will not discuss religion at dinner."

I didn't argue. But only because I agreed with her. Gwen adopted each new religion with missionary zeal, and listening to her proselytize gave me indigestion. "Whatever her religion, she's the only close family Grace has on her father's side."

"You're not serving tofu turkey, are you?"

"No."

With a second long-suffering sigh, Mother said, "I'll check on other flights."

"Mother, about that insurance."

"I already told you. Laurie was insured. Lorna promised she'd tell us all about it. We're to be at her apartment tomorrow at two o'clock. You can pick me up at half past one."

"Thank you."

"Also, Hunter Tafft may stop by."

"Hunter's going to Lorna's?" Bringing a lawyer with us didn't exactly set a friendly tone.

"Don't be ridiculous. Hunter's coming to your house. This afternoon. He can explain what you need to do to place a lien." The woman did not give up. She'd determined that Hunter and I would live happily ever after together, but there were issues. My issues. Trust issues. Did-I-really-want-to-be-the-fourth-Mrs.-Hunter-Tafft issues. I'd broken things off. Meanwhile Mother had visions of me and Hunter at dinner dances at the club, charity galas, skiing in Vail, summer vacationing in Harbor Point or the Cape, and taking occasional trips to Europe. She imagined companionable breakfasts with coffee and fresh croissants, holding hands as we walked Max, and the occasional quiet night at home spent cuddling on the couch.

In my experience, marriage—especially marriage to a man in our set—was nothing like that. Why couldn't she mind her own business? "Hunter's coming here?"

"Yes."

"Today?"

"Yes."

On cue, the doorbell rang.

"I'll get that." It was Aggie's turn to trill. She couldn't help but overhear my conversation with Mother and she held out hope that I would come to my senses and fall head over heels in love with a certain silver-haired, silver-tongued lawyer. She put down the bread, gave Max a warning look—his life wasn't worth living if he swiped it off the counter—and hurried into the front hall.

"Mother, there's someone at the door. I have to go."

"Is it Hunter?" She couldn't keep the satisfaction out of her voice.

"Probably. I can't imagine anyone's just dropping by in this weather."

"I'll let you go, dear. Goodbye."

I hung up the receiver, pushed the bread, cheese, and butter to the back of the counter (where Max couldn't reach them), and made my way to the front hall where Aggie was helping Hunter out of his overcoat.

He spotted me and smiled. "Hello."

I smiled back. And smoothed my hair. And smoothed my skirt. When a man as handsome as Hunter Tafft smiled at you, it was hard not to melt like the snowflakes in his shining hair. "Hello to you too."

"I was just making lunch." Aggie's gaze bounced between

COLD AS ICE   **117**

Hunter and me. She smirked, looking unreasonably pleased.

I had no choice but to invite him. "Please join us."

"If it's no trouble."

"No trouble at all." Aggie's smile was beatific.

We walked back to the kitchen, where Max stood on his hind legs and reached for the bread with his front left paw.

"Max!"

He stared at Aggie for a full two seconds before dropping to the floor.

"Bad dog!" She shook her finger at him.

Max blinked, unconcerned, then meandered over to Hunter and rubbed his doggy head against Hunter's gray pants. Max's version of a hug.

Hunter scratched behind Max's ears. "I wouldn't mess with her, buddy."

Max wagged his stubby tail. He knew who ran the house and it wasn't Aggie or me.

"Let me wipe down this counter." Aggie sent a do-it-again-and-die look Max's way then grabbed a paper towel and a spray bottle of something piney. "I'll have lunch ready in a jiff."

Hunter claimed a stool at the island. "Tell me what's going on."

As Aggie buttered bread, positioned slices of cheese, and heated soup, I told him everything. The loan, the need for it to be repaid, Aggie's trip to look for equipment, Laurie's icy death, and Mother's assurance that Laurie's life had been insured.

"May I see the file?" he asked.

"You should probably be on retainer."

He grinned and held out his hand. "That will be one dollar."

I reached for my handbag, withdrew my billfold, and gave him the bill. Hunter had charged me a dollar for legal advice in the past. "This time I actually want to pay you. Whatever your regular hourly rate is."

"You can't afford my rate."

"Oh?"

"Dinner."

I looked at my lap where my hands were clasped. It was Mother who had visions of companionable breakfasts with coffee and fresh croissants and vacations on the Cape. Not me. Hunter had three failed marriages to his name. I had one. There was too much baggage. And, while I loved a good croissant as much as the next woman, the other parts of being with Hunter—the club parties, the subtle competition with other wives over everything from waistlines to cars, the one-upmanship over children's accomplishments, the quiet pressure to fit in—weren't remotely appealing. "That's not an hourly rate."

"Believe me, it's a bargain."

I looked up, looked at him. For the first time ever, he looked less than one hundred percent confident. He looked like a man and not a high-priced lawyer. Like a man who could be wounded by rejection.

"Dinner as friends."

He winced. "Dinner as friends?"

"Lunch is ready." Aggie held two plates topped with cheese sandwiches and steaming bowls of soup. She put them down in front of us then went to the backstairs and called, "Grace, lunch is ready."

Grace careened down the back steps and stopped short. "Mr. Tafft. Um, hi."

"Hello, Grace. It's nice to see you."

"Nice to see you too, Mr. Tafft." Grace cut her gaze toward me and I read the question in her eyes. Why was Hunter having lunch in our kitchen?

"Hunter is looking at some documents for me," I explained.

"As long as we can decide on a fee."

I glanced at Grace. I couldn't let the bank go under.

Couldn't lose her legacy from her father. Not from one bad loan. If Hunter could help, I'd have a hundred dinners with him. As friends. "I agree to your terms."

He lifted his spoon. "Well then, as soon as I've finished lunch, I'll look at that file."

Grace joined us at the island and Aggie conjured up a plate for her.

"Did they cancel school?" Hunter asked.

"No. I went and saw a friend in the hospital. The roads were bad, so Mom said I could stay home for the rest of the day." She bit the corner off one of the triangles of her sandwich.

"How's your friend?" asked Hunter

Grace chewed and swallowed. "Not good."

"I'm sorry to hear that." Hunter lifted a spoonful of tomato soup to his lips and blew.

"A boy broke her heart," Grace added.

"Boys do that sometimes." Hunter glanced my way. "Girls too."

I took a large bite of sandwich.

"There are more consequences for girls," said Grace.

"Consequences?" I asked around a mouthful of bread and cheese.

Aggie, who was washing the soup pot, froze.

Hunter froze too, his sandwich halfway to his mouth.

Grace nodded emphatically. "If a boy and a girl fool around—" her words struck ice into my heart "—he gets a pat on the back and she gets called a slut. That's a double standard."

Hunter didn't argue. I didn't either. Aggie rinsed the pot.

I reached for a coffee cup. There wasn't one.

Teenagers and sex. When I was a teenager, Mother's birds-and-bees talk was something akin to "do not, under any circumstances, have sex before marriage." If I did have sex, no nice man would want me for a wife. I would shame my family.

I'd get pregnant, have an illegitimate child, and be forced to give up her grandchild for adoption. That or I'd get syphilis. Her strategy was to make sex so terrifying that I'd wait till marriage. Her strategy worked.

With Grace, I'd taken a different approach. My birds-and-bees talk compared sex without love to junk food. Empty. And not good for her. And please, please don't. Listening to her, it dawned on me that my talk might be lacking. Seriously lacking. Mother's terror-inducing talk was far superior.

"You're right, Grace. It is a double standard. It's not fair. But keep in mind that it's not just boys who call girls sluts." I glanced at Aggie. "Would you please make some coffee?"

"Why do girls do that to each other?"

Hunter shifted on his stool. This wasn't the luncheon conversation he'd bargained for.

Aggie pushed Mr. Coffee's button. "They call each other names because sometimes the only way they can feel better about themselves is to tear someone else down."

"It's confusing."

I could clear up her confusion. Don't have sex.

"Have you read a *Cosmo*?" she asked.

I had. And if you asked me, Helen Gourley Brown had a lot to answer for. It was one thing if Libba wanted to diddle with lots of men. She was an adult. But a teenager aspiring to be a *Cosmo* girl? My teenager? Sweet nine-pound baby Jesus. "*Cosmo* pushes the envelope. Real life isn't like that."

Grace looked doubtful.

Hunter looked uncomfortable.

Aggie busied herself with pouring a cup of coffee.

I swallowed. "In real life, people get their hearts broken. Most people—certainly most women—can't reduce sex to something meaningless."

Hunter cleared his throat and his cheeks flushed. I'd never

seen him blush before. "Teenage boys are governed by hormones, not feelings, Grace."

"I know that—" She did? I needed that coffee. "—but—"

"No buts," said Hunter. "Boys. Hormones. Bad news."

Aggie deposited a steaming mug in front of me. "Coffee, Mr. Tafft?"

"Please, Aggie."

Grace kept her gaze fixed on Hunter. "Are all boys like that? Can't they change? And why is sex okay for boys but not for girls?"

Hunter's unflappable sangfroid flapped like a flag in a stiff wind. He cleared his throat. He regarded his lap. He shifted on his stool. He even wiped his brow.

It was moments like this when I wished I hadn't run over Henry. Girls needed their fathers. Although Grace's father had spent his whole life governed by his hormones, so he might not have had a good answer.

"It's just different." Hunter's voice was not his own. It was much higher. He cleared his throat a second time. "And boys grow out of it."

Sometimes. I thought it, I didn't say it.

Grace looked down at her soup, hiding an epic eye roll behind lowered lashes.

I sipped my coffee, munched on my sandwich, and cast about for a topic other than sex.

"Did you hear Mom found another body?" Grace beat me to the new topic. But I'd gladly discuss poor Laurie rather than sex.

"I heard something about that," said Hunter.

"In the freezer at the club." Grace produced a shiver. "At least this time Mom's not a suspect."

So far. If Detective Peters found out about the insurance money and how badly I needed the Michaels to be solvent again, he'd put two and two together and reach five.

"Who do you think did it?" Hunter directed his question to me.

"No idea. Not Tom." Please not Tom. Please not Tom. "There was a bookie wandering around the club."

"A bookie?" His brows rose.

"I heard Mr. Michaels was having an affair and Mrs. Michaels wouldn't give him a divorce." Grace's words were disturbing. Her tone more so. She sounded exactly like Mother.

I gaped at her. "Where on earth did you hear that?"

"The grapevine." Now she sounded airy. Like Mother when she was being high-handed.

"Gossip and murder investigations don't mix." What a lie that was. Murder investigations were gossip fodder.

Aggie nodded. "Your mother is right, Grace. Gossip can muddy the waters." She didn't add that the grapevine had convicted me of killing my husband. I'd still be judged guilty by the members of my set if the murderer hadn't made a mistake.

Hunter, wisely remaining silent, popped the last bite of sandwich into his mouth and chewed.

Now that I'd told her not to mix murder and gossip, I had to ask. "With whom does the grapevine say Mr. Michaels was having an affair?"

Grace patted her lips with a napkin. "Isn't my telling you just passing on gossip?"

Yes. Dammit. "Tell me anyway."

"Jenny Woods."

"Mrs. Michaels accused Jenny of that. She denied it."

Graced smiled. A smile far too old for her years. "At the country club, right?"

"Yes."

"If someone accused you of sleeping with their husband in front of a room full of people, wouldn't you deny it?"

Hunter choked on a sip of coffee.

I stared at the stranger sitting at the kitchen counter. Where had my sweet little girl gone?

The stranger crossed her arms and waited for an answer.

"I would never sleep with someone else's husband." That was the absolute truth. But my response didn't answer her question. Would I lie? The more pressing question was had Jenny lied?

ELEVEN

I lifted the brass knocker on Mother's front door at precisely one thirty. The cold of the metal cut through my gloves, and I released the lion's ring quickly. *Thunk*!

Mother allowed me entrance with a quick scan of my ensemble—or what she could see of it beneath my coat. "Pants?"

Mother wore a tweed skirt and a cashmere twin set. Her feet were encased in fur-lined booties.

"Yes. Pants." Their wide cuffs hid my snow boots. "If we get stuck, I don't want to be floundering around a snow drift in a skirt."

She sniffed, but we both knew if we did get stuck she and her skirt would stay in the car and I'd push. "Was Hunter helpful?"

"Very. He went through the file and he's checking into placing a lien."

Mother positively beamed. "He's such a dear man. You could do worse." What she meant was I could not do better. "You should invite him to Thanksgiving dinner."

"I am sure he has plans, and I am not ready for a relationship." We'd been over this a million times.

Tsk. "He won't wait forever."

"That's a chance I'll have to take."

"I just want you to be happy." Her usual line was "you're not getting any younger."

I blinked back my surprise at the change. "Thank you."

"A woman needs a man." That was an expected line. One I'd heard ad infinitum.

She had my best interests at heart. My best interests as she saw them. Enough already. "Are you telling me that if something happened to Daddy, you'd get married again?"

"Heavens, no! But your father and I have been together for forty-five years."

"And?"

"And no one could replace him. If something happened, I'd find a nice man to take me to dinner and the symphony and the movies but no more."

"And what's wrong with me doing that?"

"You've got half your life in front of you. Do you really want to spend it alone?"

The tendons in my shoulders and neck tightened. "Right now, I'm happier being alone. You have to respect that."

Mother pursed her lips. She did not have to respect my wishes and my failure to fall in line with her plans was a terrible annoyance. She pointed at the closet. "Please get my coat. The mink." She was not ceding her argument, just saving it for another day.

We stepped outside and an icy wind attacked us.

Mother glowered at the drive. "You brought that car?"

My Triumph, undeserving of the sneer on her lips, awaited us.

"I did."

"I thought Grace's car was better in snow."

"It is. That's why Grace is driving it. She went sledding."

We drove (slid) to a trio of condominium apartments overlooking the Plaza. The longest short drive of my life. Mother's little gasps of alarm tightened my shoulders till they rose to my ears. The gasps were just amuse-bouches for her comments. *Why aren't you braking? That car is about to hit you! How long has it been since you drove in snow?* By the time we reached our destination my teeth were on edge.

If the city streets were a nightmare, the drive that looped in front of the buildings was a dream. A completely cleared dream. I dropped Mother at the front doors of the center building, parked the car, and sat. Blessedly alone. Mother being annoying—epically so—meant nothing in the face of getting information from Lorna. I got out of the car and hurried to the center building.

When I entered, a rush of delicately scented warm air greeted me. Pine and nutmeg and cinnamon. Their scents conjured up the holidays of my childhood and some of the tension left my shoulders.

More tension dissolved when the doorman grinned at me. "Hello, Miss Ellison." Jimmy had been calling me "Miss Ellison" since I wore Mary Janes and smocked dresses to visit my grandparents who'd lived on the seventh floor. Jimmy had taken such good care of them that both Mother and I still remembered him at Christmas.

I grinned back. "Good afternoon, Jimmy." The man was surely a septuagenarian by now. He deserved the more dignified James. But Jimmy he had always been. And Jimmy he would always be. To me and to everyone who lived there. The residents of his building didn't like change.

"Mrs. Walford tells me you're here to see Mrs. Michaels." Traces of the Deep South still lingered in Jimmy's voice. "I'll call the elevator for you."

Before he could push a button, the elevator doors slid open and Jenny Woods stepped out.

She was dressed for the weather. Snow boots, fox jacket, gloves, hat, and pants instead of a skirt. Her cheeks were rosy pink and her eyes sparkled as if she'd just received excellent news. She stopped, her eyes widening. "Ellison. What a surprise.

I didn't think anyone would be out today." Jenny turned to Mother. "How nice to see you, Mrs. Walford. How are you?"

"Fine, thank you, Jenny. And you?"

"Fine. Fine. Except for all this snow."

"It's early in the season," said Mother. "It will melt in a few days."

"I hope you're right." Jenny looked through the glass doors and shivered. "I must say it's a treat not to worry about shoveling the walk or the drive." She'd purchased the only condominium to come on the market over the summer in a bidding war that resulted in a number of disgruntled bidders. "How are the roads?"

"Not good," I said.

"Drat. I simply must get to the market."

The market? Full makeup, a fox jacket, and perfectly coiffed hair for the market? I didn't believe that for a minute.

"You're very brave to go out for a can of soup." Mother's tone suggested she had doubts about Jenny's destination as well.

Jenny's eye twitched. Guilty conscious or a dust mote? "I'm afraid the cupboard is bare." She winced and placed a hand on her belly. "And my stomach hurts. I need a stockpile of chicken noodle just in case I'm coming down with something."

Mother took a step backward.

Jenny shifted her hand from her midsection to her left arm. "What brings you out on such a raw day?"

"Lorna Michaels," I replied.

"Ahh. Poor Laurie." The absence of emotion in Jenny's voice told me what she really thought. "Such a tragedy."

"Indeed." Mother's voice was as flat as Jenny's.

It was my turn to chime in. "I feel just awful for Tom and Trip."

We nodded in unison, seemingly as unmoved by Laurie's

death as the Fates. What a trio. Clotho, Lachesis, and Atropos—the spinner of thread, the measurer of thread, and the cutter of thread. Of the three of us, who was who?

"You found her?" Jenny offered me a sympathetic moue.

Mother grimaced. She did not approve of my finding bodies.

"No. I was in the kitchen when the sous-chef found her."

"But you were there. How distressing for you." The moue ceded to a wrinkled brow.

"It was horrible." "Horrible" didn't begin to cover Laurie's frozen stare or her lavender hue. The shiver that skated across my skin had nothing to do with the weather.

Jenny reached out, took my hand, and gave it a firm squeeze. "I'm sure it was." She released my hand and glanced outside, where the sun had broken through the clouds and the whole world sparkled. "I won't keep you. I know Lorna probably needs your support."

"You didn't like Laurie?" It was an incredibly blunt question. Only Mother could get away with such directness.

Jenny was struck dumb. She opened her mouth then closed it. Then she fanned her cheeks. "Is it warm in here?"

"No." Mother narrowed her eyes and waited.

Jenny returned her gaze. For a moment. But no one could best Mother. Jenny gave in. "No," she admitted. "I didn't like her."

Mother nodded. Slowly. "You should know, there's talk floating around about you and Tom."

Some of the high color leached from Jenny's cheeks and her eyes widened. "You mean people are saying I killed her."

Mother clasped her mink-covered chest. "Good heavens, no! But they are saying you had a reason to want her dead."

Jenny glanced first at the elevator then through the front doors as if she was considering making a run for it. But she stood her ground. She even managed an insouciant shrug. "I'm not the only one."

I stared at the woman I thought I knew. By admitting she wanted Laurie out of the way, was Jenny admitting to an affair with Tom? Or something more? And who else wanted Laurie dead?

I had to ask. "What do you me—"

Jenny held up a hand, cutting me off. "I'm sorry, but I simply must run. Thanks so much for letting me know about the gossip, Mrs. Walford. I hope you'll help me nip it in the bud."

Mother answered with a tight smile.

"Ellison, simply marvelous to see you." Jenny stepped toward the front door. Jimmy stepped out from behind his desk and opened the door. And she was gone.

Mother and I exchanged glances then she gave me a near infinitesimal nod.

"Jimmy—" I called upon the power of all those Christmas tips "—is Miss Woods seeing anyone?"

Jimmy ran his fingers inside his collar. "I don't rightly know."

"Oh?"

He glanced around the small lobby as if he expected the president of the condo board to be lurking behind the potted palm.

I lowered my voice. "You can tell us."

Mother pretended interest in a still life she'd seen a thousand times.

Jimmy's eyes scanned the lobby. "Mr. Michaels has been visiting his mother a lot lately." His voice was no more than a whisper.

Mr. Michaels was in a financial bind. Visiting the one woman who could bail him out made good financial sense.

Jimmy looked left then right. "But the elevator doesn't stop on Mrs. Michaels' floor."

A soft hiss of breath escaped Mother's thinned lips. "What is wrong with young people? In my day, we—"

I pushed Mother toward the elevator. "Thank you, Jimmy. We should head on up to Lorna's. She's expecting us."

Mother looked mad enough to spit golf tees, but she didn't argue.

The doors slid open. We stepped inside. I pushed a button and the doors slid shut.

"You didn't need to go on about adultery in front of Jimmy." It was a reasonable point.

"Hmph. Does Jenny do drugs?"

I gaped at Mother. "Not that I know of. Why?"

"Her pupils looked odd."

Wide. Certainly wide. But odd?

The elevator arrived on Lorna's floor. We walked down the hall to her apartment and silently communicated as to who would knock. Raised eyebrows. Tilted chins. Me.

Lorna answered the door and beckoned us inside with a smile. "How nice of you to come out on such an ugly day."

The weather could have been a hundred times worse and I'd have still appeared on her doorstep. She had information I needed.

"Ellison, dear, would you put the coats on the bed in the guest room?"

I took Mother's mink to the guest room where the walls and drapes and bedding matched—daisies and poppies and lilies of the valley in delicate shades of blue and peach and yellow. Lorna had embraced English country style. There was an Axminster carpet on the floor, the bedroom set was Chippendale, and I'd bet all that fabric was Liberty. Wedgewood pots on a plant stand in front of the windows held actual lilies of the valley. They filled the room with their sweet scent.

I dropped Mother's coat on one of the twin beds, took off my own fur, and laid it next to hers.

"Ellison, what's keeping you? Lorna made tea."

"Coming." I hurried to the living room where a Spode teapot, joined by matching cups and saucers, waited on a tray. A variety of cookies—the Pepperidge Farm Capri mix—were displayed on a plate.

Both Mother and Lorna sat on a chintz sofa, Mother in her tweed skirt and cashmere twinset, Lorna in a velvet caftan that would make Aggie cry with envy. Their ankles were neatly crossed. Their expressions politely expectant. They could not drink tea until I joined them.

I chose a club chair and sank into its downy depths.

Posture, Ellison. Mother didn't actually speak. Well, she spoke with her eyes. They narrowed slightly.

My spine straightened. My shoulders squared. And I leaned forward, fighting the sucking comfort of the chair. I even donned a smile.

Lorna picked up the teapot with a hand roped by age and spotted by the sun. It was a hand a turkey vulture would be proud to have. "Frances, you're lemon and two sugars, yes?"

Mother nodded. "Yes, thank you."

Lorna poured, doctored Mother's tea, and handed her the cup.

"What about you, Ellison?"

"A touch of milk, thank you."

She prepared a cup for me and then herself.

When we all had tea, perfectly brewed of course, I said, "We're so sorry for your loss."

Lorna's expression didn't change. Not one whit. "Yes, well. Dust to dust." Then, as if realizing she sounded unreasonably harsh, her forehead wrinkled. "Poor Trip. It must be awful to lose one's mother so young."

"Losing a mother is painful at any age," said Mother.

Lorna nodded her agreement. "Life is so difficult for young people these days. And for their parents. Children have temptations we never dreamed of." She patted her mouth with a lace-edged napkin. "How is Grace doing with the loss of her father?"

Oh. Wow. The teacup in my hand rattled and I moved in slow motion, setting the delicate china down on the coffee table before it ended up in my lap. How was Grace doing? In the month of November alone, Grace had been arrested, shot a man, had a wild party, and had her heart broken by Lorna's grandson. And the month wasn't over yet. "Grace is getting along fine."

"There you have it." Lorna looked almost triumphant. "As long as Trip has Tom, he'll be fine."

Who was I to argue? I cleared my throat and shifted on my downy chair. "Lorna, I hate to bring this up—"

"The insurance?" Lorna bestowed a queenly smile upon me. "I already told Frances, Laurie was insured."

Here came the delicate part. "Are you sure Tom was paying the premiums?" My voice sounded tremulous.

"I'm sure he wasn't."

Thank God I'd put that teacup down. It would have fallen just like my stomach. I gripped the arm of the chair. "Pardon?"

Lorna inclined her head, a queen mildly curious about her subject's distress. "I paid the premiums. I had to. Laurie couldn't be counted on to pay anything."

I breathed again.

Lorna continued, "That woman was putting my son in the poorhouse."

I was careful not to catch Mother's eye. Lorna was very much of the my-child-is-a-saint school of mothering. Any problems between Tom and Laurie were, by default, Laurie's fault.

Mother shook her head sadly. "How awful for poor Tom."

Lorna nodded her agreement then leaned forward. "She gambled."

Mother reached over and patted Lorna's arm. "What a cross to bear."

Lorna put down her teacup, clasped her hands in her lap, and donned a brave face. "It was all Tom could do to pay the country club bill."

Such an admission did not make Tom look blameless for Laurie's death. "I'm sorry to keep returning to this, Lorna, but I want to make sure I understand. Tom owned the policy, but you paid the premiums?"

"Yes, dear." Which meant if Tom had killed his wife, there would be no payout.

"Who do you think killed her?" asked Mother. She must have awakened on the wrong side of the bed that morning and decided to be especially blunt.

Lorna took a contemplative sip of tea. "I heard Prudence Davies threatened her."

I nodded. "That's true. I was there."

Lorna shook her regal head. "I've never liked Prudence. Not even when she was a child."

Agreed.

We discussed Prudence's many character flaws for several minutes—an activity I would have enjoyed immensely were it not for the effort required to maintain good posture in a chair that demanded lolling.

Mother glanced at her watch. "Ellison, we should be going."

I leapt to my feet. "Let me take the tea things to the kitchen for you, Lorna."

"Don't be silly, dear."

"I'm up." I put the empty cups back on the tray and carried it to Lorna's small bright kitchen. The Pepperidge Farm container sat open on the counter with two dirty teacups next to it. The tea towels hanging from the oven handle were slightly askew. Other than that, it looked like a kitchen ready for a photo shoot.

I put the tray down next to the used cups and returned to the living room. "Lorna, thank you for the information and the delicious tea."

"Lapsang Souchong."

"Oh?"

"The tea. It was Lapsang Souchong." She glanced toward the kitchen. "I've been trying different types of tea in anticipation of your visit. I decided on that one."

"It was delicious." It was nowhere near as good as a cup of coffee.

"Ellison, get the coats."

I did as Mother asked and we air-kissed our way out of Lorna's apartment.

TWELVE

Mother and I stepped into the elevator. I pushed "L" and she pulled on her gloves. "Lorna's holding up well."

Aside from the looming inconvenience of a funeral, Lorna seemed entirely unaffected. "Yes. She is." My voice was dry.

Mother smoothed the wrinkles from her gloves. "This must be so trying for her."

So trying that she'd spent her morning sampling tea.

"I'm sure she'll get over it." By five o'clock tonight.

The doors slid open and we entered the lobby.

Outside, the sun had given way to clouds and there were new flakes falling from the sky. "If you wait here, I'll pull the car up."

Ever gracious, Mother nodded her assent. "Thank you."

The cold stole my breath. I gathered my coat more tightly around me and hurried to the car.

Behind my Triumph, someone was warming up their Audi coupe. The car was a lovely shade—somewhere between aquamarine and silver. Despite the freezing temperature, I slowed my steps and peeked in the passenger's window. A gray interior or black?

My steps stopped altogether, as if my feet were frozen to the pavement.

Jenny was inside the car and she was slumped over the steering wheel.

I tapped on the window.

She didn't respond.

I tapped harder. Difficult to do wearing leather gloves. I slammed the heel of my hand against the window.

Nothing.

I tried the door.

Locked.

Dammit. What was wrong with her? I hurried around the back of the coupe and yanked on the driver-side door handle.

The door opened smoothly

"Jenny. Are you all right?"

She didn't move.

I poked her shoulder.

She didn't move.

She couldn't be dead. There was no blood. No knife protruding from her chest. No tell-tale scent of almonds (I leaned forward and sniffed).

"Jenny!" The birds in the oaks towering above me squawked and took flight. Jenny remained silent and still.

No! Not again. It could not be. My knees turned to jelly and clutched the roof of the car. This wasn't happening. Not to someone I liked. She'd taken something and fallen asleep.

"Jenny!" The circling birds cawed their displeasure. To hell with poking. I shook her shoulder. Hard.

Nothing. Nothing except for a dreadful slackness. I released her and she slumped to the side. Jenny was dead.

Nausea wrung my stomach like a wet washcloth. I turned away from my dead friend. Lapsang Souchong and two Milano cookies (Lorna insisted I eat the second cookie) discolored the snow. They were joined by lunch and breakfast. My stomach heaved until there was nothing left but bile.

Dammit. Dammit. Dammit.

I fumbled in my purse and closed my gloved fingers around a handkerchief. I wiped my mouth. And my eyes. And my cheeks. The tears kept coming, almost painful in the cold.

With the soiled hanky crumpled in my fist, I stumbled toward the lobby.

Jimmy opened the door. "Miss Ellison?"

Mother's brows rose. "Don't tell me. That ridiculous car of yours won't start."

"Not exactly." I swallowed the bile lurking at the back of my throat. "The car is fine. Jimmy, we need to call the police." I rattled off Anarchy's number.

Jimmy dialed.

"What's happened?" Mother demanded. "What's wrong?"

Maybe I was mistaken. Maybe Jenny had just passed out. I sealed my lips. I couldn't say it out loud. Not yet. Instead of supplying Mother's answer, I used the wrinkled hanky to wipe the mascara from under my eyes.

"Ellison Walford Russell, what the hell is happening?" Mother crossed her arms, narrowed her eyes, and waited.

"It's Jenny Woods. I found her slumped behind the wheel of her car." I couldn't say it. There was simply no way I could articulate the words.

"Jimmy, is Dr. Fitzwater home today?" Mother asked.

"A doctor can't help."

The air around Mother stilled. Stilled but charged. The calm before a storm.

I wiped my eyes again (they wouldn't stop leaking) and made my mouth form syllables. "I think she's dead."

Mother staggered.

I caught her elbow, led her to a settee, and crouched next to her when she sat. "Would you like a glass of water?" I wanted one—if only to rinse the awful taste from my mouth.

Her cheeks were pale, but she found the inner fortitude to say, "No. I do not want a glass of water." Her shoulders squared and she glared at me. "That's two this week, Ellison. If you keep this up, we won't have any friends left."

Two bodies in a week. Was it only Wednesday when Laurie's body had turned up in a freezer? "It's not my fault. I'm not killing them."

Mother buried her head in her hands. "People are starting to avoid you. You'll adopt a bunch of cats and grow old alone."

"Don't be ridiculous," I snapped.

"I've got a detective on the phone." Jimmy held the receiver aloft.

I stood and took the phone from his outstretched hand, nodding my thanks. "Anarchy, it's Ellison."

"This isn't Jones."

I recognized the voice and my lungs deflated. Dammit. Anarchy's partner already thought I was a meddling socialite. A meddling socialite who was capable of murder. "Detective Peters?"

"Yeah."

"I think you'd better come. Or send someone. You could send someone."

"What seems to be the problem, Mrs. Russell?"

"I found a body."

The man grunted and I thought I heard him say, "Of course you did." A second grunt. Maybe a bit of blue language. Whatever he said was muffled as if he had his hand over the phone's mouthpiece. "Where are you?"

I gave him the address.

"Figures."

"What's that supposed to mean?"

"You don't find people in dingy alleys, do you?" I could imagine him in the squad room with his rumpled tie and squinty eyes and aura of cynical exhaustion.

I gritted my teeth. Usually I found bodies at the country club, or at galas, or in my yard. Today, I'd found a body—

Jenny—at the most luxurious apartments in the city. Rarely did I venture into parts of town where one might expect a shooting or—my gaze shifted to the parking lot and the Audi coupe that held Jenny—an overdose.

"We'll have a patrol car there shortly."

"Thank you." Never had an expression of gratitude sounded less sincere. "Goodbye."

I handed the phone back to Jimmy and he put the receiver on its cradle. "What happened, Miss Ellison?"

"I don't know." I looked straight into Jimmy's kind eyes. "Did Ms. Woods do drugs?"

Mother's hiss of disapproval was probably audible all the way to the third floor.

"No, ma'am. Least ways, I never saw anything like that."

The truth sat in the front row, bouncing in its seat with its hand thrusting into the air, just waiting for me to call on it.

I ignored it. "Mother, do you have Sharon and Jack's number?"

"At home in my book." Mother's address book, spiral bound with a leather cover, held every phone number or address one might ever want. All written in pencil (easily erased if the number changed). It was no surprise that she had Jenny's parent's winter number. "They left for Palm Springs the first of the month."

"We should call them."

"And tell them their daughter's dead?"

The truth, still bouncing in its desk chair, added, "Ooo, ooo, ooo! I know what happened!"

"Wouldn't they rather hear from us?" I couldn't imagine Detective Peters included kindness or empathy in his death notifications. He seemed more of a where-were-you-when kind of cop.

"No, Ellison. That's a job for the police." She smiled at

Jimmy from her place on the settee. "Maybe no one ever need know you found Jenny."

The truth's eyes were enormous. It bounced harder and waved its hand wildly. It wouldn't wait much longer.

"She took one too many valiums." Mother nodded sagely, certain of her omniscience. "There's no reason you should be associated with her death."

"You heard Jimmy. Jenny didn't take drugs."

"Don't be silly, Ellison." Mother glared at me. "Valium isn't a drug. It's a prescription."

Jimmy's mouth dropped. I gaped. Even the truth stopped its infernal bouncing. We were united in our surprise that a seemingly intelligent woman could make such a pronouncement.

"Mother, prescriptions are drugs."

"No. Heroin is a drug. Prescriptions are medicine."

Such thinking landed my friend Jinx in rehab.

The truth was done waiting. It climbed out of its chair and stood atop its desk. "I know! I know! I know!"

Whatever the truth was, I knew I wouldn't like it.

"She was murdered!" Having imparted its message, the truth resumed its seat and clasped its hands on the desk like a model student.

Dammit. The truth was a pain in the ass. It was my turn to smile at Jimmy. "Did anyone visit Jenny this morning?"

Jimmy cupped his chin in his fist and thought. "Not rightly sure."

"Who came to the building who doesn't live here?"

Now Jimmy rubbed his chin, considering. "Mr. Tom—" my heart sank "—Mr. Sherman Westcott, Mrs. Davies, a gentleman who didn't belong, and a lady I didn't know. She said her name was Edna Smith."

"Who were they here to—"

"Where's the body?" Detective Peters blew into the lobby with a gust of frigid wind and the smell of cheap cigars.

With a glance, Mother took in his wrinkled coat, his mustache in need of a trim, the shine reflecting from the top of his round head, and the way his remaining hair brushed his collar, and her lip curled.

Oh, dear.

"Who are you?" she asked in her best lady-of-manor voice.

"Mother, this is Detective Peters. He works with Detective Jones. Detective Peters, this is my mother, Mrs. Walford."

"Where is Detective Jones?" Mother's tone was wistful, almost as if she missed Anarchy. It was official. Hell had frozen over.

"He's investigating the last body Mrs. Russell found." Peters' words made me sound guilty. They were as good as a thrown gauntlet.

Mother stood. From the silver helmet of her hair to the powdered tip of her nose, from the collar of her mink to her fur-lined boots, everything about her said wealth and privilege. Everything about her said Peters' challenge was accepted. She inclined her chin. "What precisely are you suggesting, Detective Peters?"

"I'm not suggesting anything. I'm saying your daughter finds too many bodies."

It was a point Mother couldn't argue.

"So where's today's?" Detective Peters looked around the small lobby.

"Outside," I told him. "In the Audi coupe."

Peters' eyes narrowed. "Another popsicle?"

Mother gasped. She didn't find gallows humor remotely amusing.

The thought of poor Jenny...frozen. My empty stomach flipped just to remind me it didn't actually need food to make me retch. "The car is running. Jenny Woods is inside."

"And who exactly is Jenny Woods?"

My eyes. Damn my eyes. They started leaking again and my throat thickened. "A friend."

Detective Peters grunted and peered through the glass doors at the still-running Audi. "Did you touch anything?"

"The outside windows and the car handle and Jenny's shoulder." I held up my hands. "I was wearing gloves."

"You couldn't find her inside?" He buttoned the top button of his coat. "It's cold as a witch's ti—"

"Watch your language, sir." Mother had not yet abandoned the fight. Mother never abandoned a fight.

Peters grunted (the grunt said, "you're a pain in my ass"). "Sorry, ma'am."

"I should think so. My daughter, acting as a concerned citizen, did her civic duty and reported a death, and the police respond with derision and outright rudeness?"

Peters didn't grunt. He mumbled. Probably something akin to "you're a pain in my ass and a bitch on wheels," but I couldn't be sure. He might have mumbled from hell instead.

"I have half a mind to call Ellison's Uncle James."

Peters looked unimpressed.

"He's a police commissioner." And not really my uncle, just one of Daddy's friends.

"A civilian appointee." Peters should have stuck with mumbling.

Mother drew herself up and stared down the length of her nose. "Then perhaps I should call the mayor."

"Knock yourself out, lady."

"Mother."

She paid me as much attention as she would pay a gnat.

"Mother, the governor runs the police department."

"Then I'll call Kit." As far as I knew, Mother had never met

Missouri's young governor.

Detective Peters didn't know that. His cheeks grew ruddy. "Are you threatening me?"

"Absolutely not, Detective Peters." There was a level of sweetness in Mother's voice that made my teeth hurt. Her meaning was clear. She'd happily call the governor (who she did not know by his first name) and complain about the way Detective Peters spoke to her daughter.

Detective Peters did not need another reason to dislike me. Somehow, I'd unknowingly provided plenty of reasons on my own. What's more, I could fight my own battles with the irascible detective. I didn't need Mother to fight them for me.

Before Peters could reply to Mother's salvo, I found my voice. "This is ridiculous. Jenny is out there and we're in here arguing. Mother, you needn't call anyone on my behalf. And Detective Peters, what if I was wrong? What if Jenny's not dead? What if she's in a coma and in need of medical attention?"

Mother didn't look remotely moved by my comments. She was probably enjoying the battle with Peters. It was so seldom she had the opportunity to go into full grande dame mode.

Detective Peters glanced outside. "The Audi coupe?"

"Yes," I replied.

He grunted (an untranslatable grunt), reached into his pocket, and pulled out a wrinkled cap. Without another word, he jammed the cap on his head and marched out into the cold.

"What a positively dreadful man." The corners of Mother's lips drooped as if she was sorry to see him go.

"Be that as it may—"

The door swung open and Anarchy strode into the lobby. Strode right to me.

Whatever I'd meant to say to Mother flitted away. Forgotten.

He searched my face. "Are you all right?"

"I've been better."

"You're hurt?" His eyes scanned my body, looking for injury.

"No. I'm just tired of finding bodies."

"Son of a bitch!" The words carried across half a parking lot and through a closed door. Outside, Detective Peters had found where I left Lorna's tea and cookies.

He stomped around the pavement, his left leg covered in snow and freezing vomit, his arms flapping like a rotund bird's wings.

"I'm afraid I was sick next to Jenny's car."

Mother giggled. It was such an uncharacteristic sound that for an instant I worried she was choking.

Anarchy's lips twitched. "I should head out there."

Anarchy was a brave man. He pushed on the door.

"Detective Jones." Mother's voice was imperious. "I'd like to go home now."

His brows rose. "Ellison drove you here?"

Mother's brows rose at his use of my first name. "She did."

"We may have questions for her. I'll see about getting a squad car to take you home."

Now I giggled. Mother emerging from the back of a squad car while her neighbors peeked through their curtains? I had to giggle.

Mother shot me a look that said all too clearly that I'd pay for my amusement. Later. When we were alone. "That is not acceptable."

"Then I'm afraid you'll have to wait here, Mrs. Walford."

He left us alone with Jimmy.

"He can't make us stay here." Mother sounded outraged. So much for the concerned citizen doing her civic duty.

"He can't make you stay here. They're going to question me. And frankly, I'd rather talk to them here than the police station.

You can call a cab."

"I won't leave you here."

"I'll be fine."

"That fireplug of a detective has it in for you."

She meant Detective Peters. Anarchy in no way resembled a fireplug.

"Anarchy will look out for me."

Her lips thinned. "Jimmy, would you please call up to Mrs. Michaels?"

Jimmy nodded and dialed Lorna's number.

Mother took the receiver from his hand. "Lorna? It's Frances. You won't believe what's happened." Mother glanced around the lobby as if a gossip columnist was waiting to catch what she said next. She cupped her hand over the mouthpiece and whispered her shameful revelation. "Ellison found another body."

Lorna said something. Or I assume she did. Mother pressed the receiver against her ear and listened.

"No. I'm not kidding. We're stuck here until—"

Mother listened with a sour expression on her face.

"That's what I'm telling you." Frustration was evident in her voice. "Ellison found a body in the parking lot and we're stuck in the lobby for the foreseeable future. May we please come upstairs?"

With the receiver pressed into her helmet of silver hair, Mother nodded. "Thank you." She handed the phone back to Jimmy and adjusted the strap of her handbag in the crook of her elbow. "Come along, Ellison."

More Lapsang Souchong? More gossip? I just couldn't. Not when Jenny slumped over her steering wheel. "I'll wait down here."

"Don't be silly."

"Mother, I'll wait here. You go on. You and Lorna can visit

without me." Mother could bemoan her daughter who found bodies everywhere she went.

"I told Lorna you were coming."

"She'll understand."

"Ellison, I insist."

I crossed the lobby and pushed the button for the elevator. The doors slid open and I held them open. "Go on up, Mother. I'm staying down here."

Mother, looking extremely put out, stepped into the elevator. "I don't know what's gotten into you since Henry died."

I could tell her, but she wouldn't like my answer. I'd changed—something in my soul had shifted—and I wasn't going back to the way I was before.

THIRTEEN

Mother had refused to talk to me in the car on the way home from Lorna's. Instead she'd crossed her arms and stared out the window at streets blanketed in snow. But her silence had lasted only a few hours.

Now she was on the phone. "I talked to your father and we're not coming for Thanksgiving."

I did not beg her to change her mind. "Where are you going?"

"Your sister's. Your father has decided we're driving." Martyrs being fed to lions sounded less persecuted.

"Driving?"

"Yes, dear."

"But Akron is eight hundred miles away." Mother got carsick. Poor Daddy.

"I know precisely how far it is."

"The speed limit is fifty-five."

"Yes, dear." Two words. Repeated. That's all it took to tell me this was somehow my fault. The car trip. The speed limit. The bodies. Everything.

"There's snow."

"Your father assures me the highways will be clear."

"Mother, if you're going to Marjorie's because I wouldn't go up to Lorna's with you—"

"Don't be ridiculous." Her words said one thing. Her tone told a different story. I was supposed to feel guilty. Very guilty.

Tail-between-my-legs guilty. I'd stood up to her and now she had to drive halfway across the country to spend Thanksgiving with the good daughter.

"When are you leaving?"

She answered with silence. I'd failed to give her the right response (the right response would be me begging her not to go).

I examined my nails. I needed a manicure. I smiled at Mr. Coffee. He smiled back, as dependable as the sun rising in the east.

Mother sighed.

Despite my best efforts to keep undeserved guilt at bay, it pricked my conscience. I locked my jaw. I would not beg her to stay. Would not.

She waited a good ten seconds then sighed again. "We leave in the morning."

I would not feel guilty. I would not. Oh dear Lord. I did. "Remember, Gwen will be here. You'll have more fun at Marjorie's."

"Is Gwen staying with you?"

"Yes." I got off my stool and stood next to Mr. Coffee. I needed him. His strength. His dependability. His coffee. And I needed to mollify Mother. At least a bit. "I need your advice."

"Yes?"

"Gwen drinks tea."

"And?"

"And I know nothing about tea."

"Buy some of the stuff Lorna served."

I could do that, but I suspected Gwen drank herbal tea, the kind that tasted like old socks. Besides, the mere thought of facing a cup of Lapsang Souchong made my stomach lurch with the memory of throwing up in a snowbank. "Good idea."

"When is she arriving?" Mother asked.

"Tuesday. She's leaving Friday."

"So that's one, two, three, four days of vegan meals." Mother was sounding less put upon. In fact, she sounded almost pleased.

"I suppose so."

"Does Aggie know how to cook tofu?"

"I'm sure she can figure it out."

"I imagine. Listen, I've got to pack if we're going to get out of town in the morning."

"Be safe on the roads."

"Of course. We're spending the night in St. Louis. I'll call you when we get there." In other words, she was washing her hands of my problems for the next week. I could handle Tom Michaels' bad loan, putting a lien on Laurie's insurance money, two dead bodies, and whatever Grace or Max or Gwen threw at me on my own.

I was fine with that. "I'll look forward to your call."

We hung up and Max nudged me. He wanted to go outside.

I rose from the stool and opened the back door.

Max surveyed the frozen tundra of his backyard, sighed deeply, and returned to his favorite spot next to the heating vent. He wanted to go outside in nice weather.

Grace breezed into the kitchen, opened the refrigerator door, and peered inside. "What's for dinner?"

"Aggie left us chili."

"Cool beans."

"No. Chili beans."

"Very funny, Mom."

"I thought so."

Her eyes rolled. I was not funny and, frankly, it was sad that I tried.

"All I have to do is warm it up." I gestured toward the stove.

"I'll do that." She spoke quickly. Too quickly.

"You make it sound like I can't even heat up a pot of chili."

"You know that crusty black stuff on the bottom of the pot? That's not supposed to be there."

"Very funny."

"That actually was funny." She lit the burner and turned the flame down so low it would take an hour (maybe two) to warm the chili then eyed me critically. "You look pale."

"It's been a long day." An understatement.

"Why don't you go upstairs after dinner and paint? I'll do the dishes."

Were all teenagers like this? Throwing wild parties one minute, being incredibly considerate the next? "I'll take you up on that."

We ate sitting on stools at the kitchen island. Using Grace's low and slow method, the chili was perfect, but I had no appetite. I pushed ground beef and beans around my bowl.

"You're not hungry?"

"I guess not."

"Go. Paint." Grace knew that painting, daubing color on canvas, was the way I dealt with strong emotion. "Unplug the phone. Neither Max nor I will disturb you unless the house catches on fire. I promise."

"You can disturb me for blood."

She grinned. "Okay. Fire or blood. Otherwise, you are strictly off limits."

I dropped a grateful kiss on the top of her head and trudged up the stairs to my attic studio, my flagging spirits lightening with each step.

I painted for hours. Winter darkness pressed against the glass, but inside there was light and color and the feel of brushes in my hand. I painted away the horror of Laurie's death, painted away some of the sadness of Jenny's death, painted away Mother's unhappiness with me. I painted until my soul felt lighter and my arm was tired.

The clock read nearly one in the morning when I made my way downstairs. I slipped into a nightgown, brushed my teeth, and noticed a stack of messages on my pillow. A large stack.

Anarchy had called. I smiled and traced his name and number with the tip of my finger then put the pink slip of paper on the bedside table.

Gwen had called. She was arriving early and bringing a friend. I took a deep breath, held it, then exhaled. Her message joined Anarchy's on the table.

Libba had called. I flipped through the messages. One, two, three, four times. I was to call her, Grace wrote in caps on the fourth slip of paper, "AS SOON AS POSSIBLE. NO MATTER THE TIME."

What now? A new man? A bad date?

Despite my aching shoulders and tired eyes, I picked up the receiver and dialed.

Libba answered on the first ring. "What took you so long?" Not so much as a hello.

"How did you know it was me?"

"Who else would call me at one in the morning?"

It was a fair question. "What's wrong?"

"Are you sitting down?"

I rested against the edge of the bed. "I am now."

"There's no easy way to say this."

My eyes were gritty with fatigue. I closed them and asked, "Say what?"

"Tom Michaels has been arrested for murder."

I slid from the edge of the bed to the floor. The loan. The bank. Grace's inheritance from her father. "Whose murder?" I asked even though I knew the answer. Knew it in a pit-of-my-stomach, visceral way.

"Who do you think? Laurie's."

Dammit.

"And Jenny's."

"Jenny's?" I pressed my free hand over my eyes.

"An obvious case of poisoning is what I heard."

I didn't bother asking from whom. "Why would Tom kill Jenny?"

"Why would he kill Laurie? He could have divorced her." Libba made an excellent point.

I dropped my head to my knees. This was a disaster.

"I can't see Tom as a murderer," she said. "He doesn't have the fortitude."

"Ugh."

"Ugh? That's all you've got to say?"

That was all my brain could manage.

"He didn't do it." There was a plaintive note in Libba's voice.

"How can you be so sure?"

"Tom couldn't commit murder."

"Ugh." It was a phrase worth repeating.

"It's just not possible," she insisted. "Tom's not a killer. I know him. Well."

Oh dear Lord. She hadn't. "How well?"

"Well."

She had. Was there any man in our acquaintance with whom Libba hadn't slept?

"Listen, Ellison. Tom is innocent. You've got to prove he didn't kill Laurie and Jenny."

"Me?" Had she lost her mind?

"Yes, you. The police think he's guilty. They're not looking for something that might exonerate him. But you will. You've dealt with lots of murders. You can do this."

I lifted my head. If I could prove Tom's innocence, the insurance money would be his and he could pay off the loan.

Aggie could help. She had actual skills. But Anarchy would be livid if we interfered in his investigation. I weighed the two. Grace's legacy from her father versus Anarchy's ire. It was no contest. "Okay."

"Okay?" Libba sounded surprised. "I have a whole speech ready."

"You don't need the speech. I'll do it."

"What are you going to do?"

Excellent question. "You were at the club on Tuesday night, right?"

"Yes."

"Write down everything you saw. Who was there, what happened in the bar."

"That's it? That's all you're doing to investigate?"

"No." Exhaustions and adrenaline mixed a potent cocktail in my brain. "I'm going to talk to Jimmy."

Fortified by three cups of coffee and a slice of toast, I arrived at Lorna's building at nine in the morning, but the man who swung open the door for me wasn't Jimmy.

George wore a solemn expression. "Good morning, Miss Ellison."

Like Jimmy, George was a retired Monarchs player. Like Jimmy, he'd known me forever. Like Jimmy, I remembered him on my Christmas list.

"Good morning, George."

"I heard you were here yesterday. Sad day." He shook his grizzled head. "Sad day."

"It was."

"How may I help you?"

"I have a question for you, George. Jimmy mentioned some of the people who visited here yesterday."

"Yes, ma'am?"

"Sherman Westcott?"

George looked down at his desk. "Yes, ma'am?"

"Does he come here often?"

"No, ma'am."

"Any idea who he sees?"

With his gaze still angled downward, George shook his head. "Don't know, Miss Ellison."

I didn't believe him. Whoever Sherman came to see valued their privacy and gave George a bigger Christmas tip than I did. "When Prudence Davies drops by, who does she visit?"

He looked up and glanced around the empty lobby. "Mr. McNamara." His voice was low. The building's inhabitants didn't appreciate their doormen telling tales.

"Rupert McNamara?" My voice was low.

George nodded.

"And Tom Michaels? Who does he visit?"

"Mrs. Michaels, leastwise that's what he says whenever he arrives."

"What about Edna Smith?"

George shook his head. "I don't know Miss Smith."

"Is Mr. McNamara in?"

"I think so." George sounded reluctant.

"Perfect. I'd like to see him. Would you please call up and see if he's available?"

George's hand hovered over the phone and the space between his brows furrowed. "You're sure?"

"Yes." Rupert was one of Henry's cronies. I'd known him for years.

George lifted the receiver, pushed a single button, and paused. "You're sure?"

"I'm sure."

George dialed. "Mr. McNamara, this is George in the lobby.

Mrs. Russell is in here and she'd like to see you." He listened, a frown on his face. "Yes, sir. I'll send her on up."

I walked toward the elevator. "What floor, George?"

George hung up the receiver. "Fifth floor, apartment A."

"Thank you."

"Miss Ellison..."

"Yes, George?"

"You're not back down here in twenty minutes, I'm coming up."

The elevator arrived before I could ask him why. I stepped inside and the doors slid shut behind me, but not before I saw George's worried gaze peering after me.

Rupert's door was open. He stood at the threshold and called my name as soon as I exited the elevator. "Ellison!"

"Hello, Rupert."

"I must say, this is an unexpected treat." Rupert wore gray flannels, a white shirt, and a Snidely Whiplash smile. "Come in!"

Rupert's apartment was decorated in black leather and brass. Stark white walls were decorated with black and white photographs. I paused. Stared. "Are those Mapplethorpes?"

"You recognize his work?" He sounded pleased.

"I met him the last time I was in New York."

Rupert stared at me. Not just stared. Somehow, he focused his whole attention on me. I felt his sudden interest, as tangible as the coat draped across my shoulders.

"He's an interesting young man."

He held my gaze. "You must tell me all about him."

Rupert's eyes glittered with an emotion I didn't care to examine.

I looked away. "There's not much to tell. An artist friend had a party and he was there. We chatted for a few minutes."

"What do you think of his work?"

"Our aesthetics are very different." Our aesthetics weren't

on the same planet. Mapplethorpe's photographs were either erotic or portraits of people whose pain radiated from their pores. Often both. My paintings were pretty.

"You must have some opinion," he insisted.

"I think he's very talented. He'll be famous."

Rupert nodded. "I agree. What brings you here?" No offer to sit, no offer of coffee, no offer to take my coat.

He wanted blunt? He could have it. "Was Prudence Davies here yesterday?"

"Yes."

Rupert was attractive. Surely he could do better than Prudence. "What time?" I asked.

"I'm a terrible host. Would you care for coffee? We can have it in the den. It has a spectacular view of the park."

Why didn't he just answer my question? "That sounds lovely, thank you."

He smiled and rubbed his hands together. "I just put a pot on. How do you take it?"

"With cream."

Something like amusement sparked in his eyes. "Just a moment."

He left me in the living room staring at pictures of haunted people who were too young to be haunted.

When he returned he carried two white mugs. "This way." He led me through the living room. "Why do you care about Prudence's doings? You know curiosity killed the cat, don't you?"

I should have been ready for his question. Why was I interested in Prudence? Because I hoped she'd murdered two people didn't seem like an answer that invited confidences. Especially not when she had braved unplowed streets to come see him.

I followed Rupert into his den and all thoughts of Prudence

and murder and bank loans disappeared.

Sweet nine-pound baby Jesus.

It was a good thing Rupert still held my coffee—I would have dropped it.

The walls were tufted red leather studded with brackets. The brackets held—I turned on my heel.

"Do you want an answer?" Rupert's tone mocked me.

I did want an answer. But how badly?

"Turn around and have a seat, Ellison." Now his tone was commanding.

I lifted my chin and turned.

"Henry always said you were the most vanilla woman he'd ever met."

If Rupert expected me to react, he was disappointed. I already knew that Henry had discussed our sex life—or lack thereof—with others.

"So this is why Prudence came." The words twisted into something ugly on my tongue.

"Sit."

There were two black leather club chairs positioned in the middle of the room with a side table between them. Rather than face the admittedly spectacular view of the park, the chairs faced the wall. The wall with manacles. The wall with a display of whips and riding crops and—good Lord, what was that?

I perched on the edge of the chair. Just the thought of what might have happened on its leather surface made me want to send my coat to the dry cleaner. As soon as I got home. No, on the way home. I could drive a few blocks without a coat. "About Prudence? What time was she here?"

"Dear Prudence."

I opened my mouth to ask a third time, but he wagged a finger at me. "First—" he waved his other hand toward the items on the wall "—how does this make you feel?"

Looking at his display of paraphernalia, my sight edged with crimson as bloody as his walls. "Angry."

He blinked. My response was a surprise.

"Men who need to dominate." I tsked and crossed my ankles. "My theory is they're compensating for some weakness." I shook my head, ignored Rupert's stony expression, and waved my hand at his devices. "Look where all this got Henry. Dead." And I was left behind to clean up his messes—like clearing Tom of murder so he could pay off his bank loan.

Rupert's lips thinned to a narrow line. "You never wondered what it would be like to give up control?"

"That assumes I had control to give." For most of our marriage, I hadn't. Henry had made all the important decisions in our lives. Right up until I accidentally made more money than he did. His response, regaining his lost control with kinky sex, was the final nail in the coffin of our failing marriage.

I took a deep breath. Like it or not, I had control now. And one thing was certain, I'd never cede so much as a smidgen of that control to a man whose idea of fun was spanking grown women. I straightened my shoulders and donned one of Mother's most freezing expressions. "Are you going to tell me what time Prudence was here or not?"

Rupert shrugged. "She arrived around ten. She left around one thirty."

That didn't give her much time to kill Jenny. But if any woman could spew poison quickly, it was Prudence. I stood. "Thank you. I'll see myself out."

"You're sure you won't stay? Afraid?"

"Of you?"

Rupert barked something like a laugh. "No. Afraid you might like it." The Snidely Whiplash grin was back. "I could make you feel things you've never felt before."

Like revulsion? "Thank you for your offer, but I must

decline." Being polite was an armor as strong as steel. I walked toward the living room with a tight smile pasted on my lips, my fingers circling the handles of my purse like a vise. If he so much as touched me, I'd swing it.

"Why do you care when Prudence was here, Ellison?"

He'd told me what I wanted to know. I didn't have to tell him a thing. "No reason."

He scowled at me. Women weren't supposed to defy him. If he wanted something, they supplied it. Easy-peasy. For him. "This—" he jerked his chin toward his red room "—stays between us."

As if I'd ever mention I'd actually been in there. "Of course."

Then I strode out the front door.

FOURTEEN

Walking out of Rupert's apartment would have been twice as satisfying if I'd been able to stride into an open elevator. Instead I pushed the button and waited.

The doors slid open and revealed Lorna Michaels. She looked, as my grandmother used to say, like something the cat dragged in. Her hair, usually a perfect steel gray helmet, was mashed flat. Her eyes were red-rimmed. The wrinkles in her face had deepened to crevasses and her shoulders were hunched like a crone's. With her black Persian lamb coat buttoned to her neck, she looked like Whistler's Mother—with less color.

"Lorna." I stepped into the elevator and took her hands (bricks of ice) in mine "Are you all right?"

Of course she wasn't. Her lips tightened and she shook her head, apparently so overwhelmed she couldn't speak.

"What can I do?"

She pulled one of her hands free and wiped her eyes with a lace-edge hanky. "Nothing. I never dreamed—" Her voice caught on the edge of a sob. "I never dreamed anything like this could happen to Tom. This is a nightmare."

"Are you on your way to see Tom in—"

"I'm on my way to the lawyer's office." She would not allow her son's name and "jail" in the same sentence.

"Where's Trip?"

She blinked. "Trip?"

"Your grandson," I prompted.

Her gaze wandered the elevator as if she wasn't quite sure where she was. Yesterday's tea-pouring tigress had been reduced by circumstances to a kitten without claws. "Trip. I don't know where he went."

She didn't know? Nor did she seem to care. There was a teenage boy out there who'd lost his mother to murder, whose father had been arrested, who needed his family. Or what was left of it, namely Lorna.

"I'll find him," I promised. Why did I make promises like that? "How are you getting to the lawyer's office?"

"I'm driving."

In her current state, she'd end up in Omaha. "Let me drive you."

She stared at me, the faded gray of her eyes so filled with worry they overflowed. "You don't need to do that."

"It would be my pleasure." I squeezed the hand I still held. "After that, I'll track down Trip."

"Thank you. You're a good friend." A tear meandered down her withered cheek. "It's times like these that I miss my husband the most. He would have known exactly what to do."

My memories of Thomas Michaels, Sr. were of a bluff man who cared about the stock market, Kansas basketball, and not much else. There was no playbook for seeing your child arrested for murder. No guide. I doubted he'd have been any better equipped to deal with Tom's troubles than Lorna. But he would have taken charge anyway.

I offered her an encouraging smile. "I don't think Tom did this."

Some of the fire returned to Lorna's eyes. "Of course he didn't."

"Can you think of anything—anything at all—that might prove his innocence?"

"This is all so—" she searched for a word "—sordid."

I didn't argue. Instead I said, "I've known you, known Tom, my whole life. I'd hate for an innocent man to be tried for murder." Plus, if Tom killed Laurie I could kiss the insurance money goodbye.

The elevator doors slid open and we stepped into the lobby.

George looked relieved to see me.

"If you'll wait here, Lorna, I'll bring the car around."

She nodded.

"Sit on down in this here chair, Mrs. Michaels." George gestured toward one of the chairs that crowded the lobby.

When Lorna sank onto the proffered seat, I hurried out into the cold.

After George loaded Lorna into the car, we drove in silence. Well, almost silence. From time to time, Lorna sighed. Had it been Mother in the car, I would have read a novel into those sighs. I was driving too fast or too slow. Why did I take the traffic way instead of Main Street? Why did I drive a Triumph instead of a large comfortable Mercedes? Preferably a white Mercedes that matched my soon-to-be husband's. I read nothing into Lorna's sighs but worry.

I saw her up to the lawyer's office, made sure the receptionist would have a cab waiting for her when she finished, and drove home with thoughts of Rupert McNamara for company.

I pulled into the driveway (I'd paid the boys down the street ten dollars to shovel it), sat behind the wheel, stared out the windshield at mounds of snow, and made a list. Ask Jimmy what time Prudence left the building, find out who Sherman and Edna Smith visited, read Libba's account of the night of Laurie's murder, and find Trip Michaels.

With a sigh, I got out of the car and marched up the front steps. The door opened for me.

Grace stood on the other side, a worried expression

wrinkling her brow.

"What is it? What's wrong?"

"I—" she shook her head as if she couldn't find any words "—he."

"He?"

She nodded with enthusiasm, as if one pronoun explained all.

"What's happened?"

"Trip's here."

Well, there was one item marked off my list. But why choose my house? "Wh—"

"He thought I'd understand because..."

Because, for a time, the whole world had been convinced I'd murdered Grace's father.

"I don't want him here," she whispered.

"You had a crush on him last week."

She glanced over her shoulder. "That was before I knew."

"Knew what?"

"About Dawn."

"What about Dawn?"

She sealed her lips and crossed her arms. She wasn't telling me.

"His mother is dead. His father is in jail. And his grandmother is with her lawyers. He's staying until I can talk to Lorna."

Grace responded with a sigh worthy of Mother.

"You can go to your room. I'll keep him company."

This was met with the eye roll it deserved. I could not be trusted with a boy.

I took off my coat and folded it over my arm.

"Aren't you going to hang that up?"

"It needs to go to the cleaners." That was all the explanation my sixteen-year-old was getting.

I suppressed a shudder and deposited the coat in the wicker send-to-the-cleaners basket in the laundry room then followed Grace into the family room.

Trip sat on the far corner of the couch staring at his clasped hands.

Gone was the cocky kid of last week. The boy on the couch looked like the last survivor of a disaster. A disaster worse than *Airport*, *The Poseidon Adventure* and *The Towering Inferno* combined. And, unfortunately for Trip, no heroic stars were coming to his rescue. Not Steve McQueen. Not Paul Newman. Not even Burt Lancaster. He was stuck with me.

"Hi," I said.

He looked up, but his eyes were blank, shocked. I doubted he actually saw me.

"Can I get you anything?"

He shook his head in mute response.

I claimed the opposite corner of the sofa. "I just saw your grandmother. She's worried about you." As fibs went, it was a small one.

Trip failed to respond.

I glanced at Grace. She'd leaned her hip against a club chair. Her arms were still crossed and the stubborn expression on her face looked as if it meant to stay. No help there.

"Your grandmother is meeting with lawyers to see about getting your dad out of jail."

"He didn't do it." Trip's tone was hopeless.

"Then the police will find who did." My tone was too perky. I cleared my throat. "We've been where you are, Trip. Trust me, Detective Jones will find the killer."

"Detective Jones didn't arrest Dad. It was someone named Peters."

Uh-oh. Detective Peters was the type who cared more about his clearance rate than catching the guilty.

If I didn't figure out who killed Laurie, the killer might never be found. "Who had a reason to kill your mom?" The question was probably cruel, but it had to be asked.

Grace's jaw dropped.

Trip's eyes narrowed.

Max, who'd been lounging in front of the fire, raised his head from his paws.

I waited.

And waited.

"Dawn's mother." His voice was so soft I barely heard him.

"Edith Hathaway? Why?"

Now Grace's eyes narrowed. "Don't you—"

Trip stared at Max. "Dawn and I—"

"Who's ready for lunch?" Aggie stood in the doorway wearing a brown wool caftan with an applique border of overflowing cornucopias. She was ready for the coming holiday and completely unaware she'd interrupted a revelation.

"No, thank you," said Trip.

"What are we having?" asked Grace.

Max yawned and stood. He was always ready for lunch.

"Quiche." Aggie glanced around the family room. Looking for the source of tension in the air?

The source sat on the couch.

"And a green salad," she added.

"That sounds delicious," I told her. "We'll eat in the breakfast room."

She nodded. Slowly. Her sharp eyes taking in every detail. Trip's slumped shoulders. Grace's crossed arms. Max's hungry grin. My—my what? Frustration? Worry? Anxiety? "It'll be ready in a jiff." She turned and left us.

I returned my attention to Trip. "What about you and Dawn?"

Grace's eyes shot daggers my way. But they were a sixteen-year-old's daggers, which, for one accustomed to Mother's daggers, were about as sharp as butter knives.

Grace could have saved her sharp edges. I was too late. The moment for revelations had passed. Trip merely shook his head—and stared at his hands.

The breakfast room faced east to allow for the morning light. But morning had passed and actual sunshine seemed like a distant dream. Color? Warmth? Gone. Instead the world outside was cast in shades of sullen gray (the sky) and white (everything else).

The mood at luncheon matched the sky.

Grace cut the tip off her slice of quiche but didn't bother lifting the fork to her mouth. Instead she stared out the window.

Trip didn't even bother picking up his fork. He stared at his lap, a picture of misery.

I took a bite and forced myself to chew.

Max looked hopeful. At the rate we were going there would be table scraps.

Aggie stuck her head in, regarded us all, and tsked. "Eat. You'll feel better." Then she fixed her gaze on Grace and waited until my daughter picked up her fork and transferred quiche from its tines to her mouth. "Trip, you too. You've got to eat."

Trip didn't react. Didn't move.

Aggie stepped forward and rested her hand on his shoulder. "Your family needs you. You've got to eat." Her voice was soft and kind, but a ribbon of steel lay hidden in all that kindness. Trip Michaels would sit at the table until he ate his quiche. End of story.

I took another bite before she turned her attention on me. "Join us for a moment, Aggie."

She raised a brow.

I jerked my chin toward a chair. A bit of bright chatter might lighten the mood, but I couldn't do it alone and Grace was no help. She still had daggers (butter knives) lurking in her eyes.

Aggie sat.

"I can't remember having so much snow before Thanksgiving." The weather was a safe topic.

"There must be sixteen inches out there." Aggie squinted at the snow as if she could measure its depth from the comfort of the breakfast room.

All eyes turned toward the window and the blanket of white covering the lawn.

"I bet you're right." Yes, inane. Yes, banal. But better than sorrow-laden silence.

"The forecast is calling for another six inches," Aggie added.

"When?" asked Grace.

Ding dong.

"I'll get that." Grace shot up from the table and disappeared through the swinging door before anyone else could react.

Aggie stood, cast me an apologetic glance, and followed her.

With Aggie gone, Trip put down his fork.

Now was my chance. "You know, if you tell me, you might feel better."

He nodded. Slowly. "Mrs. Hathaway was mad at my mom because—" He rubbed his eyes and I nearly leapt over the table and throttled him. Just spit it out already. "Because—"

"Mom!" Grace burst through the door. "Aunt Gwen is here."

Lord love a duck. I could not catch a break. Trip's gaze returned to his lap, and he didn't look as if he'd be parting his lips again anytime soon. I pasted a good hostess smile on my face and stood. "Coming."

Gwen waited for me in the foyer. And she did not wait alone. A woman I'd never seen before stood next to her. The woman looked normal. Thank God. When Gwen said she was bringing a friend, I half expected a bald twenty-year-old in a saffron robe.

"Gwen." I stepped forward and kissed the air next to her cheek.

She pulled me into a bear hug. That was new. In none of her iterations—not as a Buddhist, nor a neo-pagan, nor a Moonie—had Gwen actually liked me. "Ellison, I hope you don't mind, but I brought a friend. This is Suze."

"The more the merrier. Welcome, Suze." Did Suze have a last name? Was the fourth bedroom completely ready? Did we have enough tofu to see us through?

Suze thrust her right hand at me. "Thanks so much for having me. I know this is a terrible inconvenience."

"Not at all," I lied and shook her hand. "Where are you from, Suze?"

"Maine."

That explained the broad "a" in having. "So you're used to snow."

"Ayuh."

I had no idea what "ayuh" meant so I smiled. "We were just eating lunch. Are you hungry? Would you care to join us?"

"We're starving," said Gwen.

"I'll have Aggie fix plates for you. Oh—" Dammit. Gwen had been in the house five minutes and already she was causing Aggie extra work. "We're having quiche Lorraine. But there's a salad."

"Quiche sounds delicious," said Gwen.

"There's ham in it. And cheese. And eggs." Meat and dairy were probably cardinal sins in Gwen's religion du jour.

"I know what quiche Lorraine is, Ellison."

There was the Gwen that stayed constant. The woman who believed her brother had married a dimwit.

"Wonderful. Aggie is a fabulous cook. Her quiche is divine." My gaze fell to the collection of luggage littering the foyer then shifted to Grace, who'd followed me from the breakfast room.

"Would you please take the bags upstairs? The blue room is ready for your aunt, and we'll put Suze in the pink room."

"Suze can stay in the blue room with me," said Gwen.

I waved away her suggestion. "The pink room is ready."

"I'm sure it is, but we can stay together. I insist."

Gwen hadn't stayed with us in a long time. Perhaps she'd forgotten the furnishings in the blue room. "There's only a double bed in the blue room."

"I know." Gwen reached out and clasped Suze's hand.

The two exchanged a charged look.

Gwen might be right about her brother marrying a dimwit. "The blue room it is. Grace?"

Grace, who'd followed the entire exchange with wide eyes and slightly parted lips, snapped her mouth shut and scooped up a few bags. "Got it."

"Are you cold?" I asked Gwen and Suze. "Do you want a cup of tea?" Hopefully Aggie had bought tea.

"Do you have coffee?" asked Suze.

Maybe the holiday wouldn't be so bad. "Always."

Ding dong.

"I'll grab that. Gwen, would you see about getting Suze some coffee?"

My sister-in-law and her...friend headed toward the kitchen. I answered the door.

Anarchy stood on the front stoop wearing a shearling coat worthy of McCloud. He smiled and I forgot all about the coat. "Hi."

"Hi. Come in."

Innocuous words that aroused sparks in the cold air seeping through the front door.

Anarchy stepped into the empty foyer, his gaze scanning the steps, the hallway, and the doorways leading to the living room and the study. All were empty. He leaned forward and brushed a soft kiss across my lips. Barely a touch, but my heart took off as if hitched to an Apollo spaceship.

My heart was needed in my chest. I put my hands on Anarchy's shoulders and pushed him away. "You arrested Tom Michaels for murder."

He nodded. "I called you after we took him into custody. I left a message."

The pink slip of paper next to my bed. "He didn't do it."

"Ellison, I can't discuss an active investigation."

All this rule following was bothersome. Besides, Anarchy was happy to discuss the case when he needed my input. If only he'd whisper, "Peters arrested him, but I have my doubts..." But he wouldn't whisper that. Ever. "Why are you here?"

"I wanted to see you."

There went my heart again, blasting off toward the moon. But there was no way on this earth or the moon that Anarchy would take time off during a murder investigation just to come see me. He was far too conscientious. "And?"

"And we're looking for Trip Michaels."

"Trip? Why?"

"We have questions."

"You want to question a teenage boy about his father murdering his mother?" I felt a stubborn expression settle onto my features. "Doesn't he need a lawyer present?"

"He's here, isn't he?"

My poker face needed work. "In the breakfast room."

Anarchy took a step toward the back of the house.

I blocked his path. "Trip's distraught. Can't you talk to him later?"

"The kid needs to be with social services."

"Why? He's staying with his grandmother." My nose itched so badly it twitched. No way was I scratching the lie detector on the end of my face. If I did, Anarchy would know I was lying. I kept my hands at my sides.

Besides, when I got everything arranged, Trip would be staying with his grandmother.

"Fine. I still need to talk to him."

"Nothing specific. Not without a lawyer." If necessary, I'd call Hunter.

Anarchy nodded in agreement. I turned and walked down the hallway, letting him follow me.

We barely paused in the empty breakfast room (empty if you didn't count Max with his paws on the table finishing Trip's uneaten quiche) before heading to the kitchen.

Grace and Aggie and Gwen and Suze gathered around the island.

"Where's Trip?" I asked.

Grace looked up from a steaming mug of hot chocolate. "He's gone."

FIFTEEN

Anarchy brought the scents of snow and leather and pine with him into the kitchen. Those scents mixed with the aromas wafting off Grace's hot chocolate and Suze's coffee. The kitchen had never smelled better.

"Anarchy, this is my sister-in-law, Gwen, and her friend Suze. Gwen, Suze, this is Detective Jones."

Gwen's brows drew together. In one of her less attractive phases (lots of body hair and no deodorant) she'd been given to calling policemen names like "fuzz" and "pigs." Hopefully, all vestiges of that stage were well behind her. "Aren't you the one who investigated my brother's murder?"

Anarchy grimaced. "I am."

Gwen extended her hand. "It's nice to meet you." They shook and Gwen's too-sharp gaze shifted between Anarchy and me. "What are you doing here now? Surely the investigation's closed."

"I'm investigating Laurie Michaels' murder." Anarchy didn't mention poor Jenny.

"Laurie Michaels? Tom's wife?" Gwen shot me a why-didn't-you-tell-me look.

I shot her a you-just-got-here-and-I-didn't-want-to-lead-off-with-murder look.

Anarchy shot us both a use-actual-words look.

"It was tragic," I explained. "Someone locked her in the freezer at the club."

"Mom found her," Grace added.

What a helpful child. "The sous-chef found her. I just happened to be there."

"Tomato. Tomahto." Where on earth had Grace picked up that sense of sarcasm?

We all stared at her.

It was Anarchy who spoke next. "Where did Trip go?"

Grace shrugged. "He didn't say."

"He had to have left tracks." Anarchy peered through the glass portion of the back door. Deep footprints crossed the lawn and disappeared into Margaret Hamilton's backyard. If Trip made it past the witch next door without being turned into a toad, an interview with Anarchy would be a cake walk for him.

Brnng, brnng.

I snatched the phone out of the cradle. "Hello."

"Ellison? This is Caro Reynolds calling."

I adjusted my tone. Less bark, more speaking-with-a-social-doyenne. "Hello, Mrs. Reynolds." No one under the age of fifty used Caro's first name. She was that intimidating.

"You must call me Caro." There was a smile in her voice. "Your mother gave me the good news."

The good news? Alarm bells rang in my ears. The only news I knew was two murders. Hardly good. "She did?" My voice was faint.

"Yes. And I'm absolutely thrilled."

She was thrilled? Whatever was thrilling, it probably wasn't two dead women. "Um..."

"It's so kind of you to step in for Laurie."

"Step in? For Laurie?"

"Yes, dear. As chairman of next year's museum gala."

Mother was lucky she was halfway across the state or there would have been another murder. Right then.

"The gala..."

"Yes, dear." A hint of impatience tinged her voice. "Such a coup to land the Chinese exhibit. It's coming to us right after the National Gallery."

I knew the gala. I knew the exhibit. What I didn't know was why Mother had volunteered me as chairman.

"We'll meet as soon as possible to go over the plans Laurie had in place. You may want to change a few things." In other words, Caro hadn't approved of all of Laurie's ideas.

"Fine." My voice dimmed to a flicker. "Fine" was barely audible.

"After the holiday then! I'll call you on Friday."

"Of course, Mrs. Reynolds."

"Caro," she corrected. "Have a happy Thanksgiving."

"You too."

She hung up the phone, and I stared at the receiver in my hand.

"Mom! Are you okay? Is someone else dead?"

I shifted my gaze to Grace and dropped the receiver into its cradle. "Not yet. Your grandmother has committed me to chairing a gala for the art museum." A headache arrived, dropped its suitcase in the foyer of my brain, and demanded I make it welcome. "What was she thinking?"

Anarchy, still wearing his McCloud coat, stared at me. "The gala for the Chinese exhibit?"

"Yes." I nodded and winced. The headache had packed hot pokers and was using them behind my eyes. "How do you know about that?"

"Some of Laurie's friends mentioned it. They said any number of women would kill to chair that party."

"Not me."

"Not you." He smiled at me and my headache receded. But then he edged toward the door. The tracks. Trip. "I'll call you later. I've got to track him down."

Trip Michaels. His problems were bigger than mine. Maybe. I sank onto a stool and buried my aching head in my hands.

Aggie (gem) put a full cup of coffee in front of me.

Anarchy slipped out the back door.

Gwen tsked.

I groaned.

"Grace, I believe I'd like to freshen up. Would you show me to our room?" At least Suze had the sense to leave me alone in my misery.

Not Gwen. She watched Grace and Suze disappear up the backstairs, cast a disparaging glance at Aggie, and said, "Ellison, we need to talk."

We need to talk. Has anything good ever followed those four words?

I steeled myself. "What is it, Gwen?"

"I'm sorry to bring this up now, but it's been weighing on me."

Well, if something was weighing on her then by all means, now, when I had an epic headache, was the time to discuss it. It wasn't as if my day could get any worse. "What's wrong, Gwen?"

"I want you to buy my shares of the bank."

I snorted hot coffee through my nose. It hurt. "No."

"No?" She scowled at me. "Why not?"

I accepted Aggie's silent offer of a dish towel and mopped coffee off my face, my sweater, and the counter. "The bank's about to go under."

"What?" The cups on the shelves in the butler's pantry rattled. "What do you mean the bank's about to fail?"

"Henry made some bad loans."

"My brother would never—"

"He loaned money—lots of money—to Tom Michaels. Not only can Tom not pay it back, he's in jail for murder."

"How much?" The saucers rattled with the cups.

I gave her the number.

Gwen crossed her arms and shook her head, the very picture of denial. "Henry would never loan Tom that much money. Everyone in town knows Tom Michaels has a gambling problem."

A, how did she know that when I didn't? B, it was Laurie who liked to gamble. "I thought Laurie was the one with the problem."

She shook her head. "It's Tom and it doesn't matter. Henry would never loan either of them enough to get the bank into trouble."

"Be that as it may. Tom Michaels and his company owe us more than one million dollars. And if he defaults—when he defaults—the bank goes under."

"Is Sherman Westcott still running things?" She made the question sound like an accusation.

"Yes."

Gwen pursed her lips. "I never liked Sherman Westcott. Never trusted him. This is his fault, not my brother's." Her brother, even dead, could do no wrong.

Sherman might be a bad banker, but was he dishonest? I didn't know. I sighed. Deeply. "It hardly matters whose fault it is. The money's gone." I could have stopped there, but Gwen deserved the whole story—soon her shares of the bank would be as worthless as Grace's. "Laurie was heavily insured. I'd hoped we could put a lien on the insurance money. But if Tom killed Laurie, the insurance company won't pay."

"We need to prove Tom is innocent." Her voice took on a Mickey Rooney let's-put-on-a-show-and-save-the-town quality.

"What if Tom did it?" My worst fear spoken aloud.

"He didn't." She curled her lip into a sneer. "I dated Tom Michaels when we were in high school. He didn't have the gumption to kill a spider, much less his wife." She paused, considering our next course of action. "We need to talk to Sherman Westcott."

"Fine." I didn't have the energy to argue. Besides, talking to Sherman was already on my to-do list.

Gwen planted her hands on her hips and scowled. "I'm telling you, if someone loaned Tom that much money, it wasn't Henry."

My head throbbed. Throbbed. "Fine, Gwen." What more did she want from me?

"I can't believe you let this happen."

I couldn't either.

Of course Sherman Westcott wasn't reachable by phone. Of course Gwen insisted that we track him down. Of course I didn't argue. Which is how Gwen and I ended up driving by the Westcotts' house. Repeatedly. Like love-struck teenagers.

"The drive is empty," she said.

No change from the previous five times we passed by.

"Where else could he be?" she demanded. "We're not going home until we find him."

"The club?" It was a shot in the dark.

"Let's go there." She glanced at her watch. "Besides, I could use a drink."

During Gwen's last visit, she'd seen me drink a single glass of wine and given me an hour-long lecture on the perils of alcohol.

My fingers tightened around the steering wheel. "Fine."

"It's cold in here." She rubbed her gloved hands on the upper portion of her crossed arms. "Can you turn up the heat?"

The heat was blasting. "It's up as high as it'll go."

She glared at the dashboard. "This is a mid-life crisis car."

I said nothing, kept my hands at ten and two, and locked my gaze on the road.

"Also, it's a summer car. You should have something more substantial for winter."

Had Mother mailed her precise instructions for annoying me? Who was I kidding? Gwen didn't need any instructions.

The club's driveway cut through the snow-covered golf course.

"I wish you would have told me about all this snow."

"We kept missing each other."

"You could have left a message."

The woman was from Kansas City. She knew the weather was iffy from November to March.

I parked the car.

"There's a closer spot."

I clenched my teeth. "This one's fine."

"Yes. But that one's closer."

"It's an extra twenty steps, Gwen."

"Fine." She shot me her my-brother-married-a-nitwit look, got out of the car, slammed the door, and strode toward the clubhouse without me. One would have thought I'd asked her to walk the length of the Great Wall of China.

I briefly (not briefly) considered driving away. I sat and daydreamed about leaving her for at least a minute—maybe five. Gwen was long-since inside before I got out of the car.

An arctic gust of wind tore at my coat and tried to steal my hat. I hurried toward the clubhouse.

"Ellison!"

With my eyes squinched against the cold and the wind, I scanned the parking lot and saw no one. The damn wind was playing tricks with my ears.

"Ellison! Help!" A person or the wind?

Again I scanned the lot. Again I saw no one. Bad things

have happened in the parking lot. That was why I parked far away from other cars. And now I was hearing things. There was no way I was wandering between cars looking for a voice in a freezing gale. If I did, someone would shoot me, or knock me over the head with a golf club, or blow up a car—my car. Instead, I hurried toward the safety of the clubhouse, proving some people (Mother) wrong. She said I never learned from my mistakes.

I paused at the reception desk. A new employee sat there. I read her nametag. "Joan, I think I heard someone calling for help in the parking lot."

Lips pursed and a hand reached for a phone. "We'll have someone look around, thank you."

There. I'd done it. Reported a potential problem without getting involved. Mother would be proud. "I'm looking for my sister-in-law. She came in a few minutes before me."

"I believe she went to the bar."

"Thank you." I took off my coat and hat and gloves and handed them to the girl who checked coats.

She handed me a green plastic chit with a number on it.

I smiled my thanks and headed to the bar.

Admittedly, the bar's view of the blanketed golf course was spectacular. There ended the spectacular.

Gwen, who'd borrowed my second-best mink, had draped the coat over the back of a chair. The lit end of her cigarette hovered near the collar. Worse (for me, not the coat), she was talking to Prudence Davies.

They both turned and looked at me.

"Ellison." Prudence offered up one of her pit viper smiles. "We were just talking about you."

There was a time when Prudence's barbs stung. That time was long gone. "Oh?" I manufactured my own lethal smile. "I was talking about you just yesterday."

She raised a single brow. If Mr. Ed raised his brows, he'd look like Prudence—horsey and curious.

"Rupert McNamara said you stopped by to see him the day Jenny Woods died."

An expression I didn't recognize flickered across Prudence's face.

"He said you left right around the time Jenny did. I'm surprised you didn't see her in the elevator."

The expression flickered again. Alarm? Worry? Fear? Prudence turned to Gwen. "This is what Ellison does. She finds a body then searches for a way to make me look guilty of murder."

Gwen looked marginally happier now that those twenty extra steps were behind her—that or the neat scotch in her left hand and the cigarette in her right had improved her mood (apparently her soy-eating, clean-living, abstention days were just memories). She wasn't remotely interested in Prudence as a suspect. "You're dating Rupert? He was one of Henry's dear friends."

"Henry and Prudence were dear friends." There was enough acid in my voice to eat through metal.

Now Gwen raised a brow. Seriously? The woman knew Tom Michaels had a gambling problem but didn't know her dear brother had slept with anyone who wore a skirt? Even Prudence.

"Really?" Gwen blew a plume of smoke at me.

"Really. Prudence and Kitty Ballew were both Henry's dear friends." Maybe—maybe—I was still bothered that my husband had cheated on me with such abandon.

The edges of Gwen's lips hardened until little lines cut valleys around her mouth. "Is this true, Prudence?"

Prudence lifted her chin. "Henry loved me."

Gwen shook her head. Denial or inability to square the image of her dear brother with a man who fell in love with a woman like Prudence Davies? "That can't be right. Henry thought you were a bony-assed harpy."

Gwen could stay with me forever if she promised to call Prudence a bony-assed harpy once a day.

Prudence's chin lifted still higher. "Henry always said you were a bitch."

This was devolving quickly. Then again, dealings with Prudence usually did.

Gwen smiled sweetly. "Henry meant that as a compliment."

"Keep telling yourself that."

The smile ran away from Gwen's face and she finished her scotch in one gulp. "I adored my brother, but I wasn't blind to his faults. He was lazy. Especially when it came to women. If he was with you, it was because you were easy." She stubbed out her cigarette with a vicious jab. "From the sound of it, you still are." Then, lifting her chin even higher than Prudence's, she collected my second-best mink and said, "Ellison, Sherman's obviously not here. I'll see you at the car."

She stalked off without a backward glance, sure I'd follow.

Prudence shook her horsey head. "God, what a bitch."

I took a step toward the door, but Prudence stopped me with a hand on my arm.

"What?"

"I didn't kill Jenny. Why would I?"

That was an excellent question. And that question was why I believed her. Sort of. I shook free of her grasp.

"If you tell anyone I had anything to do with Jenny's death, I'll sue you for libel."

It was my turn to lift my chin. So I did.

I stopped by the coat check and collected my best mink, my hat, and my gloves, and took my time putting them on. Some small best-unexamined part of me didn't mind that Gwen waited in the cold.

Joan stepped out from behind her desk. "We checked the

parking lot. There was no one there."

"Well, that's a relief. It must have been the wind."

Joan was too polite to let her opinion show on her face, but I saw her real thoughts (that Mrs. Russell, she's nothing but trouble and nutty as a fruitcake to boot) lurking in her eyes.

"Thank you for looking." I stopped and adjusted my hat in the mirror—Gwen could pace those twenty steps a bit longer.

I stepped out into the cold expecting an angry sister-in-law and a deadly glare. I got neither. Gwen wasn't pacing. Far from it. Instead, my second-best mink lay in a heap on the frozen pavement.

SIXTEEN

I stood just outside the door to the club and gaped, my feet frozen to the pavement not by cold weather but by cold blood in my veins.

Gwen could not be dead. She couldn't. Not in the parking lot. Not in my second-best mink. Not when she'd become an almost decent human being.

A smattering of sleet hit my face, reminding me to move my feet. With my head spinning and my cheeks burning, I stuck my head inside the door and bellowed, "Joan! Call the police and an ambulance."

Nothing.

"Joan!" I bellowed louder. Loud enough for the drinkers in the bar to hear me. Loud enough for Mother to hear me on her road trip. And she was simply appalled that I was yelling at the club.

Finally, Joan stepped out of her office and glared at me. From thirty feet away her eye roll was obvious. Cuckoo-for-Cocoa-Puffs was at it again.

I adjusted my volume to a mild roar. "My sister-in-law is lying on the pavement. Call an ambulance."

Joan nodded once (a put-upon, I-need-a-job-where-women-don't-bellow-at-me nod). "I'll call for help right away." She disappeared into her little office.

I hurried out into the cold. Tiny face-stinging needles of freezing rain welcomed me back. Worse, the sleet had formed a layer of ice on the pavement.

I walked with care. Slowly. Those extra twenty steps took forever.

"Gwen!" I knelt beside her.

My sister-in-law groaned. Corpses didn't groan.

She was not dead. Not dead was good. Not dead allowed breath back into my lungs and returned my heart to the semblance of a normal beat. I closed my eyes and said a silent thank you to whatever being had spared her life.

Gwen groaned a second time.

"Are you shot?" I demanded. "Did someone sneak up behind you and hit you over the head?" I didn't see any blood, but that didn't mean it wasn't there.

Gwen's eyes fluttered. "What are you talking about?"

"Who did this to you?"

"You did." There was real venom in her voice.

I sat back on my heels. Gwen had suffered a traumatic brain injury. There was no other explanation. I might, on occasion, have thought about bumping off my sister-in-law, but only when she'd been particularly insulting, and I'd never even considered killing her in a parking lot. If I was going to kill her (Never. Ever. Not.), I'd poison her dirty-socks-flavored tea and wave toodles over my shoulder as I walked out the door. "Me?"

"You're the one who insisted on parking halfway to Timbuktu. I slipped on the ice."

The scotch she drank before walking on ice was probably my fault too. I clenched my hands into fists. I had a choice. Bicker with the woman on the pavement or take the high road. The high road was Eleanor Roosevelt's road. It was Mother Teresa's road. It was Golda Meir's road. Strong women who would never argue with their fallen sisters-in-law in a sleet-filled parking lot. "Let's get you out of the cold." I unclenched my fingers, crouched next to her, and offered a hand.

"If I take your hand, we'll both end up on the pavement." She shifted and a grimace darkened her face. "Besides, thanks to you, I'm injured."

High road. High road. "Where are you hurt?"

"My ankle." She reached up and touched the back of her head. "And my head."

I made a sympathetic noise in the back of my throat. "It's freezing out here. I really think we should get you inside."

Gwen's eyes narrowed. "Henry always said you were useless in a crisis. Why didn't you bring help?"

"Help is on its way."

"Fat lot of good that does me now. This pavement is freezing."

High road. High road. I schooled my face into a polite mask. One that hid my true desire—to slap her upside her already injured head.

"There it is!" She sounded triumphant.

"There what is?"

"The expression. The Ellison-is-a-saint expression. It drove Henry crazy."

The Ellison-is-a-saint expression? I'd call the way I'd smoothed annoyance off my face the if-you-weren't-family-I'd-leave-you-to-freeze-alone-in-this-parking-lot expression.

"Gwen, I know you're in pain, but—"

"Give the martyr act a rest, Ellison."

High road. High road. Except the low road was looking better and better and keeping a smooth expression on my face took such effort the muscles in my cheeks shook.

"It's your fault he's dead."

My mouth sagged open. Did she really blame me for her brother's death? Of course she did, she blamed me when she slipped on the ice. Not even Mother Teresa would take the high road in a situation like this. "How dare you!"

Gwen snorted.

Henry had thought his sister was Mad-Hatter crazy. He had disapproved of her life. He had said disparaging things about her clothes, her opinions, and her intelligence. He had laughed at her. Often. I longed to tell her all that. And more. Other than hurting her, what good would telling do? I bit my tongue.

"What are you mumbling?" she snapped. "I ode?"

I was mumbling "high road."

Gwen's nose was the color of a ripe tomato. Her eyes were squinty with either anger or pain. Her skin looked pale against the dark fur of my second-best mink. A wave of pity made the high road easy. "Nothing. Just mumbling."

"Figures. Useless."

The blare of an ambulance's siren saved me from answering. I stood and flagged down the driver.

He parked next to Gwen.

"I can't believe you called an ambulance." She shot me a murderous glare—sharper than Grace's, but not nearly as deadly as Mother's. On a scale of one to I'll-kill-you-while-you-sleep, I gave it a six.

"They'll take you to the hospital." Where—I crossed my frozen fingers—hopefully she'd remain until it was time for her to return to wherever she came from. Pasadena. Maine. Hell. "My sister-in-law hit her head," I told the man tending to Gwen. "Hard. She's been saying horrible things. So unlike her."

He nodded. "I'll get a neck brace."

Now Gwen's glare was every bit as deadly as Mother's. Maybe even deadlier. This glare was somewhere between a nine and a lock-my-door-and-put-a-chair-under-the-knob-before-I-go-to-bed. Good thing she'd be at the hospital while I slept.

I smiled. Sweetly. The high road had led me to this moment. I intended to enjoy it. "I'll run home and get Suze. We'll come check on you—" a gust of wind treated me to a thousand stinging needles of sleet "—if the roads are passable. If not, we'll come in the morning."

"You planned this."

The EMT shifted his gaze between us.

"Gwen, you fell. How could I possibly plan that?" I lowered my voice to a stage whisper. "She's been drinking."

"One drink! I had one drink." Gwen's voice fought a losing battle with a frozen gust that had swept across the entire state of Kansas to steal our breaths.

"An old-fashioned glass filled with straight scotch." I spread my fingers, demonstrating the level of scotch. It wasn't much of an exaggeration and the warm glow of satisfaction that came with saying the words aloud offset the cold.

With gentle fingers the man snapped an enormous white brace around Gwen's neck. "Ma'am, we're moving you to a stretcher."

"Don't you worry, Gwen. Mother is on the board at the hospital. They'll take good care of you."

Gwen's eyes narrowed to slits. "Your family is so civic-minded." The sneer in her voice was as biting as the wind. She looked up at the EMT. "Her sister married a man who manufactures condoms. His top-seller is the King Cobra."

While Marjorie's husband's business caused Mother endless embarrassment, I didn't care if my brother-in-law made condoms or galoshes. "You know, Gwen, you're right. I never thought about it, but manufacturing condoms is something of a public service."

Gwen muttered a few words entirely unbecoming of a lady—crazy, catty, or otherwise.

The men moving her onto the stretcher regarded us with amused expressions in their eyes. They'd go home and tell their wives or girlfriends about their trip to the country club and the awful women they'd helped. For now, they loaded Gwen into the ambulance. One climbed into the back with her, the other put his hand on the door.

"Wait!" Gwen's voice had a quaver in it. "You're coming, aren't you?"

"Of course. I told you, I'll stop at home and pick up Suze. We'll be there." I paused. "If the weather allows."

The driver closed the door on Gwen, but not before I glimpsed her eyebrows, somehow raised and pulled together, and her lips, stretched toward her ears. The woman was terrified.

Dammit. I didn't want to feel empathy or sympathy or anything but annoyance. I jammed my hands in my pockets, hunched my shoulders against the cold, and followed the driver to his door. "At the hospital, tell them she's related to Frances Walford. They'll know what to do."

"Yes, ma'am." He climbed into his vehicle and drove away, leaving me alone in the icy parking lot.

I did what I said I'd do. I went home for Suze.

I found her in the kitchen with Libba. The two of them were seated on stools at the kitchen island with their hands wrapped around mugs of Aggie's hot chocolate. That explained the smell of chocolate that permeated the kitchen, but not the aroma of mint.

"Where have you been?" Libba's tone was just shy of belligerent.

"The club." I sniffed. Where was the mint? "What are you doing here?"

"I did what you asked. I wrote everything down." She loosened her grip on her cocoa and held up a sheaf of papers.

"Thank you." I'd deal with Libba's tell-all later. "Um, Suze?"

Suze giggled. She hadn't struck me as a giggler. "Yes?"

"Gwen slipped and fell on the ice. She twisted her ankle and hit her head."

Suze stopped giggling.

Libba started giggling. She wrinkled her nose and her shoulders shook with mirth. "Sorry." She held up hands to fend off our judgment. "Nervous response."

I ignored Libba and her nervous response. "I don't think it's serious, but they've taken her to the hospital to check her out."

"The hospital!" Suze rose from her stool and swayed.

"Don't worry," said Libba. "Ellison goes every week. She gets prefernatal treatment." She shook her head. "Preferenced." She shook her head harder. "Preferential. That's it. Preferential treatment."

What exactly was in those hot chocolates?

"If you'd like to see her, we should go. The streets are getting slick."

"Yes. Of course I want to go."

"I'll go too," said Libba.

Oh joy. "There's no room in the car." Three adults were one too many in my Triumph.

"We'll take mine," Libba insisted. "I'll drive."

Not happening. Whatever was in those hot chocolates wouldn't mix well with city streets. "We'll take yours and I'll drive."

Libba stuck out her tongue. "Be that way."

"I'll get my coat," said Suze. She only staggered a little bit when she walked.

"What are you drinking?" I demanded.

"Hot chocolate," Libba replied.

I narrowed my eyes. "And what else?"

"Marshmallows."

Very funny. "And?"

"Peppermint schnapps," Libba admitted.

That explained the minty scent in the kitchen. "I own schnapps?"

"I brought it with me."

Of course she had.

Libba lifted her chin. "Don't be such a stick in the mud."

"Don't be such a lush."

Suze hiccupped. "I'll be right back." She clambered up the back stairs.

"Nice. Making a guest use the servants' stairs."

Did everyone on the planet want to pick a fight with me? "I did not make her use those stairs."

Libba shifted her gaze toward heaven (an expression just shy of an eye roll) and sank back onto her stool. "Your Swedish ivy looks depressed."

The ivy sat on the table by the window. It didn't look depressed. Or happy. Or angry. It looked green. "Pardon me?"

"Your ivy. It's sad. What's its name?"

"Its name?"

"Yes, Ellison, plants need names." She regarded the ivy. "She looks like an Agnes to me."

Agnes from Sweden? Not Ilsa or Freja or Elin? "Why Agnes?"

Libba shrugged and took another sip of her hot chocolate. "She looks like an Agnes. Have you been talking to Agnes regularly?"

"I don't talk to my plants." I talked to my coffee maker.

"No wonder Agnes is depressed."

Oh good Lord. Enough. I walked over to the back stairs and called, "Suze, are you ready?"

"First you make her use the back stairs, now you're bellowing like a fishwife."

"Coming," Suze called back.

I turned my attention to Libba. "What in the world is wrong

with you?"

"Schnapps. It makes me mean."

"Then don't drink it."

"That ship has sailed, sister."

Suze's footsteps rang on the stairs before I could think of a snappy comeback.

We drove to the hospital in relative silence—nothing but the *whoosh* of the defroster, the *swish* of the wiper blades, and the pops of my knuckles whenever I tightened my death grip on the wheel.

I let Suze and Libba out at the entrance to the lobby and parked the car. When I entered, they were nowhere in sight.

Swallowing a would-it-have-killed-them-to-wait sigh, I approached the information desk. "Good afternoon, I'm looking for my sister-in-law, Gwen Russell. She came in through the ER. Has she been admitted yet?"

The woman behind the desk gazed up at me through Coke-bottle glasses. "Room 270. I just checked for some other ladies."

"Thank you."

I trudged up a flight of stairs and found Gwen's room.

Libba leaned against the wall outside the door. Her brows were drawn and her arms were crossed.

"What's wrong?" I asked.

"Did you know that—" She pushed her hair away from her face then covered her eyes with the palms of her hands. "Did you know that—"

"That Gwen and Suze were a couple?"

She re-crossed her arms and stared at me. "It doesn't bother you?"

"Not really." It obviously bothered Libba. But she adored men. "I figure love is love. I do worry this is another one of Gwen's phases. Suze seems like a nice woman. I'd hate for her to get hurt."

"Hmph."

"Hmph?"

"Maybe you're not such a stick in the mud."

"Gee, thanks."

"I can't wait to hear what Frances says."

The thought made my blood run cold.

"We should go get coffee or something." Libba jerked her head toward the door. "Suze is scolding Gwen."

That I had to see. I tapped lightly on the door and stepped inside.

Suze sat next to Gwen's bed. The two held hands and Suze stared at Gwen with open adoration. I wanted to tell her to be careful, that Russells treated other people's hearts with reckless disregard. I wanted to tell her that Gwen had been through countless fads and phases. I wanted to tell her revealing so much emotion was dangerous. Instead, I donned a polite smile. "How's the patient?"

"She'll be fine." Suze used her free hand to wipe her eyes. "But they're keeping her overnight for observation."

"Good news." I smiled at my sister-in-law. "How's the ankle?"

"A mild sprain." Gwen's lips pursed and the skin under her eyes looked tight. Her face was a billboard for you're-interrupting-please-leave. Forget the please. Leave now.

I backed toward the door. "Libba and I are grabbing a cup of coffee. May I bring you anything?"

"No." They spoke in unison.

"I'll be back in a little while."

Neither seemed to care.

I stepped back into the hallway where Libba waited. "Let's go for coffee."

Libba fell into step beside me. "What does Grace think of all this?"

"All this?"

"Gwen and Suze." She nodded toward a group of people waiting for the elevator. "Stairs or elevator?"

"Stairs." The elevators were glacially slow. "Grace and I have not discussed their relationship."

"Are you avoiding the issue?"

I stopped and looked her in the eye. "No. I'm not. There's no issue. Gwen and Suze's relationship is none of my business. Nor Grace's. And even if it were, I'm more concerned with two murders and the state of the bank."

"Okay." She tugged at my elbow and we resumed walking.

I might have said my focus was on the murders, but my thoughts remained with Suze and Gwen. "Have you ever been in love?"

"Hundreds of times." Flippant. Figured.

"I mean it, Libba. Have you ever been head-over-heels, can't-sleep-at-night, head-spinning in love?"

"Hundreds of times," she repeated. "You?"

I kept my gaze on the steps in front of me. It wouldn't do to trip. "No."

Libba stopped in her tracks. "You loved Henry in the beginning. I know you did."

"That was more of a we-want-the-same-things-and-it's-the-right-time-of-our-lives-to-get-married love. Plus, Mother approved. At that time in my life, Mother's approval was important." I lifted my gaze to the oatmeal-colored walls. "There was no depth to our feelings. Henry and I were destined for failure."

I felt her gaze on my face but refused to turn and look at her.

"What brought this on?" she asked. "The detective?"

Anarchy? No. No. Not yet anyway. I hurried down the last few steps. "Of course not the detective. It was the way Suze looked at Gwen. I've never looked at anyone like that."

We moved from the stairwell toward the lobby and the coffee shop.

"Once." Libba's voice was so soft I almost didn't hear her. "It was a long time ago."

I searched my memories for the one man who Libba might have cared for and found nothing. "Who?"

"It doesn't matter. He broke my heart." She lifted her chin and led the way into the coffee shop. "I don't want to talk about it. Are you sure you're not in love with Detective Jones?"

"Positive." I was also positive it was time to change the subject. "Did you bring your recollections from the night Laurie was killed?"

"They're in my purse."

"Good. I'll read them over coffee and you can answer any questions I might have."

"Over coffee? I think my memories call for martinis."

Too bad for Libba, the coffee shop didn't serve vodka.

SEVENTEEN

Libba had used a legal pad for her opus and torn out the completed pages. The top of each yellow page was ragged and the papers were wrinkled and soft from their stay at the bottom of her purse.

The man drinks too much. It's embarrassing—I looked up from the first line. "Are you sure these are the right pages?"

She rested her arms on the table and peered at me as if she was Mrs. Franks, the fifth-grade teacher who'd scared the bejesus out of my ten-year-old self. "Those are the only pages. You've got them out of order."

If the pages weren't in order, I could not be blamed. They'd been in my possession for less than a minute.

"They're numbered. You have to start with page one." She exactly captured Mrs. Franks' you're-on-my-last-nerve tone too. "Give them to me." She held out her hand.

I returned the sheaf to her and smiled at the waitress with the beehive hairdo who stood next to us with a pad and pencil at the ready.

"Two coffees please."

Libba glanced up from shuffling papers. "What kind of pie do you have?"

"Apple, cherry, coconut cream."

"Coconut cream, please." Libba returned her gaze to the mess of paper spread in front of her. "Here." She thrust one of them at me. "Here's page one."

"Thank you," I said to the waitress.

The page that Libba held out was wavy, as if someone had used it as a coaster for a sweaty glass. Scotch on the rocks was my guess. I took the paper from her and read her big, loose, loopy script that ignored the lines (Mrs. Franks would have given her an "F").

The bar was crowded. I remember thinking it was odd for a Tuesday night. Usually there are a handful of regulars and it's easy to get a drink. I had to wait.

Laurie was there. She looked at me and my dress with that sour-pickles expression of hers and said, "I think you're so brave, Libba."

I pretended not to know what she meant. "Oh?"

"Your fashion choices."

I was wearing a Mary Quant jersey mini-dress. Hardly cutting edge or brave. I smiled at her. "You're brave too."

She smoothed the seams of her hideous plaid skirt (mustard and baby poo—I kid you not) and adjusted the line of buttons on her cardigan. "Whatever do you mean?"

"It takes real courage to choose frumpy."

We didn't talk after that.

Jenny Woods was there too. Now, she looked fabulous. She had on a pair of black slacks and a black silk shirt (I bet it was Gucci) and this medallion necklace...I wish I could ask her where she got it.

I looked up.

Libba was constructing a castle out of plastic creamers.

"Do you describe what everyone is wearing?"

"Just the women."

Oh joy. I returned to my reading.

Lorna Michaels was there, but she wasn't with Tom and Laurie. She was at a table with your parents. Lorna had on a Chanel suit. That suit was probably fifteen years old, and she still looked better than Laurie.

Laurie stalked over to Tom and they started whispering, but I could tell they were furious with each other.

Trey Marstin was there. God, that man's hair. He's not fooling anyone. He looks like he's wearing a Yorkie on his head.

Who else was there?

The Ledbetters, the Hardys, the Westcotts…

I looked up from Libba's list of couples and thanked the waitress for my coffee. "The Westcotts were there?"

"You sound surprised."

"Sherman Westcott has been trying to reach Tom. Did you see them talking?"

"No." Libba picked up a fork and stabbed at her pie.

I took a sip of heaven. What was Sherman up to? I skimmed the rest of the list.

"You read fast." Libba pointed her fork at me.

"It's a list of names."

"Skip that. Here, here's page two."

I took the second page from her.

I'd finally been served a stinger when this woman walked in. I'd never seen her before. Not unattractive. Brown hair. Tweed suit. But a suit with some style. Not like something Laurie would wear. Also, she wore the most fabulous earrings. They were gold lion heads. She was looking for Laurie. Said it was imperative that she talk to her immediately.

Someone pointed out Laurie and Tom and she marched on over to them.

Her cheeks were flushed—the woman's, not Laurie's—and she looked angry.

She had a few words with them. Loud words. Something about blame and fault. Everyone was listening. They pretended they weren't, but you know how people are. They were listening like mad.

Finally, Tom suggested they speak in private.

Laurie led the woman off and I assumed he'd follow, but he didn't.

"What time did Laurie and the woman leave?"

"Nine thirty, give or take ten minutes."

As soon as she was gone, Tom and Jenny started talking. Whispering, really. Not discreetly. But everyone was so intent on getting the bartender's attention that perhaps I was the only one who noticed.

When I got a chance, I asked Tom who she was and he told me Trip had broken up with her daughter.

Which, if you ask me, is crazy. My mother would have no more confronted any of my ex-boyfriend's parents than she would fly to the moon on one wing. You don't fight Grace's battles.

I tried not to. I looked up and smiled at my oldest friend. "Did Edith Hathaway leave the club when she left the bar?"

"Is that who she was? I have no idea."

"Were the Westcotts seated with anyone?"

"No." She closed her eyes. "They were off in the corner by themselves."

"Did you ever, over the course of the evening, hear Laurie accuse Jenny of sleeping with Tom?"

"No." She handed me page three.

After the crazy lady left, Tom and Jenny kept their distance from each other. Jenny actually chatted with Trey. He kept fingering his gold chains. It made my skin crawl.

Tom went over and talked to Lorna. I remember that because neither of them looked happy. He even raised his voice. I heard him. Something about Lorna minding her own business. She was probably scolding him about being obvious with Jenny. That or the argument with the crazy lady.

I drank my stinger and thought about going home, but

Rupert McNamara came in and he's always good for a—

I raised my head so quickly it was a wonder I didn't give myself whiplash. "You and Rupert?" Ew. Ew. Ew.

"No. Never. We just flirt. Why?"

"Keep it that way."

Libba raised an inquisitive brow.

If gold chains made her skin crawl..."He has proclivities. Just trust me." I returned to page three before she could ask me how I knew about Rupert's proclivities.

Rupert and I were talking about what was better, summer or winter, when Prudence interrupted us. That woman has a face like a horse. Have you noticed?

I had.

At any rate, she dragged him off—probably for a quickie in the coat room—and I was at loose ends again. The room thinned out, but I couldn't tell you who went home. The older people certainly. Maybe. Possibly. I think I saw your Mother, but I wouldn't swear to it.

Jenny escaped Trey. I don't know where she went. She just disappeared. If you can believe it, while she was gone, Trey hit on me. As if!

The page ended and I looked up.

Libba had page four ready for me.

The man drinks too much. It's embarrassing.

"Why are you pursing your lips?"

"I'm not." I was.

"I'm sure it's not because you think I drink too much."

"Of course not." Sometimes she did. "Mother set me up with Trey. At a brunch. I walked out."

"I remember you telling me."

I nodded. "He tried to sell Daddy on investing in a chain of hookah stores."

Libba choked on a bite of pie. Then she choked on the ice

(the crushed kind that belongs in snow cones) in her water. Then she knocked over my water.

I saved the pages. The waitress mopped the table. Libba mopped her eyes. "Your father and hookahs?"

"Don't choke again," I cautioned.

"No." Libba was rendered near speechless by the thought of my staid father and an old-fashioned bong.

"Did anyone follow Laurie when she left the bar?"

Libba shrugged and shook her head. "Don't know."

"Was Tom there when you left?"

She nodded and reached for her water glass.

"And that was around ten?"

"Ish," she croaked.

"Who else do you remember being there?"

"Jenny wandered back in. She sat down at a table with Tom. I remember thinking it wasn't very smart of them." She wrinkled her nose. "Indiscreet even. Beyond the two of them, I'm not sure." She offered up an apologetic moue. "I'm not much help."

She certainly hadn't cleared Tom as a suspect. If anything, the opposite. "Don't be silly. This is tremendously helpful."

"Do you think Suze is ready to leave?" Libba wiped a few stray drips of water from the table with a paper napkin.

"I hope so." I shifted my gaze to the weather outside. The other side of the plate window looked foreboding and dark. Dark enough that Libba and I were reflected in the glass.

"If she doesn't want to leave, I may take a cab. You can drive my car home." Libba waved the wadded napkin at the soaked front of her sweater. "In fact, I'm going. Being wet is miserable, the weather looks awful, and I want to be dry. If you have any questions about the rest of the pages, call me."

We stood and I dropped a bill onto the table.

"Thanks for the pie."

"My pleasure. Thanks for taking time to write everything down."

She kissed the air next to my cheek. "I'll talk to you later. Toodles."

She slipped into her coat, hurried through the lobby, pushed through the revolving doors, and leapt into a waiting cab.

I moved more slowly. According to Libba's notes, Tom had ample opportunity to kill his wife. Then again, so had most of the people who'd been in the bar that night. But it was Tom I cared about. It was Tom who needed an ironclad alibi. Too bad the one woman who might have provided one was dead.

I paused in the lobby, opened my pocketbook, and searched for a lipstick. Whatever color remained on my lips after my parking lot adventure had transferred to the cup in the coffee shop. Checkbook. Billfold. Compact. Comb. Where was the lipstick? There! I jammed Libba's papers into my purse, pulled out the tube, hooked my handbag over my elbow, opened the compact, peered into its tiny mirror, and applied Peachy Pink to my lips—

Whomp!

I stumbled forward and applied Peachy Pink to my chin.

"Oh my gracious. I'm so sorry. I wasn't looking where I was going. I—" Edith Hathaway stood in front of me, her face a study in contrition. "You."

I closed my lipstick, dropped it into the depths of my purse, and dug for a hanky. Even with lipstick smeared on my face and my hair destroyed by the sleet in the club parking lot, I looked better than Edith. She had rings under her eyes that would do a raccoon proud, not only was her hair limp but it looked dirty, and her skin had a yellow tone. "It's nice to see you again," I said. It would have been nicer if she hadn't whacked into me. "How's Dawn?"

She glanced around the near empty lobby (weather has a way of emptying hospitals of visitors). "They're keeping her on a psychological hold," she whispered. "It was keep her here or transfer her to a specialty hospital."

A specialty hospital. Edith meant a hospital for people with mental disorders. Libba would call it a loony bin. But Libba's idea of mental health was a friend, a conversation, and a pitcher or three of martinis. Mother would lower her voice, say "that place," and wrinkle her nose with distaste. They both thought of depression as a personal weakness. I gave up on finding the hanky, reached out, and squeezed Edith's cold hand. "I'm sure they're taking good care of her."

"She wants to go home. I want her to go home. But what if she—" Her voice caught.

What hell. If she took Dawn home and the child killed herself, Edith would live with corrosive guilt forever. The poor woman.

"What can I do?"

She blinked. Surprised by my offer.

I was surprised too. Those words came out of nowhere.

"I came down to get a cup of coffee and go right back to the room, but if I could just sit." There was longing in her voice. "I need a few minutes alone. A cup of coffee in a real cup. A sandwich. Just half an hour. Would you visit with her?"

How could I refuse Edith a thirty-minute respite? "Of course. I'd be delighted. Same room?"

"Yes." Tears filled her eyes. "Thank you."

"You're welcome."

"You might want to—" She touched her chin.

The lipstick. "Thanks."

I stopped by a bathroom, rubbed the Peachy Pink off my chin, took a wet towel and addressed the mascara smudges under my eyes, and powdered my face. I also applied a comb to my hair.

When I pushed open the door to Dawn's room, I looked almost presentable.

Dawn looked up from reading a *Seventeen* with Caroline of Monaco on the cover. She dropped the magazine on her lap. "Mrs. Russell."

"How are you, Dawn?"

"Fine, thank you. How are you?"

A rote reply.

"I've had better days. My late husband's sister fell in the parking lot and hit her head."

The girl stared at me. I'd gone off script.

I tried again. "The weather is awful."

She glanced toward the window.

"And I keep finding bodies." Where had that little confession come from? I sank into the chair next to her bed.

"And I thought I was having a bad week." A hint of humor glinted in Dawn's eyes.

"Yours is still worse than mine. I hate being in the hospital."

"Everyone does."

A fair point.

"Your mom is grabbing a sandwich." Just in case she wondered why I'd shown up in her room.

"And she was afraid to leave me alone for more than five minutes." There was a cynical tone in her voice that didn't belong.

"Mothers worry." That was an understatement. "It's what we do."

Dawn's eye rolls weren't nearly as dramatic as Grace's. Or perhaps she saved the drama for her mother. "You know when the worst thing in the world happens?" She didn't wait for my answer. "In a way, it's freeing. Nothing worse can happen."

I didn't have the heart to tell her the universe always—always—had a card up its sleeve.

Survive *The Towering Inferno* and get hit by a bus.

Get impeached from the presidency, get phlebitis, and then, according to rumor, go broke.

Find a body, then find ten more.

"Don't you agree? Nothing worse can happen." The cynicism had disappeared from Dawn's voice and been replaced by a youthful need for reassurance.

I gave her what I hoped was an encouraging smile. It made my face hurt.

"What's the worst thing that ever happened to you?" she asked.

"I found my husband's body."

"And you're fine now."

The kid had a point. I was fine. In fact, I was better now than I had been before I ran over Henry's corpse. "I am."

Dawn looked down at the princess's sun-kissed face and a tear plopped onto the magazine cover. "I got pregnant."

Words failed me.

"It was Trip's."

I reached towards her hand, but she moved it away. Another tear plopped. And another. The lowest headline, "Tips to Beat Test Panic," was getting soaked.

"I couldn't tell my mom. I couldn't. I knew she'd never look at me the same way again." She wiped her eyes. "She told me Trip was no good like a million times."

"What did you do?"

"I told Trip and he told his mother. She took me."

"Took you?"

Dawn nodded. "To get an abortion. I'm not eighteen, so I had to have parental consent. She said she was my mother."

I leaned back in my chair. If some woman took Grace to get

an abortion without my knowledge or consent, I'd...I'd kill her. The woman, not Grace. I lowered my gaze to my lap.

"You think I'm a murderer."

"No, I don't. You're not." I thought she was a frightened child who'd played at being an adult.

"I killed my baby." Her tears were falling freely. Princess Caroline was getting soaked. "The guilt ate at me and I couldn't tell my mom and Trip didn't care. Not one bit. I even called Mrs. Michaels."

I looked up. "What did she say?"

"She said a baby would have ruined my life and that she did me a favor."

"That's it?"

"She said she was late for her bridge game."

What a cold-hearted bitch. Arguably she deserved to be frozen into a popsicle. "Honey, I'm so sorry."

"It's not your fault." There was a you-just-don't-get-it edge to Dawn's voice.

"I'm sorry you had to go through this. I'm sorry Mrs. Michaels didn't listen to you. I'm sorry...I'm sorry you're so sad."

Dawn's nose was red now. She sniffled.

"Here." I handed her a Kleenex.

She wiped her eyes then blew.

"Everything seemed so hopeless."

"I know." Her hand was still out of reach or I would have held it tightly. "But it's like you said, when the worst happens and you survive, you know you can survive whatever comes next."

"That's what the shrink says."

The shrink. She was on a psychiatric hold. Of course she had a shrink.

"Do you believe that?" I asked.

"I guess I do. Mom knows everything and she still loves

me." She moved her hand toward mine.

I clasped her thin fingers. "That's what mothers do. They love their children no matter what." I would have gone on, but Edith Hathaway, who had every reason to kill Laurie Michaels, walked in.

EIGHTEEN

On the way home I concentrated on the road. Had to. The streets weren't streets. The streets were skating rinks. And I was not a good skater.

Suze had the good sense to sit in silence. That or, if her clenched fists were any indication, she was too afraid to distract me.

We reached home in one my-nerves-are-shot piece and slipped-slid our way to the front door.

"Careful, the steps are icy," I warned.

Suze clutched the handrail and, somehow, we made it unscathed into the warmth of the foyer.

"We're home," I called.

No reply.

The scent of something delicious in the oven led us to the kitchen, where Grace had the phone pressed against her ear. "Hold on. Mom just walked in." She smirked and held out the receiver.

I took it from her. I glanced around the kitchen. Aggie, Grace, and Max watched me carefully. "Hello."

"Ellison, it's Anarchy."

There it was—the fizziness that sparkled in my blood whenever he called. I took a deep calming breath. Now was not the time for fizzy. Now was the time to tell him that there were suspects beyond Tom Michaels. Suspects he'd never considered.

"Hi. Let me change lines." I focused my gaze on Grace. "I'll take this in the study. Please hang up when I pick up."

My daughter's smirk deepened. She looked at Suze and said, "It's Mom's detective."

I rolled my eyes (how often does a mother get to do that?) and hurried to the study.

With the receiver on Henry's desk clutched in my hand, I spoke into the phone. "I've got it, Grace." I heard the click of her receiver into its cradle and said, "Hi." Now that we had a modicum of privacy, I was as tongue-tied as a teenager on a first date.

"Your detective?"

Of course he'd heard that. "Kids." That one word conveyed that Grace possessed an active imagination and that I was entirely innocent when it came to thinking of him as my detective. I wasn't. "My sister-in-law fell in the parking lot at the country club today." It was an awkward way to change the subject, but the alternative would color my cheeks scarlet for days.

"Is she all right?"

"She is, but she's still in the hospital. They're keeping her for observation." If I closed my eyes I could still see my second-best mink on the frozen asphalt and taste the terror on my tongue. "For one awful moment, when I saw her lying on the pavement, I thought she was dead."

"That would have made three bodies in one week. A new record?"

Everyone's a comedian. "She hit her head. That's all." I'd dipped my toe, now it was time to take the plunge. I squared my shoulders. "I visited Dawn Hathaway after we got Gwen settled."

"The girl from Grace's party?"

"Yes." I leaned against the desk and rubbed my eyes with my free hand. I had to tell him. Had to. It wasn't just that I wanted Tom cleared. It wasn't. Laurie deserved justice. "Dawn told me that Laurie Michaels helped her get an abortion."

"Oh?" There was a dangerous edge to his voice.

"Dawn's mother found out."

"What are you saying?" The edge was still there. Sharper now.

"I'm saying Edith Hathaway might have killed Laurie. She had a reason. A good one. And she was at the club the night Laurie was murdered."

"There were lots of people at the club that night."

"But Edith's not a member, and by all accounts she came in looking for Laurie."

Anarchy sighed. It was the sigh of a man who'd fought and lost the same battle many times. "Ellison, you have to stay out of this investigation. Two people are already dead."

"So you don't think Tom did it?"

"I did not say that."

"Good as. You have Tom in custody. You wouldn't worry about me investigating if you were sure you had the murderer locked up. And I'm not investigating. I'm just asking questions."

"What do you think investigating is?"

A vision of Sherlock Holmes with his magnifying glass, deer-stalker hat, and oversized coat rose before me. It was quickly followed by a vision of Poirot stroking his waxed mustache and exercising his little gray cells. I was nothing like them.

"Investigating involves canvasing neighborhoods, interviewing witnesses, and identifying suspects."

"Two out of three require questions."

Silence seemed the best response.

"I worry."

My heart warmed and a certain fizz returned to my blood.

"A lot," he added.

I pressed my hand against my heart. The fool muscle had

doubled its number of beats per minute. "I—" Words failed me. That or I was out of breath from my racing heartbeat.

"Just stay out of the investigation."

"Okay," I agreed. "If you promise to take a closer look at Edith."

"Done."

It was time for a change of subject. "When are you leaving for San Francisco?"

"I'm not."

"You're not going home to your family for Thanksgiving?"

"No." His tone did not invite further questions.

"Where are you having dinner?"

He was silent a shade too long. "With Peters' family."

I didn't believe him. "Have dinner with me instead."

"With you?"

"Well, with me and Grace and Suze and Gwen. Aggie is cooking." I didn't want my lack of culinary abilities to be the reason he said no.

"It's a family dinner."

"Hardly." Suze wasn't related to anyone, and Gwen, well, she was the kind of relation one could do without. "It would be much nicer if you were here. Although, I should warn you, Gwen blames me for her fall, so she may not be very pleasant."

He chuckled. "Like I said, a family dinner."

"Please come." How much I wanted him at my table surprised me. I crossed my fingers and waited.

"What time?"

"Between five thirty and six for cocktails. Dinner's at seven."

"I'll be there. Remember. No investigating."

"I'll remember."

"Jones!" Peters' voice carried through the phone lines.

"Listen, I have to go. I'll talk to you later."

"Okay. I'll see you Thursday."

Anarchy hung up the phone, but not before I heard his cranky partner say, "Something, something, Hathaway."

I stayed there, leaning against Henry's desk, thinking about Anarchy at my table. The thought made me smile.

Brnng. Brnng.

I stared at the phone, unwilling to interrupt my dream of Anarchy in my dining room, his brown eyes twinkling in the candlelight.

Brnng. Brnng.

Brnng. Brn—

Silence. I sighed.

"Mom!" Grace's voice carried from the kitchen. "It's for you."

I sighed again and picked up the receiver. "Hello."

"Ellison, it's your mother."

Uh-oh. She was in a mood. Her tone told the story.

"You need to work on Grace's phone manners."

"I'll do that." Right after I finished crocheting a hundred potholders. "You made it to St. Louis."

"We did, but your father was wrong about the weather. We're stuck here."

"But you're safe."

"We are. We're staying near Plaza Frontenac." No wonder she didn't sound more upset. She had a Saks and a Neiman Marcus to keep her company. "Your father says with the storm moving east, the roads will only get worse. We're coming home."

"Oh?"

"We'll be at your house for Thanksgiving after all."

Oh dear Lord. Mother and Suze? Mother and Anarchy? "Wonderful."

"Also, I talked to Lorna. She's going through such a terrible time right now that I invited her."

"That might not be such a good idea." I spoke through gritted teeth.

"Why not?"

"Anarchy Jones is coming to dinner."

"Why?"

"Because I invited him."

"Don't be smart with me. Why did you invite him?"

"We're not doing this, Mother." We were not discussing the way I felt about Anarchy, or how unsuitable a police detective was for the daughter of a scion, or the unfortunate fact that Anarchy had arrested a few people Mother called friends.

I could feel her disapproval travel the frozen roads from St. Louis to Kansas City.

"Lorna is one of my oldest friends and she's going through hell. You can un-invite him."

"Or we can all act like adults."

"Don't be ridiculous. Lorna's bringing Trip."

When I didn't answer, she kept talking. "If we're lucky, Tom will be out on bail and you can ask him about the insurance money."

I pinched the bridge of my nose. "Anarchy is joining us for dinner on Thursday."

"Your father and I will discuss our plans." In other words, she'd rather brave ice-covered roads from St. Louis to Akron than sit down to Thanksgiving dinner with Anarchy.

"Let me know what you decide."

She hung up—an emphatic hang up—without saying goodbye.

Guilt immediately washed over me. Mother was family. Lorna was going through a terrible time. Trip had just lost his mother. Their holiday promised to be dreadful.

So of course Mother invited them to my house.

The thought strengthened my wavering resolve.

I was already poking about trying to clear Tom of the murder. Wasn't that enough?

What's more, I'd found Anarchy another suspect in Edith Hathaway. A suspect with both motive and opportunity. If I could link her to Jenny, Anarchy would have to take my suspicions seriously. Maybe I could—there had been an Edna wandering about the building the day Jenny died.

I opened Henry's desk drawer, pulled out the phone book, squinted as I looked up the number, and dialed.

Jimmy answered the phone.

"Jimmy, this is Ellison Russell calling. Do you remember Edna Smith who was there the day Jenny died?"

"Yes, Miss Ellison."

"Can you describe her to me?"

"She was just a regular lady."

Hardly a useful description.

"Was there anything special about her?" I pressed. "Anything you remember?"

He fell silent.

I gave him a moment to think.

"Her earrings."

"Her earrings?"

"Yes, Miss Ellison. Her earrings were gold lions. Heads. I'd never seen anything like them before."

"Thank you, Jimmy." I hung up the phone and hurried back to the kitchen, where my purse rested on the counter.

I dug through it, pulling out my lipstick, my comb, my billfold, a receipt, my compact, and finally Libba's pages. My finger traced down the pages.

There!

I'd finally been served a stinger when this woman walked in. I'd never seen her before. Not unattractive. Brown hair. Tweed suit. But a suit with some style. Not like something

Laurie would wear. Also, she wore the most fabulous earrings. They were gold lion heads. She was looking for Laurie. Said it was imperative that she talk to her immediately.

Edith Hathaway and Edna Smith were the same person. All I had to do was tell Anarchy. Of course, I'd also have to tell him I'd asked more questions (within fifteen minutes of promising him I wouldn't).

Later that night, after Suze turned in, I tapped on Grace's bedroom door.

"Come in."

Grace, who usually wore short nighties, had on a flannel Lanz nightgown. She was curled up in bed with the covers pulled up to her gown's lace yoke and she held a book.

"What are you reading?"

She turned the book's cover toward me. *The Tropic of Cancer.*

Oh dear Lord. "Is that for school?"

"It's for our banned book class."

I blinked. "Your what?"

"Our banned book class. We've already read *Catcher in the Rye* and *Huck Finn*. After this, we're reading *The Awakening* by Kate Chopin."

The Frances Walford in me itched to march straight down to that school—the school to which I wrote exorbitant tuition checks—and demand a change in the syllabus. The artist in me told Frances to calm down.

"I don't think I've ever read that." I nodded toward the book in her hands.

She wrinkled her nose. "Not my favorite."

I took another step into her room. "I saw Dawn today."

Grace hadn't been moving, but she stilled. "How is she?"

"She's still in the hospital." Another few steps brought me to the bed. I sat at its foot. "She's on a psychiatric hold."

"Oh."

I studied my daughter's face. It was blank. Whatever she was thinking or feeling she kept well hidden.

"She told me what happened."

Grace's eyes widened slightly. "She did?"

I nodded. "I hope you know you can tell me anything. I'll never stop loving you. Never stop supporting you."

Grace looked down at her comforter. "She didn't want her mother to be disappointed."

"I understand that. Disappointing mothers can be painful." I knew that only too well. "But I guarantee you, Edith Hathaway would not have stopped loving her daughter. If she'd known Dawn was pregnant, she would have helped her find a solution. Hopefully one that didn't lead to Dawn taking a bottle of pills."

Grace shook her head. "Mrs. Hathaway would have made Dawn have the baby. She believes abortion is murder."

Maybe. "If there's one thing I've learned in my life it's that iron-clad convictions fall by the wayside when the circumstances are personal." The question was, had Edith's convictions slipped enough to commit murder herself?

"What do you mean?"

"I mean that people's core beliefs about race, religion, politics, abortion, or even sex get reassessed when there's a family crisis."

She nodded. Slowly.

"Do you think Edith—" Did she think Edith had killed Laurie? I swallowed and began again, "Do you think Edith would—"

"Do I think Mrs. Hathaway would have made Dawn have the baby?" Grace finished my question. The wrong way. "I do. I also think she'll hold this against Dawn. Forever." Grace glanced down at the rather salacious book in her lap. "According to Dawn, her mom is kind of crazy about chastity."

Not something I cared to talk about. Which meant I probably should.

"We've never really talked about sex." It was a topic guaranteed to embarrass us both.

"Yes, we have." Grace's cheeks flamed as red as the twisting stripes in her nightgown.

"I'm not talking about mechanics. I'm talking about the rest."

"The rest?"

"There's more to sex than tab A and slot B, Grace."

The color of her cheeks deepened.

I glanced at the ceiling. Sadly, there were no parenting tips written there. "It seems as if we're bombarded by the idea that sex is the equivalent of a casual game of tennis. You find someone to play with, hit a view volleys, shake hands when it's over, and walk away." I brushed a stray lock of hair away from my eyes. "Maybe some people can do that. Most can't."

Grace watched me warily.

"For most people, sex involves emotion. It did for Dawn."

Grace's lips thinned, and any thoughts she had, she kept to herself.

"Neither Dawn nor Trip were thinking about consequences. Not pregnancy, not emotional fall-out." I paused, ready for questions about consequences or emotions or even preventing pregnancy.

"Did you and Daddy have sex before you got married?"

I wasn't ready for that. "No," I squeaked.

"No?"

"No." My voice was stronger—firmer—now.

"So you were a virgin?"

"Yes."

"Did you ever want to do it with anyone else? Before Daddy?"

How had I lost control of the conversation so quickly? "That's really none of your business" was the easy answer. And the wrong answer. All the parenting books and articles I'd read said an open and honest dialogue about sex was the way to go. I swallowed. "Yes."

"But you didn't?"

"No."

"Why not?"

I paused. The glib answer—your aunt was having enough sex for both of us—was a bit too honest and hardly appropriate.

"I was scared."

Grace waited.

"I was scared of getting pregnant. I was scared I'd catch a disease. I was scared of what Mother would say to me if she found out. But most of all, I was scared of the way I'd feel. The first time was supposed to be important, and what if he didn't really care about me? What if all he wanted was sex? What if afterwards he ignored me or told his friends or dated one of my friends? I wasn't ready."

"Do you regret not doing it?"

"No." So much for honesty. The itch on the end of my nose was entirely bearable. "Like I said, I wasn't ready." That was the truth.

"Who was he?"

"Grant Wycliff." I'd whiled away countless hours of pre-calculus class doodling "Ellison Walford Wycliff" and "Mrs. Grant Wycliff" surrounded by hearts and flowers in my notebooks. "No one important. I haven't seen him in years." I'd whiled away countless hours of my marriage—especially after I discovered Henry's cheating—wondering what if.

"Why not?"

"He went away to Yale, married a girl from Darien, and never came back."

"Did you love him?"

"At the time, I thought I did."

"Did he love you?"

"I wasn't sure." I glanced back up at the ceiling. Still no parenting tips written there. "If we'd really loved each other, being apart for a few years wouldn't have mattered."

"I want my first time to be with someone I love."

"I want that for you too."

She nodded. "Do you ever miss Dad?"

If ever there was a question that deserved honesty. "Sometimes." When there was a thorny parenting question.

"I miss him. Thanksgiving will be our first big holiday without him." She wiped at her eyes then lifted her chin. "But I like Detective Jones, and I'm glad you're moving on."

My heart broke into little pieces. "Come here."

She leaned forward.

I leaned forward.

We hugged. Our arms wrapped tightly around each other. The scent of her Herbal Essences shampoo and Tame Crème Rinse a reminder that she wasn't a little girl anymore. Someday she would fall in love.

I held her tighter.

NINETEEN

The day before Thanksgiving, I didn't have time to break my promise to Anarchy. There was Gwen to be picked up from the hospital, three last-minute trips to the market (that's what happens when dinner for four becomes dinner for nine), then Gwen wanted a frosty malt from Winstead's and nothing else would do.

Fortunately, despite the sullen skies and moaning wind, nothing fell from the sky to the ground. No snow. No sleet. No freezing rain. The main streets were lined with exhaust-blackened snow, but they were clear.

Grace arrived home from school shortly after noon (early dismissal) and I sent her on the fourth market run (Aggie used almost all the butter for the pie crusts, leaving none for mashed potatoes or bread dressing or biscuits).

Aggie, her voluminous peacock caftan covered by an enormous white apron, waved mixing spoons around like a demented conductor with a cursed baton.

"I can help," I offered.

Aggie snorted.

"I can help," said Suze.

Aggie stopped waving her spoon and eyed Suze with interest. "Can you cook?"

"I went to culinary school."

"Grab an apron."

Which left me to entertain Gwen, who was ensconced in the

family room with her feet on an ottoman, her frosty malt on the side table next to her, and the television tuned to *As the World Turns*.

She shifted her gaze away from the television. "Nancy Hughes reminds me of our mothers."

"Who?"

Gwen pointed at the screen. "Nancy Hughes. She's the family matriarch."

Ah.

Gwen sucked on her straw. Sucked hard. Hard enough to collapse the plastic. Frosties and straws didn't always play well together.

"Do you want a spoon?"

She shook her head and used her cup to point at the woman on the television. "Stayed home, raised her kids, volunteered at the hospital."

Add the Junior League and the country club and that was Mother and every single one of her friends.

Gwen sucked on her straw again. "What a waste of talent."

It was lucky Mother wasn't around to hear Gwen. Frances Walford would hardly appreciate her life being called a waste. Mother loved her life, and if she experienced strange stirrings, a sense of dissatisfaction, or (god forbid) yearnings, she didn't admit to them. I knew for a fact Mother had read Betty Friedan's *The Feminine Mystique*. I knew because she warned me not to take its message to heart. She said it would destroy my marriage.

Mother had been right.

"Have you made any progress finding out who killed Laurie Michaels?"

"I have."

Gwen blinked. Twice. She even looked mildly disappointed, as if she'd been looking forward to telling me how useless I was.

"Who?"

"A woman named Edith Hathaway."

"Why did she do it?"

"Laurie did something damaging to Edith's daughter."

"A mother protecting her young. I like it."

I didn't. Dawn needed her mother. And, thanks to me, Edith Hathaway might soon be in jail. I could understand murdering Laurie. In Edith's shoes, I'd have been tempted to do the same. But why Jenny? "It's a tragic mess."

Gwen shrugged. "I thought you were going to say that Sherman Westcott had done it."

"You don't like Sherman." It was a statement of fact.

"No."

"Why not?" I asked.

"He's a liar and a cheat."

"Then why did Henry hire him?"

Gwen stared at me—a shade too long. "On occasion, my brother made mistakes."

I took the high road and ignored the not-so-subtle suggestion that marrying me was one of Henry's mistakes. "How do you know Sherman is so awful?"

"I just know," she said with all the mulishness of a girl twenty-five years her junior.

"Your not liking him isn't enough to accuse him of murder." I settled into the club chair next to the couch. "Even if Sherman did want Laurie dead, he wouldn't want Tom arrested for murder. If the bank goes under, he'll lose his job, and believe you me, I'll make sure everyone knows this is his fault. He won't find another job in banking anytime soon."

"There are all sorts of reasons Sherman could have killed Laurie." Gwen put down her frosty and crossed her arms.

"Such as?" I asked.

"Maybe they were having an affair."

"Have you seen Sherman Westcott lately?"

"Maybe Laurie knew his deepest, darkest secret."

His deepest, darkest secret? "This is everyday life, not *As the World Turns.*"

"Maybe he killed Laurie hoping to save the bank, never dreaming Tom would be arrested."

"The police always look at the spouse first." This I knew too well. "Between the debts and the insurance money, Tom would be a suspect even if he'd been three states away when Laurie died."

Gwen glared at me. "Maybe he was embezzling from the bank and Laurie found out."

"How would Laurie find out about that?"

"I don't know." Gwen's eyes narrowed. "She just did."

I refrained from replying.

On the television, Mr. Whipple scolded someone for squeezing the Charmin.

"If this Hathaway woman is innocent? What then?" she demanded.

"Then we keep looking," I replied. "The bank examiners won't swoop in the day after Thanksgiving." I sounded more optimistic than I felt.

Gwen's face settled into a bleak mask. "What if they do?"

Through all of her iterations, Gwen had remained blithely unconcerned with filthy lucre. That no longer seemed to be the case. "How much do you need?"

"Pardon me?" Gwen raised a single dismissive brow.

"You're selling your shares. You must have a reason."

"Which is none of your business." Her words and her tone were the verbal equivalent of a slap across the face.

I even raised my palm to my cheek.

Ding dong.

I stood.

"Won't your housekeeper answer the door?"

"Aggie's cooking." Besides, answering the door was an excellent reason to escape Gwen's company. "I'll get that," I called into the kitchen.

I left Gwen alone with Nancy Hughes, hurried to the front door, and pulled it open.

Hunter Tafft stood on the front stoop. "Ellison."

"This is a surprise." An understatement.

"I'm sorry to show up without calling first, but we need to swing by the bank."

"Oh?" My voice was faint.

"I have questions for Westcott."

"You do?"

"He's in his office now. I called."

"That bad?"

A grim expression settled on Hunter's face. "That bad."

"Let me get my coat." I reached into the front closet and grabbed the first coat I touched.

If Hunter thought my wearing Graces' shearling was odd, he kept his opinion to himself.

"Aggie," I called down the hall. "I'm going out for a bit."

I climbed into Hunter's Mercedes and he closed the door behind me. When he'd settled behind the wheel, I said, "Tell me."

He scowled at the windshield. "It's easier to explain with the documents handy."

Fine. Be that way.

We drove to the bank in tense silence and arrived just as Sherman was leaving. He wore a black homburg, a gray overcoat, and a somber expression. He looked like a staid banker. Or an undertaker.

He stopped when he saw us getting out of the car.

"Ellison." He did not sound pleased at my arrival. "Tafft."

He jerked his chin in Hunter's direction. "I'm just on my way out."

"I'm sure you can spare a few minutes," I said. It was me talking, but I channeled Mother. Her strength and her scariness.

Sherman's lips thinned, but he nodded his assent. He led us into his office and settled behind his desk. "What's this about?"

"I gave the Michaels' file to Hunter Tafft. He's been reviewing it for irregularities."

Sherman paled and his hand closed around the lip of his desk as if he needed something solid to steady him. "Irregularities?"

"Yes."

Sherman's steady chin quivered. The man might not be a murderer (probably wasn't a murderer), but Gwen was right about the liar and cheat part of her assessment. There was something in that file Sherman didn't want found.

And Hunter had found it.

"You gave confidential bank documents to Hunter Tafft?" Sherman's voice was stronger now. He shifted his glare between the two of us as if he was a principal and Hunter and I were naughty children.

"I put him on retainer."

"Without the board's approval?"

Hunter cleared his throat. "Grace Russell owns 51 percent of the shares. Gwen Russell owns another 20 percent. If the family wants to hire a lawyer to review a file, they'll hire a lawyer."

"This is highly unusual."

"No. It's not. What's highly unusual is that you had a problem loan of this size and you didn't bring it to the board's attention."

Sherman's cheeks were ruddy—the exact color of aged bricks. He stood, looming over us. "Ellison, a word in private?"

"I think not." I glared up at him.

"I insist."

I channeled more of Mother. "Let's remember who signs your checks."

Sherman Westcott deflated like a pricked balloon.

"Sherman—" I kept my voice cold and even "—what's in that file?"

The banker shook his head. "You'll fire me."

"I found it, Ellison." Hunter sounded implacable.

Sherman collapsed into his chair.

"What did Hunter find in those files?" I asked.

"Nothing. Tafft is wrong."

And people said I was a bad liar. Maybe he wasn't lying. Maybe he was delusional.

"The bank made capital loans to Tom's company." Hunter's voice was dry and impersonal.

Sherman stared at the polished surface of his desk.

"But he didn't spend the money on capital."

Just as Aggie suspected.

"Of course he did." Sherman's objection was patently ridiculous.

"He inflated the price of equipment." Still dry. Still impersonal.

Sherman shifted in his chair. "I knew nothing about that."

"It was your job to know." My voice was neither dry nor impersonal. It was outraged. If the bad loan had been discovered by bank examiners, Sherman's reputation would be ruined. He'd never get another banking job. His best bet for saving his job and his reputation had been Tom paying back the loan. Was Gwen right? Had Sherman killed Laurie? My hands tightened to fists. "If it was Tom who was dead and not Laurie, I'd suspect you of murder."

Except if Tom was dead, he couldn't pay off his note.

Sherman's expression was stark. "I didn't kill anyone."

"You colluded with Tom Michaels," said Hunter.

Sherman looked up from his desk and sent a beseeching gaze my way. "He ran into a rough patch. He assured me he'd make good on the loan."

A rough patch? The man had a gambling problem.

"How much did he kick back to you?" Hunter sounded mildly curious.

Kickbacks?

Sherman shifted his gaze to Hunter. Desperation lurked in the banker's eyes.

Kickbacks.

"I know a police detective. In fact, he's investigating Laurie's death. I am positive he'd be interested in this." I reached for Sherman's phone.

"Wait!" Sherman's voice squeaked. "Tom gambled."

I didn't move, my hand poised over the phone. "And you loaned him money."

"The people he owed—" Sherman returned his gaze to his lap "—they kill people."

And Sherman had paid off Tom's debt with the bank's money. I stared at him. The words I needed—words that would adequately express my anger and disgust—escaped me. I settled for narrowing my eyes and shooting one of Mother's death stares his way.

"Tom and I are old friends."

"You risked our family's bank for an old friend?" And kickbacks. "Why?" Disbelief twisted my voice into one I didn't recognize. The twist in my voice had nothing on the twist in my stomach. It felt positively green. "You're a thief."

Sherman dropped his gaze, planted his elbows on his knees, and let his head fall into his hands.

"Did Henry know?" I demanded. Sherman's answer

mattered. A lot. I took a breath and smelled Love's Baby Soft. The scent lingered on Grace's coat.

Sherman didn't move. It was almost as if he hadn't heard my question.

I leaned forward. "Did my husband know?" Was Grace's legacy worth saving?

Sherman answered me with a miniscule shake of his head. "He knew the loan was troubled. He didn't know why."

Thank heavens. But was Sherman telling the truth? About any of it?

I picked up the phone.

"If you call the police, the examiners will be at the bank by Monday." The man was calling my bluff.

I inserted my finger in the hole in the dial.

"I mean it, Ellison." Sherman held out his hands. Begging. "Think about Grace. She'll lose the bank."

My hand paused. For an instant. Then I dialed the second digit.

"You can't do this!" He rose from this chair.

"She can," said Hunter.

Hunter was right. "I can." I kept dialing.

"I'll go to jail."

"You should have thought about that before you loaned the bank's money to a man with a gambling problem." I narrowed my eyes. "You should have thought about that before you took kickbacks."

Sherman sat down hard. As if his legs could no longer support him. "You're ruining my life."

How many times had Grace said exactly that?

Be home by curfew. You're ruining my life.

You cannot spend the night at Peggy's when I know for a fact her parents are out of town. You're ruining my life.

It's lovely that you're a vegan this week, but Aggie isn't

going to cook to suit you. You're ruining my life.

As overdramatic as the phrase sounded coming from a teenager, it sounded even worse coming from a grown man. Sherman Westcott's life might be ruined, but I had not done the ruining. Across from me, the solid, staid banker was collapsing in on himself. His strength traded for fragility.

"What did you think would happen, Westcott?"

"I thought Tom would pay back the loan, I'd close the file, and no one would ever know."

Hunter's lips thinned. "When things went south? When you admitted, at least to yourself, that the loan was bad? What did you expect would transpire?"

"I don't have to answer that." Sherman drew himself up, sat straight, glared at Hunter.

"I'd like an answer." My index finger was in the dial, but it wasn't moving. "Think of it as practice for the police."

Sherman looked suddenly furious. "I thought you'd cover the note."

I could have done exactly that. But sinking my savings into a troubled bank hadn't seemed the wisest way to ensure Grace's future. Yes, I wanted the bank saved. But not because it was a good investment. I wanted the bank saved because it was Grace's legacy from her father.

That legacy seemed a lot less important now that two women were dead. I finished dialing Anarchy's phone number.

"Jones."

"Would you please come to the bank?"

"What's wrong?"

"I—" I glanced at Sherman Westcott. "Don't be angry."

"Are you sitting there with a killer?"

"I don't know. Maybe."

"Are you in danger?"

"No."

"I'm on my way." He hung up the phone.

Sherman scowled at me. "I could just leave."

"You could. No one's keeping you here."

"You'll send the police to my house." Sherman's voice was whiny and his coat gaped around him as if the dark wool had expanded by three sizes and the man had shrunk by six.

"I will."

"If you'd just covered the note." More whining.

"I think we're better off not talking," I said.

Sherman sank farther into his chair, a man diminished by his choices.

Hunter stuffed papers into his briefcase.

I looked over my shoulder for Sherman's secretary. I needed coffee.

She was nowhere to be seen.

I stood. "I'll be right back."

Hunter raised a brow.

"Coffee," I explained.

He nodded.

"You?"

"No. Thanks."

I'd poured myself a cup and was headed back to Sherman's office when Anarchy blew into the lobby like a gust of wind. He strode toward me. His hands circled my upper arms and his coffee-brown gaze searched my face. "Are you all right?"

"I'm fine."

His gaze continued searching—my eyes, my hair, my lips— as if he doubted my word. "What happened? What's going on?"

"Sherman Westcott is waiting for you."

"Sherman Westcott?"

"He runs the bank. You need to talk to him."

"You've been asking questions." His eyes narrowed.

"Not like you think. Sherman and Tom Michaels defrauded

the bank."

Anarchy blinked. "What?"

"I wasn't interfering in your investigation." Much. "The bank loaned Tom an enormous sum of money to buy capital equipment. Not only did he not buy the equipment, he gave a kickback to Sherman."

Anarchy's lips thinned to a grim line. "Did Laurie know about this?"

"I have no idea."

"Do you think Westcott killed her?"

"He was at the club the night she died." I shook my head. There were too many people who'd wanted Laurie dead. And what of poor Jenny? Who had killed her? And why? Had she seen something the night Laurie died? "I don't know. Maybe. Maybe not."

His lips quirked. "That's definitive."

All I wanted was to step closer to him, lean my forehead against the broad expanse of his chest, and slide into the comfort of his arms wrapped around me. Instead, I dredged up a smile. "He stole from Grace. I'm not exactly unbiased."

He shifted his gaze from my face to the wall of offices.

"Go."

"You don't want to come?"

"If I never see Sherman Westcott again, it will be too soon." I meant what I said. He'd lied to me. He'd stolen from Grace. He might have killed Laurie. And Jenny. "Hunter Tafft is in there."

Anarchy's eyes narrowed and he nodded. Slowly. Then he brushed a kiss across my forehead.

"What was that for?"

"You being you." Without another word, he walked away.

TWENTY

"Grace, if you wear that your grandmother will have a coronary. Please find something at least five inches longer."

"Mom." She made "Mom" into a complaint.

"You know better."

"Fine," she huffed.

With the stomping of her feet on the stairs echoing in my ears, I checked the downstairs. A fire crackled merrily in the living room hearth and floral arrangements graced the library and coffee tables in the living room as well as the bombe chest in the foyer and the dining room table. The red wine was decanted and the whole house smelled of roasting turkey.

I followed my nose to the kitchen. "Aggie, I can't thank you enough for being here."

"This worked out fine." Aggie looked up from basting the turkey. "My sister always serves at noon so she can get to bed early."

"Does she work the day after Thanksgiving?"

"No. She shops."

Oh dear Lord. The day after Thanksgiving was the one day I wouldn't shop. The crowds were terrible. The parking was worse. And just try and find someone to offer actual sales assistance. "That's very brave of her."

"She'll have all her Christmas shopping done by noon then go out for a big lunch." There was an unfamiliar wistfulness in Aggie's voice.

"You should go with her."

Aggie shook her head. "You have house guests."

"We can muddle through for one morning. Grace can make eggs and bacon. I'll make the coffee and put the bread in the toaster."

"I'd love to go with her." Longing replaced wistfulness.

"Then go. Shop till you drop."

The smile Aggie gave me reminded me what real thanks looked like.

"Do you need any help in here?" I asked.

"No. I've got everything under control."

She did. A pot of water on the stove bubbled in anticipation of potatoes. Mince and pumpkin pies rested on the counter, pushed back far enough to be out of Max's reach. Cookie sheets filled with root vegetables waited to be roasted. A mason jar held flour and water for gravy. And silver platters and bowls stood at the ready.

I served a buffet for Thanksgiving. Life was easier that way. Everyone could pick white or dark meat. Oysters or no oysters in their bread dressing. No gravy, gravy on just the mashed potatoes, or gravy on everything.

"Go get yourself a drink," Aggie directed.

I didn't argue. Tonight promised to be epic, and not in a good way.

I returned to the living room, where a bar table held chilled wine, a bucket full of ice, water, seltzer, tonic, limes, lemons, and every liquor under the sun.

Wine or scotch?

Ding dong.

My decision would have to wait.

I opened the door to Mother and Daddy. Mother whooshed into the foyer, allowed Daddy to take her coat, and took a careful inventory. The flowers on the chest, the gleam of well-polished furniture, the sparkle of the crystal chandelier. Everything was perfect. She would not find fault.

Or so I thought.

"Ellison, the house looks—" Her gaze caught on the front stairs and stayed there.

Gwen and Suze descended. Holding hands.

"Harrington, I need a scotch."

Daddy followed Mother's gaze and his eyes widened. But my father was a man of action: he handed me the coats and hurried off to pour Mother two fingers of single malt.

Mother's mink and Daddy's camel hair smelled of Joy, Mother's perfume. That was the only joy in the foyer.

Mother's face looked hewn from marble.

Gwen looked oddly triumphant.

Suze shifted her feet as if she wanted to run back to the blue room and lock the door.

"Mother, you remember Gwen. And this is her friend, Suze. Suze, this is my mother, Frances Walford."

"A pleasure to meet you, Mrs. Walford." Suze extracted her hand from Gwen's and held it out to Mother.

"Call her Frannie," instructed Gwen. "Everyone does." If they had a death wish. No one called Mother "Frannie" except for Daddy.

Mother, looking very much like a Mrs. Walford and not a Frannie, shook Suze's hand. "A pleasure."

Then Mother turned to me. "What's this I hear about Sherman Westcott being arrested?"

"What?" Gwen stared at me open-mouthed.

"For embezzlement."

A flush rose on Gwen's cheeks. "And you didn't tell me?"

"I thought we could get past the holiday." I'd thought wrong.

Ding dong.

Saved by the bell.

With Mother and Daddy's coats still folded over my arm, I opened the front door.

Lorna and Trip Michaels stood on the other side.

I forced a welcoming smile.

Lorna had aged twenty years in a few short days. Her face was lined with worry. And when she pulled off her gloves, her hands looked like brittle bones draped with spotted crepe.

Trip looked younger. A child rather than a young man. His swagger and confidence stripped away by his mother's murder and his father's arrest.

Grace appeared at the top of the stairs wearing a Laura Ashley frock that covered her from chin to ankle, a character from *Little House on the Prairie* rather than my daughter.

"Grace," I called. "Would you please take the coats?"

She traipsed down the stairs, gave me a be-careful-what-you-wish-for moue, and gathered two minks, Daddy's camel hair, and Trip's pea coat over her arm. "Which room, Mom?"

"Pink."

She nodded and took the coats upstairs.

"There's a fire in the living room. And I believe Daddy is already working on drinks." I ushered everyone out of the foyer.

We entered the living room and Daddy handed Mother three fingers of scotch.

A second old-fashioned glass holding a second three fingers waited for him on the bar. "What can I get everyone?" he asked.

The kids settled for soft drinks, Gwen asked for a glass of red wine, Suze and I opted for white, and Lorna requested a dry martini. "Bone dry," she told him.

Daddy's idea of a wet martini included whispering the word "vermouth" over the rim. A dry martini was straight vodka with an olive.

Aggie, in her formal black caftan, passed around rumaki

and crab puffs.

Max followed along behind her in hopes someone would drop something.

Mother's gaze settled on Grace. "Is that the dress I gave you?"

"It is, Granna."

Mother wrinkled her nose. "I didn't think it would look quite so rustic."

Neither Grace nor I could come up with a response.

"Gwen," said Daddy, "I heard you took a spill at the country club. Glad to see you up and about."

"Thank you, Harrington. The pavement was slick, and Ellison insisted on parking miles away from the door."

"Ellison has had some bad luck in that parking lot. I reckon she likes her car to be clear of anything that might obstruct her view."

God bless Daddy.

Trip sipped his cola. Lorna guzzled her martini and held up her empty glass. "Harrington, that was delicious. Would you please fix me another?"

If Daddy had any opinions about a grown woman drinking vodka like water, he kept them to himself.

Mother was not so circumspect. "Are you sure, dear? Wouldn't you rather have a wine spritzer?"

Lorna curled her lip. "No. I would not rather have a wine spritzer." Her voice was snide, with a mind-your-own-business note that was unmistakable

Mother's face froze. No one spoke to her like that. Ever. "Now, Lorna—"

"Don't 'now, Lorna' me. Do you have any idea what I've been through this week?"

Mother sent an arctic glance my way. A glance that said clearly, my daughter has put me through more than your son ever dreamed of. "I believe I do."

Daddy poured Lorna another martini.

In the annals of horrible holiday parties, this evening already ranked high. One day, Grace would tell her children about the awful Thanksgiving dinner of 1974. It couldn't get any worse.

Ding dong.

It got worse.

"Excuse me," I said to the room at large, then I hurried and answered the door for the remaining guest.

Anarchy stepped into the foyer and handed me a bottle of Veuve. "Happy Thanksgiving."

"Thank you," I murmured. I should have given him a warning, offered him an out. "Lorna and Trip Michaels are joining us for dinner. Mother invited them."

He winced.

I hadn't told him about Mother either.

"Would it be cowardly to run?" His eyes twinkled.

"I wouldn't blame you." I glanced at the door to the living room. "Lorna's drinking and doesn't have much control over her tongue."

"I can take it."

"Your funeral." I gazed up into his eyes. "I am sorry about this."

He brushed my cheek with the back of his fingers. "Don't worry about it."

I took his coat, hung it in the hall closet, and squared my shoulders. "Ready to brave the lion's den?"

"Ready."

We walked into the living room, where Lorna was proclaiming Tom's innocence (loudly) to Gwen and Suze. Mother and Daddy were quizzing Grace about her grades. And Trip was sneaking something stronger into his soda.

Everyone stopped what they were doing when they saw Anarchy.

Grace, God love her, broke away from Mother and Daddy and crossed the room to greet him. "I'm so glad you're here." She reached up on her tiptoes and kissed Anarchy's cheek.

Daddy followed her, extending his hand. He would not snub a man who'd saved his daughter's life.

The two men shook hands.

Mother looked less pleased. Just-swallowed-a-frog less pleased.

Lorna scowled at the man who'd arrested her son and held up her glass. "Harrington, I believe I'll have another drink."

We did not linger over cocktails. It was as if every person in that living room had decided getting the evening over quickly was the best plan.

I led my friends and family into the dining room, where candlelight gilded the walls and a buffet groaned with Aggie's delectable dinner.

"Ellison, this looks marvelous," said Suze.

"It's all Aggie. Please—" I nodded toward the turkey "—start the buffet."

Suze and Gwen prepared plates, then Trip and Grace.

"Lorna, your turn."

Lorna glared at me but helped herself to turkey, roasted vegetables, both kinds of bread dressing, cranberry sauce, mashed potatoes, and gravy. Except—

The gravy missed her plate. Entirely. She poured gravy onto my silk Dupioni curtains. She poured gravy onto the Oriental carpet beneath her feet. She poured gravy onto the buffet table. Her plate and her person she missed entirely.

"Holy Mother of God!" Mother's face was frozen in a rictus of horror.

"Aggie!" I cried. "Grace, go get some towels."

Grace ran for the kitchen and Max snuck into the dining room. He was only too happy to lend a tongue and immediately set himself to cleaning the carpet.

Aggie and Grace appeared with tea towels. Lots of them.

"The buffet, Aggie. Please." There was no point in daubing at the curtains. They were ruined. I'd have to call a decorator. The thought made my eyes water and my throat swell.

"Ellison, are you all right?" Anarchy appeared at my side.

"I'm fine." I swallowed the I've-got-to-hire-a-decorator-induced lump in my throat. "Perhaps someone might take the gravy boat from Lorna."

It was at that moment that Lorna looked at me, her eyes bleary with three martinis (that I knew of). "Ellison, you're out of gravy."

I closed my eyes and remembered my grandmother's lessons. She'd taught me that if a guest in my home drank from their finger bowl then I should drink too. "Aggie, is there more gravy in the kitchen?"

Aggie looked up from mopping congealing gravy off the buffet table. "Yes."

"Lorna, please have a seat. Aggie will bring you some gravy in just a moment."

Lorna sat.

Mother glared.

The rest of us went through the buffet and took our seats.

"Daddy, a prayer?"

My father cleared his throat. "Kind heavenly Father, we thank you for this food, this family, and these friends gathered together. Please guide us as we search for patience—" everyone at the table looked at Lorna "—and understanding, and bless this food to the use of our bodies, we ask in Christ's name. Amen."

The food was marvelous. The conversation less so.

The weather was the safest topic, and we milked it through most of the meal.

"Has anyone read the new Ludlum?" asked Daddy.

Asking a table full of women if they'd read the latest thriller wasn't a question likely to evoke much discussion, but Suze surprised me. "*The Rhinemann Exchange*? I've read it."

Daddy smiled at her. "What did you think?"

"I love novels about the Second World War." She took a sip of wine. "But I'm a history buff in general."

Daddy was too. The two together were off to the races. Conspiracy theories, and battles, and the Desert Fox. God love them, they got us through the rest of dinner.

When Lorna finally put down her fork, I rang the silver bell by my right hand.

Aggie appeared and cleared the table.

"I'll help," said Grace.

I didn't stop her. I wished I could clear a few dishes and escape the table too.

Mother shot me a look. Why was my daughter clearing plates with the help?

I ignored her. Instead, I asked, "Who would like pie? Mince, pumpkin, or a little bit of both?"

Four pumpkin. Three mince. Two little bit of both.

"Everyone wants whipped cream?"

Of course everyone wanted whipped cream.

"And coffee? Who will have coffee?"

"Do you have tea?" asked Lorna.

Aggie paused, her hands full with a silver bowl of leftover roasted vegetables. "We do."

"I'll have tea."

A few moments later, we all stared at enormous slices of Aggie's homemade pie. Dollops of whipped cream floated atop each piece and steaming cups of coffee sat at our right hands.

Except for Lorna's. She had tea.

She took a sip and spit it back into her cup. "What is this?"

"Tea."

"What kind of tea?"

"We brought it back from Fortnum and Mason," said Grace.

"Yes. But what kind?"

"Darjeeling," I guessed.

"I only drink Lapsang Souchong. Ever."

"I'm terribly sorry. I don't think we have any."

Lorna pushed her cup away.

My smile covered my clenched teeth. Lorna's son was in jail for murder and she was dining with the man who'd arrested him. She deserved a bit of patience and understanding, but the gravy on my curtains had used up most of both.

"Drink your tea when you get home, Lorna. The pie's divine."

Thank you, Mother!

Lorna sniffed as if pie was a poor substitute for Lapsang Souchong. But she ate every bite.

When every bite of pie had disappeared, I stood.

Mother patted her lips with her napkin. "You know, dear, I never eat and run, but I think perhaps your father and I ought to take Lorna and Trip home."

I could have kissed her. "I'd love for you to stay."

"Not tonight." Mother shook her head and I almost believed she felt regret. "Dinner was marvelous. My compliments to Aggie. Grace, will you fetch the coats?"

I nodded my approval and Grace was off faster than Laura Ingalls running through a field of wildflowers.

A moment later we stood in the foyer as Mother and Lorna slipped into their minks.

"Lorna, Trip, thank you for coming."

Lorna settled her bleary gaze on me. "Thank you for having

us."

The rote of polite goodbyes carried us through the next few minutes.

I closed the door on them and leaned my forehead against the frame. "What a night."

Suze and Gwen inched toward the stairs.

"Go put your feet up," I told them. "I won't be long behind you."

They climbed the stairs, leaving me alone with Anarchy and Grace.

"You look like you could use another cup of coffee," said Anarchy.

"Yes. But first I want to see how bad the curtains are."

We filed back into the dining room where Max had his paws on the table as he licked a dessert plate clean.

"Bad dog!"

He looked up from licking as if my scolding was a mildly interesting idea, something to consider and reject.

"Off!"

With a long-suffering sigh he returned his paws to the floor.

A quick glance at the drapes told me they were a total loss. Lord, what a night. I stacked a few licked-clean plates, picked up Lorna's full teacup, and carried everything into the kitchen.

Aggie stood at the sink washing china. "If you'll put those on the left."

I deposited the dirty dishes on the counter.

"You look done in," said Anarchy.

"No joke, Mom. You look wiped out." Grace pushed through the swinging door from the dining room with a handful of dirty old-fashioneds and Lorna's purse hanging from the crook of her arm. "This is it for the living room, but Mrs. Michaels forgot her purse."

I rolled my eyes.

"I think that's the first time I've ever seen an adult that drunk."

There was a reason they didn't allow kids at club cocktail parties.

Grace put the purse down on the counter.

I stared at it, too tired to shift my gaze. "We'll return it tomorrow."

"You ought to go sit down," said Grace.

My bones ached, and as much as I wanted to collapse on a couch with my head on Anarchy's shoulder, I wanted to crawl into bed more.

"I'll help you clear then I'm hitting the road."

Who could blame him? "It wasn't much of a holiday."

"Are you kidding?" Anarchy smiled at me. "There's no one on earth I'd rather spend Thanksgiving with."

Grace rolled her eyes.

I thought about what Anarchy said as I was falling asleep. It warmed me from the inside and I drifted off with a smile on my face. I might have fallen asleep just like that, a sappy smile on my lips as I clutched a pillow to my chest. I might have, but, in a revelation more jarring than getting hit in the face by unexpected sleet, I realized who'd killed Laurie and Jenny.

TWENTY-ONE

I spent the night staring at the ceiling, weighing pros and cons and flimsy evidence. Weighing anger and disappointment and the value of a promise.

When the light outside my window brightened to a soft gray, I dragged myself out of bed and called Mother.

She was not pleased to hear from me. "Do you have any idea what time it is?"

"Yes." Then I told her everything.

"What are you going to do?" she asked.

I told her that too.

"I'm coming with you."

"That's not a good id—" I bit my tongue. "Thank you. I'd appreciate that. I'll pick you up at nine."

Our to-do list was short. Return Lorna's handbag.

That and confront a murderer.

I got dressed, stumbled down to the kitchen, drank two cups of coffee, and ate a slice of leftover pumpkin pie. I drank a third cup of coffee.

Procrastination, thy name is Ellison.

At a quarter till nine, I pulled on my coat. "I'm returning Lorna's handbag."

Neither Max nor Grace seemed very interested.

I lingered. "I love you."

"Love you too, Mom." Grace didn't look up from her book.

I didn't have to do this. I could just tell Anarchy my

suspicions. But what if I was wrong? I shuddered to think. "What are you reading?"

"*Heart of Darkness.*" Grace raised her gaze from Joseph Conrad. "Did you think Trip was acting weird last night?"

"Weird?" I echoed.

"Yeah."

"He was sneaking rum into his cola. Does that count as weird?"

"Never mind." With that, she went back to reading about good and evil, sanity and insanity, and the horrible idea that effort and struggle and love counted for naught.

I picked up my bag and my keys and Lorna's bag, a lovely black crocodile purse with brass hardware. "Bye, honey. I'll see you later."

I motored to Mother's.

She climbed into my car without complaining that it was too small, too cold, or too sporty. Instead, she settled into her seat and held Lorna's bag on her lap.

We arrived, parked in front, and hurried inside. "Good morning, Jimmy," I said.

"Good morning, Mrs. Walford, Miss Ellison."

"Did you have a nice holiday?" I asked.

"I did. I did. How about you?"

"It was memorable." There was an understatement. "Mrs. Michaels forgot her purse last night." I nodded toward the extra bag clutched in Mother's left hand. "Would you please let her know we're here?"

Jimmy picked up the phone, dialed a number, and relayed my message.

"Mrs. Michaels says to come on up."

We rode the elevator to Lorna's floor.

Not a single word from Mother. Not one. She'd never been silent for so long.

I knocked on Lorna's door.

Lorna answered. She looked as gray as the weather. Gray as the quilted house coat she wore. Gray as Mother. "Frances, Ellison, aren't you nice to return this?" She took the bag from Mother's hand. "Come in. I'll make you some coffee."

"Please don't make any on my account." I stepped inside. "There's more coffee than blood in my veins this morning."

"You're sure?" Lorna shuffled toward the kitchen. "It's the least I can do after last night."

"I'm sure. I just came to return your purse and ask you a question." If I could find the courage. "Is Trip here?"

"That's your question?"

"No. Just wondering."

Lorna waved us toward the seating arrangement in the living room.

I chose an armchair and sat.

Mother sank onto a loveseat across from me.

Lorna sat next to her. "Trip went out with some of his friends. He said something about picking up his car from your house. Now, what's your question?"

I glanced around Lorna's English country apartment. Nothing had changed since the last time I visited her. The chintz, the flowers in the window, the scent of lilies of the valley and tea. I took a breath and looked into Lorna's slightly bloodshot eyes. "Why did you kill Jenny Woods?"

Lorna stared at me without moving. There was no rise and fall of her chest, no blink of her eyelids, no movement in her face. "I don't know what you're talking about."

Was I wrong? My evidence wasn't really evidence. My evidence consisted of empty teacups and a lie. "You only drink Lapsang Souchong."

Lorna remained frozen.

Mother, whose hands were neatly folded in her lap, shot me

a murderous glare.

I wasn't wrong. "The day Mother and I came to visit you said you'd been trying new teas."

Lorna blinked but said nothing.

I took another deep breath and continued. "You made up trying new teas to explain the dirty cups I saw in your kitchen."

Finally Lorna moved. She narrowed her eyes. "Don't be ridiculous." She turned and glared at Mother. "I can't believe you're allowing your daughter to speak to me this way."

Mother's lips thinned.

"Where would I get poison?"

I glanced at the flowers rioting in front of her southern window. "The day Mother and I stopped by—" I squared my shoulders "—Jenny was here before we were and you gave her tea made with water you'd used in a vase that held lilies of the valley." Even now, the lilies of the valleys' delicate bells gleamed white against the greenery.

"You've lost your mind." Lorna's body was rigid with outrage. She looked down the considerable length of her nose. "How dare you?" She turned again to Mother. "We've been friends, best friends, for sixty years. You can't believe this nonsense, can you?"

Mother went from gray to green, a delicate celadon hue.

"Your friendship with Mother is the reason I came here instead of going to the police."

Lorna's lip curled. "What exactly would you tell them, Ellison? That I left teacups on my counter?"

"I'd tell them you believed it was Laurie not Tom who had the gambling problem. I'd remind them you were at the club the night Laurie was killed. I'd tell them you'd do anything to protect your son—" I glanced around her apartment "—and what wealth you have left."

Lorna covered a yawn with the tips of her fingers as if I

were boring her.

I wasn't finished. "I'd tell them you killed both Laurie and Jenny."

A second yawn.

"I'm giving you the opportunity to turn yourself in. Please, take it."

Lorna shook her head. A grande dame rejecting my sad attempt at justice. "You have a vivid imagination."

"Would you really let your son go to jail for something you did?" Mother's question hung in the air.

Lorna deflated. Slightly. "You believe her, Frannie?"

Lines I'd never noticed before were etched deeply into Mother's face. She pinched the bridge of her nose. "I don't want to."

"But?" Lorna's voice was small.

"In all the years I've known you, in all the years we've been friends, you've never drunk anything but Lapsang Souchong. Nor have you cared if someone preferred a different tea. You've only served that one tea for decades. Everything Ellison says makes sense."

"Well." Lorna sat very straight.

"It's because of our friendship that Ellison is here now. I told her it would kill you to be hauled off to jail in the back of a police cruiser. She's offering you the chance to avoid that indignity. Turn yourself in."

"Or what?"

"Or I'll go to the police and tell them everything." Somehow I kept my voice steady.

Lorna's lips thinned and she glanced down at her hands. "Are you sure you don't want some coffee?" Where was that sense of humor last night when the most interesting things uttered at my holiday table were total snowfall guesses for the month of November?

There was no way Mother or I were consuming anything in Lorna's apartment. "I'm sure."

Lorna donned a chilly smile. "It seems we're at an impasse."

"Please." A plaintive note snuck into my voice. "Don't make me call the police."

Lorna smoothed the fabric of her robe across her lap. "I'm too old to go to jail."

"Think of it as keeping Tom out of jail." I glanced at Mother. "Mother would never let me be imprisoned for something she did."

Lorna looked down at her hands. Hands I'd always thought looked like a vulture's talons. Her nails were filed to a point and painted blood red. "We can't all be Frances Walford."

Mother's back stiffened and she looked at her oldest friend with an expression that said she didn't know her at all.

"The prosecutor will probably appreciate your coming forward."

Lorna sat in silence.

I didn't breathe. Didn't move. "Please."

Lorna shifted her gaze to Mother and the two women stared at each other. Silent communication between almost sisters—more than sisters. The two of them had picked each other. A family by choice rather than the accident of blood.

The moment lasted an eternity.

Then Lorna sighed. "You win."

I never won.

"Why Jenny?" I asked. "Did she see you kill Laurie?"

"That woman." Lorna's face twisted into something ugly. "She was putting my son in the poorhouse. I followed her into the kitchen. Someone had left the freezer unlocked and she stuck her head inside. All it took was a quick shove. Then I locked the door."

"Why Jenny?" I insisted.

"She knew." Lorna's back slumped against the couch.

"And you killed her."

"I didn't want to."

The three of us sat, considering her last words.

"Would you like a ride to the police station?"

"No." Lorna looked up from her hands. There were tears in her eyes. "I believe I'll confess to my grandson first. I'd rather he heard this from me."

Poor Trip. His grandmother had killed his mother, which, I supposed, was better than his father killing his mother.

"You'll turn yourself in? Within two hours? You promise?"

Lorna glanced at Mother. "I promise on the friendship your mother and I have shared that I'll turn myself in. Tom will be free." Her eyes narrowed and she shifted her gaze my direction. "And you can get your mitts onto Laurie's insurance money."

Ouch. I stood abruptly. "Thank you. I'll see myself out."

I waited for Mother in the hallway for at least ten minutes. When she did appear, there were tears in her eyes and she looked old. Mother never looked old.

We left. I counted the elevator's slow passage of floors till my feet touched the lobby. I saw Mother safely into the passenger's seat then I climbed behind the wheel.

Next to me, Mother's silence was a tangible thing. As solid and real as the gear shift. As cold as the frost on the windows.

I drove to her house and she got out of the car without saying a word to me. Not a word of censure. Not even goodbye. Forgiveness would be a long time coming.

Max met me at the front door. He rubbed his gray head against my leg. A doggy hug. Perhaps he sensed I needed one.

I scratched behind his ears and swallowed the tears that clogged my throat.

"Quite a dinner you hosted last night." Gwen spoke from the top of the stairs.

"The food was good." I could say that. I'd had nothing to do with the food.

She sniffed. "You ran out of gravy."

In that moment, I understood why killers killed. I forced a smile. "What are your plans for the day?"

"Suze wants to see the Nelson."

God bless Suze. A nice long trip to the art museum that removed Gwen from my home was perfect. "Good for you. I believe I'll paint."

I escaped to my studio. Paint and a blank canvas helped me put my emotions—sadness, rage, fear—in order. The painting I created wasn't pretty art. It was dark and disturbing and a reflection of the questions in my head. Had Lorna turned herself in yet? What was wrong with my karma that I kept finding bodies? Just how angry would Anarchy be with me?

A little more than an hour later, Grace called up the stairs. "Mom."

"Blood or fire, Grace?" Those were the two reasons I could be disturbed when painting.

"Neither," she called. "Granna's on the phone. I think you'd better take it."

With a sigh, I plugged the phone into the jack and picked up the receiver. "Hello."

"Lorna's dead."

I sat down. Without the benefit of a chair. On the floor. "What?"

"Lorna. Is. Dead."

"How?" I couldn't quite catch my breath.

"She killed herself." The sadness in Mother's voice broke my heart. Had she guessed Lorna's plan? "She must have done it right after we left. Trip found her."

Oh dear Lord. What had I done? "How do you know?"

"Her neighbor across the hall called me."

"I am so sorry." Mother had lost her oldest friend. "How?"

"Poison in her tea." Mother's voice cracked. I could picture her, seated on the couch in her living room, her ankles crossed and a handkerchief clutched in her free hand.

"Should I come over?"

"No, Ellison. I don't want to see you right now."

The sting of her words stole my breath and before I could speak, Mother hung up the phone.

Ding dong.

The bell echoed through the foyer, up the stairs, and between my ears. He was here. I knew it in my bones.

My stomach entered free-fall.

I shuffled downstairs with all the enthusiasm of a man walking to the gallows.

By the time I reached the foyer, Grace had let Anarchy inside.

They both looked up at me as I descended the steps.

Grace looked curious. Anarchy looked...I couldn't read his face.

"Ellison, we need to talk."

An awful, I'd-been-caught-doing-something-terribly-wrong adrenaline surge chilled my fingers and dried my mouth. I'd broken my promise. I'd interfered in his investigation. And Lorna was dead. "The study?"

"After you."

"Grace, would you please bring coffee?"

Grace searched my face. Whatever she saw there softened her expression from curiosity to concern. "Sure, Mom."

I led Anarchy to the study, closed the door, and waited for him to excoriate me.

"How did you know about Lorna Michaels?" he asked.

"I don't know. It just came to me as I was falling asleep. It was the tea. When Mother and I went to see Lorna, there were empty cups on the counter. She said she'd been trying new varieties. After last night, I knew that was a lie." I sank into one of Henry's leather club chairs. "She was at the country club the night Laurie died and she and Jenny lived in the same building."

"And you didn't tell me." Anarchy stood, looking down at me.

"No."

"You went to confront a murderer by yourself." His voice was razor sharp.

"Mother went with me." That sounded pathetic. "She's an old lady. Was an old lady."

"Who'd killed two much younger women."

I looked up from my study of the carpet. "I didn't drink her coffee."

Anarchy's hand covered his forehead and eyes, then moved south and covered his mouth, as if his palm could block the words I knew were coming.

I waited.

And waited.

Nothing.

"What will happen to Tom?"

"We're still holding him. Do you want to press charges?" A sharp voice and sharper planes on his unforgiving face. There was no warmth in his eyes. No quirk on his lips.

My late husband's anger had been a fire-breathing beast. The hot fire of his ire had blistered my ears more than once. I looked up at Anarchy and realized his anger was as cold as ice.

"Tom? Charges?"

Anarchy nodded. Once.

Tom might not be a killer, but he'd still defrauded the bank. "No charges if he'll pay off the loan."

"I suggest you get Tafft working on that immediately." He was definitely furious.

Tap, tap.

"Come in."

Grace pushed open the door. There were two mugs of coffee in her hands.

I accepted the cup with cream. "Thank you."

Anarchy took the second cup. "Thanks, Grace."

With a curious look over her shoulder, she left us.

"You should have told me." Anarchy's voice was steely.

"I've known Lorna since I was born. I thought she'd do the right thing." I held the mug tightly, grateful for its warmth in my hands. "She promised me she'd turn herself in."

"She didn't."

"No."

It was coming. A speech on divided loyalties. How I'd put my family's history with Lorna above his investigation. Above justice. How I'd done exactly what I promised I wouldn't do—I'd interfered in his investigation. And now Lorna was dead.

He put his untouched coffee down on the coffee table. "Do you have any idea what I felt when I heard you'd been to her apartment this morning? When I read her note?"

Her note? I shook my head, afraid to speak. In my chest, my heart was breaking apart. Tiny piece by tiny piece.

"Terror." He leaned forward, took the mug from my hands, and put it on the table. His hands circled mine. "She could have killed you."

"She didn't."

He nodded, his lips a grim line, his eyes shuttered. "You should have called me."

"I—" I had no words.

"You made a choice. You knew how I'd feel and you still put your family's history with Lorna Michaels above the law."

I still had no words. I needed words, dammit!

He dropped my hands.

Even if I'd somehow found a few words, my ability to speak had disappeared. Held hostage by a swollen throat. I spoke with my eyes. *Please don't say this is over. I care about you. This— us—we might be real.*

He stood. "This. Us. It isn't going to work."

He strode across the room and disappeared into the front hall. A few seconds later I heard the front door open and close.

He'd gone.

I raced to the window and peered out at the driveway. Anarchy climbed into his car. For a moment he sat there, not moving.

For a moment I hoped he'd get out of the car and come back to me.

Hope is the cruelest of emotions.

The moment passed and he drove away.

The jagged shards of dreams I didn't know were mine swirled around me. They pricked my armor, my skin, my heart.

Forgiveness would be a long time coming.

JULIE MULHERN

Julie Mulhern is the *USA Today* bestselling author of The Country Club Murders. She is a Kansas City native who grew up on a steady diet of Agatha Christie. She spends her spare time whipping up gourmet meals for her family, working out at the gym and finding new ways to keep her house spotlessly clean—and she's got an active imagination. Truth is—she's an expert at calling for take-out, she grumbles about walking the dog and the dust bunnies under the bed have grown into dust lions.

**The Country Club Murders
by Julie Mulhern**

THE DEEP END (#1)
GUARANTEED TO BLEED (#2)
CLOUDS IN MY COFFEE (#3)
SEND IN THE CLOWNS (#4)
WATCHING THE DETECTIVES (#5)
COLD AS ICE (#6)

Available at booksellers nationwide and online

Visit www.henerypress.com for details

Henery Press Mystery Books

And finally, before you go...
Here are a few other mysteries
you might enjoy:

IN IT FOR THE MONEY

David Burnsworth

A Blu Carraway Mystery (#1)

Lowcountry Private Investigator Blu Carraway needs a new client. He's broke and the tax man is coming for his little slice of paradise. But not everyone appreciates his skills. Some call him a loose cannon. Others say he's a liability. All the ex-Desert Storm Ranger knows is his phone hasn't rung in quite a while. Of course, that could be because it was cut off due to delinquent payments.

Lucky for him, a client does show up at his doorstep—a distraught mother with a wayward son. She's rich and her boy's in danger. Sounds like just the case for Blu. Except nothing about the case is as it seems. The jigsaw pieces—a ransom note, a beat-up minivan, dead strippers, and a missing briefcase filled with money and cocaine—do not make a complete puzzle. The first real case for Blu Carraway Investigations in three years goes off the rails. And that's the way he prefers it to be.

Available at booksellers nationwide and online

Visit www.henerypress.com for details

PROTOCOL
Kathleen Valenti

A Maggie O'Malley (#1)

Freshly minted college graduate Maggie O'Malley embarks on a career fueled by professional ambition and a desire to escape the past. As a pharmaceutical researcher, she's determined to save lives from the shelter of her lab. But on her very first day she's pulled into a world of uncertainty. Reminders appear on her phone for meetings she's never scheduled with people she's never met. People who end up dead.

With help from her best friend, Maggie discovers the victims on her phone are connected to each other and her new employer. She soon unearths a treacherous plot that threatens her mission—and her life. Maggie must unlock deadly secrets to stop horrific abuses of power before death comes calling for her.

Available at booksellers nationwide and online

Visit www.henerypress.com for details

MURDER IN G MAJOR

Alexia Gordon

A Gethsemane Brown Mystery (#1)

With few other options, African-American classical musician
Gethsemane Brown accepts a less-than-ideal position turning a
group of rowdy schoolboys into an award-winning orchestra.
Stranded without luggage or money in the Irish countryside, she
figures any job is better than none. The perk? Housesitting a lovely
cliffside cottage. The catch? The ghost of the cottage's murdered
owner haunts the place. Falsely accused of killing his wife (and
himself), he begs Gethsemane to clear his name so he can rest in
peace.

Gethsemane's reluctant investigation provokes a dormant killer
and she soon finds herself in grave danger. As Gethsemane races to
prevent a deadly encore, will she uncover the truth or star in her
own farewell performance?

Available at booksellers nationwide and online

Visit www.henerypress.com for details

LOWCOUNTRY BOIL

Susan M. Boyer

A Liz Talbot Mystery (#1)

Private Investigator Liz Talbot is a modern Southern belle: she blesses hearts and takes names. She carries her Sig 9 in her Kate Spade handbag, and her golden retriever, Rhett, rides shotgun in her hybrid Escape. When her grandmother is murdered, Liz hightails it back to her South Carolina island home to find the killer.

She's fit to be tied when her police-chief brother shuts her out of the investigation, so she opens her own. Then her long-dead best friend pops in and things really get complicated. When more folks turn up dead in this small seaside town, Liz must use more than just her wits and charm to keep her family safe, chase down clues from the hereafter, and catch a psychopath before he catches her.

Available at booksellers nationwide and online

Visit www.henerypress.com for details

Made in the USA
Coppell, TX
11 June 2022

78736725R00151